SWEET AS CANE, SALTY AS TEARS

SWEET AS CANE, SALTY AS TEARS

A NOVEL

KEN WHEATON

978-1-6246-7246-0

This edition published in 2014 by Open Road Integrated
Media, Inc.
345 Hudson Street
New York, NY 10014
www.openroadmedia.com

For Mama and them.

AUTHOR'S NOTE

A word about "yall." While most consider y'all a contraction of you all, I consider it one word and treat it thusly. Please indulge one person's crazy mission to change the language.

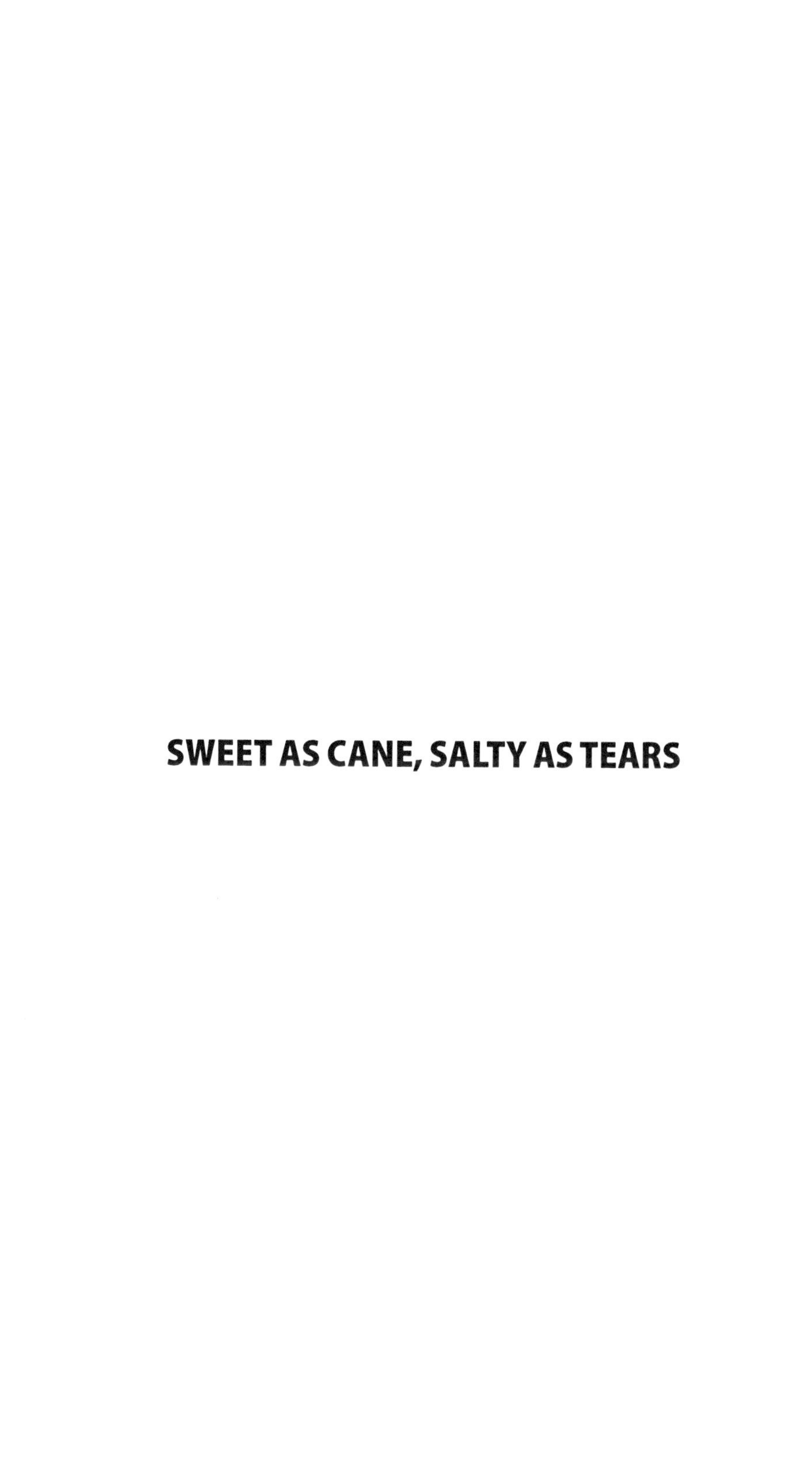

SWEET AS CANE, SALTY AS TEARS

PROLOGUE

In this one, I'm about thirty pounds heavier, my stomach pushing out at the waistband of my mom jeans. My ass has been replaced by rumps, two of them, defined by the granny-panty lines etched into the denim.

But these things don't concern me. That stomach, those hips, that ass—they've been around. They've accomplished things, brought life into this world. They're not anything to be embarrassed about. It's what women my age look like.

This isn't a nightmare. Not yet. We'll see. If my mom jeans fall off in front of coworkers—hell, if I'm seen by my coworkers wearing mom jeans—I'll have to reconsider.

No, dream-me isn't mortified by her weight; is beyond the age where she bothers with the mental calculations to determine how long she needs to exercise to cancel out the beer she's drinking, the carb-rich potatoes she's picking out of the mounds of boiled crawfish.

"Eat till you shit," someone says. Karen-Anne, my younger sister. A face from two decades ago is grafted on top of a generic lady-body, like something turned out by one of those FBI computer programs used to guess what a kidnapped child would look like twenty years after disappearing into the night.

I raise a bottle of Miller Lite to my sister. "Eat till you shit!"

"Awwwwww," a child's voice says. "Yall said a bad word."

This voice comes from behind me, so I turn to see which kid it is, but he's off and running toward the house, his face hidden. Still, dream-me knows the child is my grandchild, even if she can't quite call to mind the child who produced it, and shouts after him, "Go play, Larry. And if I hear you repeating that word, you gonna shit, too."

Dream-me has the thick Cajun accent she grew up with. Her hair is cut short, a sensible do for a fifty-year-old woman. It's dyed dark black to obscure any trace of gray. She is smiling, laughing along with the adults gathered around the table.

They're all slightly giddy, buzzed on light beer, boiled crawfish, and a breezy spring day. The sun shines bright in the Louisiana sky, pale blue and unmarred by clouds. A few of them wear hoodies—either camouflage or LSU purple—68 degrees striking them as cold. We are at dream-me's place. Outside of dreams, I've never seen it, don't know where in the real world it could exist. But I've been here often enough now to recognize it as my own. The table loaded with crawfish is set on the lawn fronting a two-story wood-frame house, between the front porch and a pond slightly larger than an Olympic swimming pool. The yard wraps around the pond and stretches half a mile or so toward a highway, across which is a levee and a river. On either side are fields high with sugarcane. It's probably the wrong part of the state, the wrong time of year for sugarcane, but this is the border of my dream home. The cane stalks lean over in the wind, rustling along with the willow tree on the right bank of the pond. A dog's bark echoes in the distance; the laughter of grandchildren drifts across the roof from the other side of the house. Their parents—our children, the connection—seem to be missing, as if the brain's processing power is maxed out on the scenery, on my siblings, on the generic representations of kids running around.

"Mama and Daddy, yall all right up there?" Kurt Junior shouts, his hands continuing to separate crawfish tails from crawfish heads.

I turn to look and there they are on the porch swing, where they always are in the dream. Still, it surprises me to see them, sitting there, looking like they looked in real life, old and scrawny and white-haired and crag-faced like those museum-exhibit photos from Dust Bowl days. Except they're smiling, happy with their cigarettes and their beer and their offspring gathered in one place.

"We fine. Yall go on and eat," Mama says.

"Just be sure to save some for us," Daddy adds, his voice strong and clear.

The propane-fueled burner hisses under a pot of water, another thirty pounds of crawfish boiling red.

"Somebody needs to see about that pot," Kendra-Sue says. As if to punctuate the thought, my older sister flicks a bit of crawfish fat at me.

"Dammit, Kendra-Sue," dream-me says.

"What you gonna do?" she says.

"Uh-oh," Karen-Anne says. "Somebody get the pineapple."

"Don't be silly," I say.

"Scared, Katie-Lee?" Kendra-Sue challenges.

"Of you? Ha!" I pitch a crawfish head at her. "Kurt Junior. Pineapple."

"Hot damn!" he shouts. "Mama! Daddy! Kids! Yall come on!"

And just like that, a circle has formed on the lawn, Kurt Junior in the middle with a football-sized pineapple in his hand, Kendra-Sue and me to either side of him. Our eyes flit from the pineapple to one another, oblivious to the crowd gathered. An expectant hush falls.

"Yall ready?" Kurt Junior asks.

We nod.

The pineapple lands on the ground between our feet with a thud, its bright scent lifting up into the air, mingling with the cayenne-, coriander-, and allspice-laden atmosphere of the crawfish boil. Kendra-Sue and I circle, making feints in its direction, eyes locked. Her foot darts in and sends the pineapple rolling, splitting the crowd arranged around us. I get to it before she does, bend over, scoop it up on the run.

But I'm immediately brought down by a full-body tackle. Stupid. Kendra-Sue hadn't intended to pick it up.

On my way down, I wrap my arms tight around the fruit. Its bark bites into my skin. When I land, its heft knocks the wind out of me and I can't hold on. It rolls out of my grasp.

"How you like them pineapples?" Kendra-Sue says, launching herself from my body.

I grab her ankle, pull her back, climb her like a rope.

"Oh no you don't," I say.

The crowd is going wild.

It's an inch from my fingertips. I stretch and stretch, *this close* to its top frond, when one of the kids steps in and kicks it away.

"You little shit," I shout, laughing.

Not thirty seconds later, Kendra-Sue and I are buried under a pile of squirming, giggling kids, our faces mashed into the grass. We're both smiling. Her beery breath is warm on my face.

"You got it?" she asks.

"Nope. Don't even know where it is."

A small, scabby knee slips down onto her cheek. "It's like playing fort, but with kids instead of blankets."

"There's so many of them," I say.

"Tell me about it."

A blistering whistle cuts the air. Daddy. "All right. That's enough fooling around. Yall kids get off there before you smother 'em." His word law, the children scatter like dandelion puffs in the wind. Larry has ended up with the pineapple, so they chase him back to the other side of the house.

Kendra-Sue helps me off the ground and we brush the grass clippings off our clothes.

"You still need to see about that pot," she says, as if she's incapable of *not* reminding me about it. And she's not. It's a dream, after all. It's in the script. The pot is still steaming, the burner still hissing.

"Kurt Junior, you want to turn that thing off and put the crawfish in the ice chest." They keep hot in there, soak up more seasoning and the stick of butter we throw in.

"Nuh-uh," Kurt Junior says, "I'm not touching his equipment. Let him come fool with that. It's my day off."

"Where is he, anyway?" asks Karla-Jean, the oldest of the girls, the only one not drinking a beer because it would make the Baby Jesus cry.

Kendra-Sue cuts me another look. "Hey, Lawrence," she shouts into the air. "Get your ass out here and see about your pot. Lawrence!"

A solitary cloud passes in front of the sun, its shadow sliding across the table, sending a shiver down my spine. From the other side of the house, one of the kids starts crying and one of the others calls her a crybaby. The cane bends over in a strong gust.

Something occurs to dream-me. "Hey, where's Kane? He's missing, too."

"Kane?" Kendra-Sue asks.

"Yeah."

"Well, Katie-Lee," she starts, but she's cut off by a loud bang.

Kurt Junior flinches.

Dream-me grows increasingly agitated. Something's not quite right.

"Where's Kane?" I ask again as the phone in the house starts to ring, the old, jangling ring of a black rotary-dial phone. "Yall haven't seen him?"

"It's okay, Katie-Lee," Karen-Anne says, putting her hand on my arm.

The phone rings louder and louder still.

CHAPTER ONE

Eleven in the morning on a Monday and it already promises to be a long week. Why shouldn't I spread the joys of my Facebook feed to my bedraggled coworkers?

I copy the photo and the caption on my screen, paste them into an email, pick a handful of lucky recipients, type in a subject line—"Try to top this one"—and hit send.

In the photo, the boy, three or four years old, I can't tell, has clearly just woken up. His blond hair, long and shaggy, sticks out in places. His right hand is balled into a fist and jammed into his eye socket, the universal gesture for "Christ, what time is it?" Still, his mouth is just beginning to curl into a sheepish smile, one that perhaps turns into a laugh. Because in his left hand he holds a dead squirrel by the tail. It's long—almost as long as the child's torso—and reddish. If I remember my Louisiana squirrels, this is a fox squirrel, a species that looks a little less like a rat than the gray squirrels in New York—but not by much.

The caption: Nonc' Charles brawt Tristan some brekfast in bed!! LOLOL!!

It's too good not to share.

"Why is that child sleeping with a rat?!? I can't unsee it. Ugh." This from Patrick, our assistant art director, born and raised in New York City and fearful of anything with four legs that isn't a cat.

My reply: "Squirrel season! It's in full swing. Fuzzy-wuzzy will be in a pot by the end of the day."

"That might be the first time I've seen *brought* misspelled that way." From Angela, the junior copy editor who is entirely too wrapped up in her job.

Reply: "Hey, they got three letters right. That's not bad for that part of the world."

"What a cute baby!" writes Molly, who's pregnant with her first child and so baby crazy she misses the point completely. "Who is he?"

Reply: "Hell if I know. A cousin or something? So many relatives popping out so many babies, I can't keep 'em straight."

For ten minutes we go back and forth. So what if we're in the production department of a weekly print magazine, an endangered species in a dying ecosystem? So what if our editors are sneaking off into meetings to examine the budget numbers and figure out how many people will be laid off this time around?

I'm wondering why Kelly, who typically shrieks loudly and laughs while typing her responses and thus alerts the bosses we're goofing off, is being so silent, when a new email drops into the squirrel call and response. I see the "From" line and my heart drops into my stomach: Kandrepont@la.charter.com. My older sister, Kendra-Sue. Her email rather than Kelly's must have autofilled.

"That's real nice, Katie-Lee. Real fucking nice. I don't even know where to start. You are fifty years old. A grown-ass woman, Katie-Lee. You are making fun of your family for being trashy and illiterate—and you don't even know who that kid is. By the way, that's one of your grandnephews. You might know that if you did more with your family than made fun of them on email and if you weren't in New York still acting like a teenage girl. Have a nice week, Katie-Lee."

I blink at the screen while resisting the urge to run or cry or puke—or to run from the office while crying and puking.

The email is a Kendra-Sue masterpiece. In half a paragraph, she's made me feel small, unclean, unworthy. She's shamed an entire office in New York. And by replying to all, she's also revealed two of my most closely guarded secrets: my age and my given name.

"We were just joking," I type. "Sorry," I add. I reply to her only.

She replies to all—which meant she took the time to copy and paste all the email addresses from the earlier exchange. "I guess I just don't get the NYC sense of humor. Whatever, Katie-Lee. I don't want to hear it."

To make matters worse, Patrick is unable to resist the urge to chime in. "Uh-oh. Katie-Lee's in troubbbllllеее!"

A new email shows up. Kendra-Sue again, now targeting Patrick. "I don't know you, you don't know me. But you're not much better than she is, making fun of people you've never met."

"Well, it'd be pretty rude to make fun of the people I know," he responds.

I stand up from my cubicle and shout across the twenty feet of beige carpet that separates us. "Damn it, Patrick! Not helpful!"

"Sorry," he says, throwing up his hands.

"Says a lot about all of you, I guess," Kendra-Sue replies.

"Nobody type a single word," I say. "Not one word. Let it go."

This, I know, will be hard for them to do. To a person, we're all last-worders. But I can't have all of them piling on. Besides, they couldn't handle Kendra-Sue.

I throw myself back into my chair, wrap a strand of hair around my finger, stick it in my mouth and chew for a good minute before I realize what I'm doing. "Jesus, Katie-Lee," I say to myself. "Jesus, Katherine," I correct.

I look at my desk phone, expecting it to ring, Kendra-Sue on the other end boiling over. Silence. I dig my cell phone from my pocket. Nothing. I text her. "I'm really sorry, Kendra-Sue. Seriously."

Nothing.

And that sets the course for the day, the hours stretching, quitting time a door at the end of a hall that just keeps getting farther and farther away. My desk phone doesn't ring. My cell phone doesn't buzz with text alerts. No new emails or Facebook updates from Kendra-Sue. Just me and my guilt, building and building. I take an extra Lexapro just to stave off a panic attack. Wouldn't do to have a fit during our Monday afternoon meeting.

Six o'clock rolls around and I can't get out the door fast enough. The others watch me as I leave, not so much because of the earlier incident, but because this, this skipping out at the stroke of six, is frowned upon. The news calls! There are web stories yet to come as the reporters file at 5:55, leaving us their mangled pile of copy before heading out for the evening. With layoffs looming, this is daredevil action, just walking out at closing time.

I could tell them I'm too old for this shit. I could tell them that when I was hired, I was told that 5:30 p.m. was the end of the working day. I could tell them that feeling guilty is for families and that no matter what corporate America would have you believe, the only people safe when the budget hits the fan are the owners. I could tell them that I'm embracing my inner millennial. I could point out that all the women with kids get to leave whenever they want because a kid is sick or a kid's school is closed or there's a school play or a soccer game or just because the brat asked her to.

I guess I could point out that when I get home to Brooklyn, I can pull up the CMS and edit and post stories from the comfort of my couch.

But I have no intention of doing so.

No, my priority is getting to Grand Central, packing myself into a 4 Train and getting back to Cobble Hill. Maybe I'll get a bottle of wine and order Thai food. Or maybe I'll get a bottle of wine and order pizza. Or maybe I'll go to Bar Tabac and get a table to myself, eat French food and order a bottle of wine. The possibilities are endless.

The wind is howling down Lexington, the first snowflakes flying sideways into my eyes as an early December storm settles over the city. I'm stuck behind two Connecticut types, waddling in their bad-fitting suits, talking loudly. "So much for Global Warming," one says. "I know, right?" the other responds. They'll be the first screaming the minute the thermometer inches over 75 and all that cholesterol starts leaking out of their pores.

After ducking into Grand Central, I find myself on a subway platform that is suspiciously uncrowded. A 4 Train pulls up almost immediately and it looks like a humane mode of transportation rather than something out of a Holocaust documentary.

I board the train, let the doors shut behind me and lean against them with a sigh. Escape.

Not quite.

To my left is a family of five, taking up the bench seats on either side of the train, a stroller in between them. The dad—a wiry thing in a Starter jacket and a wifebeater, a scrawny little shit with the sort of facial hair and ink-work that is cutting-edge fashion in trailer parks and meth labs across the country—is making a sandwich on the cup holder of the stroller. He drops a piece of salami on the floor, looks down at it and kicks it under the seat with the heel of his shoe.

"Papi," says the elder of two boys sitting across from him, "I'm done with this." He waves a Sun Chips bag at his dad, who takes the bag and throws that too under the seat. Where does he think he is, Coney Island? I half expect a seagull to swoop down from somewhere.

Many of us are watching, some even mustering the courage to shoot nasty looks at the family. Not this girl. I'm too old, too white, too chicken. Take your pick. I may be disgusted, but I know better than to get involved. Even if Papi were capable of shame, his wife has that look in her eyes, like she's just daring someone to say something to her man.

The woman standing next to me just might give Mami what she wants. She's dressed in a fire-hydrant-red pantsuit, topped off with shoulder pads and platinum hair, like she just escaped from 1989. I can feel her tensing up, steeling herself. Something tells me these are her people and she's embarrassed by what's going on. She's shaking her head and glaring at Papi. Once he notices, he leans back for a second as if thinking over his next move. Between Union Square and Brooklyn Bridge, obviously struck by inspiration, he yanks the baby out of its stroller, sniffs its butt and says, "Woooooooooo!" loudly before stripping her down and changing her shitty diaper.

He throws it under the seat.

"Ess-cuse me," the woman next to me says. "This is *not* your house."

He looks at her, she looks at him. The train falls silent.

"Whatever," he says, then picks up the diaper.

We pull into the Brooklyn Bridge stop, all of us slightly optimistic that a small battle has been won on behalf of civility. The doors slide open, Papi smiles at the woman next to me and, just before they slide shut again, pitches the diaper out onto the platform.

"Animal," the woman says.

"What you said, bitch?" says Papi's wife.

"You heard me," replies the woman. I have to give it to her. For a midthirties, professional in a lady suit, she has balls.

But Mami is having none of it. "You get a job in Manhattan, you think you better than us?"

A screaming match escalates, one so loud that at the last few stops in Manhattan, commuters on the platform don't dare board. As we leave Bowling Green and descend beneath the East River, Business Lady, having at this point given up all pretense, says, "See these poles? Guess your daughter better get used to 'em, because that's where she's gonna be in twenty years. Better hope she's not ugly like her Mami, cuz she sure won't make any money with a face like that."

Mami stands up and charges. Instinct takes over and I do what feels right, crouch into a squat and cover my head with my arms and hands. It never occurs to me to try to stop this fight, to stick an arm into this whirling dervish of Puerto Rican fury as it moves from our end of the train to the other, as older passengers cry out for peace and the younger passengers whip out cell phones and cry out for more. When we hit Borough Hall, I exit the train as soon as the doors open, leaving the fight, now in Round Two, behind me. After running up the stairs, I stand on the corner of Court and Joralemon, taking deep breaths. Snow is beginning to fall, fat clumps drifting down, already sticking to parked cars.

"Get a grip," I whisper to myself. "No reason to be upset." And there isn't. Not really. The fight was simply an occurrence. It had nothing to do with me. These things happen. But for some reason, I can hear Kendra-Sue's voice in my head, calling me a chickenshit, asking why I didn't say anything to Papi, why I didn't step in to break up the fight.

I take a deep breath. Hold it. Let it go. Only one thing to do.

▫ ▫ ▫

The smell of the Brazen Head—old wood, spilled imported beer, a chafing dish of all-you-can-eat wings—has a calming influence on me. I grab a seat at the corner of the bar closest to the door, a sea of after-work defense lawyers separating me from the regulars at the other end of the room playing darts and slowly working their domestic beers. This corner has somehow become an unofficial safe zone for the few single women of a certain age who have the audacity, the daring, to venture out alone in search of a drink or two in a social setting without getting hit on.

"Hey honey, red wine?" asks Michelle, already grabbing the dusty bottle of Shiraz that seems to be touched only when I'm in the house.

"Jack Daniels, if you please."

"A David Allan Coe reference," she says, raising her eyebrows. That she knows this is one of the reasons I love this place. "Must have been a hell of a day."

"That it was."

She puts some ice in a glass and starts to pour. "Work?"

"Sister."

She stops pouring, as I figured she would, dumps the contents of the rocks glass into a tumbler and fills the thing up to the top. Michelle shares an apartment with her own sister.

"On me," she says. "I'll be back in a bit to talk."

She doesn't make it back. Not really. Between taking orders and chatting up sizeable tips from her male patrons, we manage only half sentences.

"Total bitch."

"Drives me crazy."

"Family."

"What are you gonna do?"

"Could just kill."

"Murder."

"How bad?"

"She told everyone at work how old I was."

"Just one second," Michelle calls to a guy at the end of the bar waving a folded twenty as if it were a dog treat and he was thinking, "Come here, girl. Come!"

"She did what now?"

I tell her, as quickly as I can, what happened. "That's a tough one," Michelle says, her Boston accent coming through. "I can see why she's pissed. But to play the age card. That's uncalled for." She pauses. "So, I gotta ask."

Years coming here and I've never slipped up on that one. And now she expects me to let it go just like that.

"Let's just say I'm old enough to use coupons at the drug store."

"Pfft," she says. "I've been doing that since twenty-five. C'mon."

I've already decided to tell her. Why not? I know how it's going to play out. She'll be shocked and go on about how good I look, how she never would have guessed and so forth. That will make me feel just a slight bit better about today, better than the Jack is already making me feel. Still, no reason not to make her work for it.

"Show me yours and I'll show you mine."

"Christ," she says. She looks around the bar, makes sure no men—or at least none that matter—are eavesdropping. "Thirty-three. Jesus year."

"Jesus year?"

"Year he died. Saved the world by thirty-three. And me?" She looks around the place. She's got other things going on—acting, comedy—but I understand all too well the panic that can start to take hold in the midthirties for those of us who haven't pursued a more traditional path through life. She pounds a shot to clear her head. "Now you?"

"Fifty," I say.

"Get the fuck out of here," she says. "No."

As predictable as it is, I get the warm fuzzies all the same.

"That makes me sick," she adds.

"What makes you sick?" A man's voice, just over my right shoulder.

Grayson, one of the bar's co-owners or partners or something.

"The usual," Michelle says, drying her hands on a bar towel and moving away. "What pigs men are," she says to us, before turning to the guy with the twenty and giving him a million-dollar smile. "Hey, hot stuff. What can I get for you?"

She lies so casually and so well, I can't help but be impressed.

Grayson straddles the stool next to mine. "Katherine," he says, leaning in to kiss me on the cheek. He looks down at the glass of Jack, my second one. "Well then. Man trouble, work trouble?"

"Little this, little that," I say, no longer interested in discussing it. I've chased it off for the time being. It'll all still be there for me to worry over tomorrow—enhanced with what will likely be a crushing hangover. The mission for the moment is to keep it at bay for the rest of the evening, maybe get drunk enough that I can rush around the corner, climb the stairs to my apartment and hop into bed before it all comes back to me and keeps me up all night. "You working tonight?" I ask, turning completely toward him, my knees bumping into his.

"Nope," he says.

"Good," I say.

Sometimes, thank God, it's easy as that.

CHAPTER TWO

Hungover at work, I'm awaiting the latest email from a contributor whom I've been arguing with all morning over his use of jargon. His line of argument is, in essence, that it's an opinion piece and that he's a very successful business-type person and a borderline genius, so just let it go already. My position is that he is an asshole without an original idea, someone whose contribution to mankind is little and his writing even less, that if I cut out the empty clichés and business speak from his piece we might be left with one sentence that says, in essence, "Using social media is the most awesome thing in the world." I don't tell him any of *that.* Instead, I've told him that there's no way his made-up words, undoubtedly things he is already attempting to trademark, are making it into the magazine. Some samples: citizumers; netotiate; adultsters.

My phone rings. It's the boss man.

"Hey," I say.

"Why am I getting an irate email from George?" he asks. He sounds beaten down, like he himself is one step away from walking out the door, never to return.

"Because George can't write for shit and he doesn't like being edited by a woman."

"All true, but why is he emailing *me*? Shit isn't supposed to roll *uphill.*"

"Sorry," I say.

"It's just I've got a ton of meetings this week and I really, really don't have time to deal."

"But c'mon. Adultsters?"

He pauses. There's still some little part of him that cares.

"Just let him slide, okay? Because if I get into it, he'll go above *my* head. And that's the last thing I need this week."

"But—"

"As a favor to me, Katherine? Please?"

"Fine," I say.

Defeated, I sulk over to Facebook.

Right there on the first page, posted by Kendra-Sue, is a photo. At first glance it could be one of her grandchildren taken with Hipstamatic or Instagram or one of those annoying phone apps that make things look old-timey. But it's not. It's Kane as a little boy, eight years old maybe, standing on the bank of a bayou, a stringer full of bluegill bream in his hands.

"Happy birthday little brother," the caption reads. "Would have been 45 today. Not a day goes by we don't think of you. Watch over us."

The photo has been liked twenty-five times and commented on by fifteen people. Another sister, Karen-Anne. My brother Kurt Junior, who's written, "Hopefully he's catching a mess of 'em up in heaven." Karla-Jean, my oldest sister, hasn't commented, but last I heard, the pastor of her weird church made them all get off of Facebook because it's a tool of the devil.

The other comments are from what I imagine are nieces and nephews and perhaps even their children. Everyone missing Kane. Praying for him. Asking him to watch over them. Jesus this. God that. These people never even met Kane! They weren't even born yet. Hell, some of them, their parents weren't even born yet. And now they're going to publicly pound their chests and make proclamations of love on Facebook? Drag religion into it? Give credit to God? For what? Taking a life?

"Katherine? You okay?"

"What?" I look up. It's Vanessa. Vanessa is an optimist. And delusional. And working on the premise that she has some semblance of control over the universe. She's the sort who cries over elections, as if the results have any effect on her and her family, supported as it is by her husband, the sort of investment banker who could buy two branches of government as easily as he could a slice of pizza. She's a few years younger than me, the closest in age in the office, and so thinks we are some kind of buddies. I have a love-hate relationship with Vanessa, in that I love to hate her.

"You're crying."

"Shit," is all I say, and hurry off to the bathroom and lock myself into a stall. I grab my phone and text furiously to Kendra-Sue.

"How dare you?!" I type, so pissed I actually use an exclamation point.

Not even a minute passes before she responds, which makes me all the more suspicious that this was some trap set up by her. "What r u talking about?"

She is entirely too old to be using textese.

"Don't pretend you don't know," I type back.

"???" is her response. Then: "U should be apologizing 2 me."

"Bullshit."

I'm waiting for another text when the phone does something weird: it rings. Kendra-Sue's name comes up, along with a picture of yet another grandkid or niece or gypsy child she found on the side of the road. I answer without thinking about what I'm going to say, without thinking that whatever it is will be said in a stall in the ladies' room at work. As if on cue, someone walks in. Screw it.

"You just happened to wish Kane a Happy Birthday the day after we get into a fight? Like you didn't do that to get back at me?" Because I'm in the bathroom, I'm whispering, which only makes me sound even more deranged, I'm sure. I'm praying that whoever walked in will be scared off, will turn right around and leave. But no such luck.

"Are you out of your damn mind?" Kendra-Sue asks.

"Tell me it's not true," I say.

"First of all, that wasn't a fight," she says. "You were making fun of your family to your big-city coworkers. Ooohhhh, look at the crazy Cajuns down on the bayou. Fight? You're lucky I didn't just post the email on Facebook for the rest of the family to see. Then again, they probably wouldn't know who you are. Not like you ever come around. Or talk to anybody."

"Don't make this about me," I say.

"Pretty sure you already did, Katie-Lee." She pauses. "Oh. I'm sorry. Katherine."

"Whatever. Fact is, we fought. And next thing I know, you're posting about Kane and his birthday on Facebook. You didn't do that last year, Kendra-Sue. Never did it before."

She laughs, not with me but at me. "Christ you're dumb," she says. "I wasn't even on Facebook last year. Fact is, we do a little something every year, I just never told you because it would upset you and because you wouldn't come anyway. Not all of us are trying to forget, some of us try to remember. Now how do you feel? Wait. Don't answer. Because I don't care."

Then she hangs up.

And there I stand in a bathroom stall with a volcano's worth of rage and nowhere to direct it. I feel like an idiot, like a cartoon character with steam spitting out of my ears and my hair on fire. I lean my head against the stall door. Footsteps approach. "Is, uh, everything, uh, okay?" someone asks sheepishly. I don't recognize the shoes—some sort of stylish sneaker—or the young voice. It must be someone from one of the other magazines on the floor.

"Does it sound like everything's okay?"

"Sorry," the voice says, then makes for the door. "Bitch," she mutters, just loud enough for me to hear.

"You didn't wash your hands!" I yell after her.

I stand in front of the bathroom mirror, surveying the damage. Red, puffy eyes. Frown lines and other assorted wrinkles more severe than usual. It's enough to make me reconsider my lipstick-only position on makeup.

And the hair.

Black with silver streaks and entirely too long for someone my age. That according to no less an authority than *The New York Times*, which devoted a 1,500-word trend piece to older women with long hair.

By the time I return to my desk, the little hand on the clock—and, yes, we still have such a clock—has worked its way to the one. I do some breathing exercises, take a Lexapro and convince myself that I can do this, I can make it through the next five hours of work. Five hours of sitting in this beige cubicle in this beige office, being accosted by the sort of communication "professionals" who can't write or think, who are sloppy and lazy, pushy and impatient. Who send emails addressing me as Carla or Tina or even Bob. Who get the name of the magazine wrong. Who obviously haven't read anything we've published in the last six months. Who follow up repeatedly, not realizing that silence means no. Who make more money than me.

Not that I'm hurting. My salary's crept up over the years and my rent has stayed the same. I'm a beneficiary of rent-control laws meant for people who are actually poor. I indulge in one big trip a year. Other than that, my expenses are low. So, not counting the retirement savings—another reason I've hung around this place—I've got a substantial mountain of cash that I'm sitting on. Hell, I've been sitting on it so long, I don't know what to do with it. It was originally going to be a deposit for an apartment. Then for a round-the-world tour. Then maybe a small condo on a beach somewhere out of the way. Or in the mountains. Then, I don't know. At this point, I'm like that dragon in that old story, just content to curl up with my hoard and sleep with one eye open to make sure a band of little people—or the government—doesn't show up to steal it away.

I surf over to my bank's website just to check my balance. Yup. Still there. Old-fashioned savings account. Safe. Reliable.

I'm about to start surfing some travel sites—it's what I do after I count my money—when I get a Facebook notification.

A friend request.

Lawrence Moore.

And just like that my hands are shaking, the base of my skull buzzing with bees, my breath coming in short, ragged bursts. Lawrence Moore, looking at me from my computer screen. High school Lawrence, wearing a football uniform, one knee on his helmet, smiling at the world, completely oblivious to what's heading his way—our way. Fucking Lawrence. On today of all days. Fucking Facebook. I've wrapped up and packed away entire decades of my life, yet here is this ghost, drifting out into the light of the day, intruding upon the present.

As if on autopilot, I shut down my computer, stand, grab my coat and make for the door. It's so early no one even looks my way. They assume I'm taking a late lunch. I walk by one of the conference rooms, the one with the plate-glass windows. All the shades are pulled down and I can hear the bosses in there mumbling in conspiratorial tones. When I hit the street, it occurs to me that Midtown Manhattan might not be the best place to calm down, and the subway is a gantlet I don't think I can survive. My phone has somehow ended up in my hand, Kendra-Sue's contact info at the ready. She's the only one I could call to talk about this, but that's not going to happen. Not today.

So my thumbs type in Candy's name, then "I need wine therapy." I wait, slumped against the patch of brick wall between the dollar-slice place and the shelter entrance at St. Agnes Church. One minute, two minutes. The phone buzzes. "Tonight?"

One word and a question mark, but I can practically hear the prepared excuses piled into it. "Tonight? I'm tired." "Tonight? It's only Tuesday and I'm having a hell of a week already and don't want to wake up hungover after listening to you complain for two hours." "Tonight? I'd say yes, but we both know I'd much rather talk about me and this already sounds like it's going to be the Katherine show."

I don't blame her. But I don't let her slide, either. "Yup. Tonight. It's either you, or I drink alone." Considering our past, it isn't very fair of me.

⊡ ⊡ ⊡

New Yorkers of certain means like to think of the Port Authority Bus Terminal as a time capsule, a last remaining bit of Old New York, the gritty, dangerous place that scared a generation of Americans off of urban areas. A place where the poor, humble, unclean, and undocumented wash up on its concrete shores, where the crazies seek refuge from the elements. Walk through the sliding doors off of 42nd Street and you're back in a pre-Giuliani paradise of drug dealers, smut peddlers, and bathroom lurkers.

Which is a ridiculous thing to long for. And it's not even true.

Gone are the peep shows and the hardcore junkies orbiting the building. Gone the cars abandoned on its approach. Port Authority may be a little rough compared to Penn Station, look derelict compared to Grand Central, but it's as much a shopping mall as the other two. Hell, they've even fancified the bowling alley, turning it into the sort of place that attracts mustachioed hipsters and their jegginged girlfriends looking for a sarcastic good time and an affordable pitcher of ironic beer.

That's not the place I walked into in January of 1980.

Twenty I might have been, a grown woman I thought I was, but Port Authority seemed set into the bedrock of Manhattan specifically to alert you that you were still a silly child and you had no idea what you were about to get yourself into. I imagine my experience was common to most refugees and runaways. Step onto a Greyhound bus in an open-air parking lot somewhere in the South or the Midwest, spend untold uncomfortable hours twisted into a seat next to a disgruntled vet or smelly old woman, taking breaks only for dirty bathrooms and vending machine snacks, and finally disembark at the concrete docks tucked away inside the great terminal's belly. We pulled into what was supposedly the shiny new North Terminal, but it already looked like something that had been through decades of hard use. My stomach was tied into knots—knots full of butterflies. The oil-stained concrete and flickering lights made me stop on the bottom step of the bus. I had no frame of reference to process what I was seeing. I'd never been in so much as a parking garage.

"Come on, lady," someone toward the back said, already embracing the role of rude New Yorker. "We got places to be."

After touching one toe down and not bursting into flame, I forced myself into the building. Inside, things did look at least a little bit new. All that marble flooring and the modern design actually put me in mind of St. Landry Savings & Loan, which had just opened its new modern building in Opelousas, a testimony to progress that would be deemed ugly and out-of-date within the decade. I slid into a phone booth, called Kendra-Sue collect to let her know I'd arrived, dried my tears, and realized I was on the verge of wetting my pants.

I'd never smelled anything like that bathroom. Not growing up in Grand Prairie feeding healthy animals or taking care of sick ones. Not in the woods after stumbling upon an armadillo that had been dead for weeks. I couldn't figure it out at first. The glass of the mirrors still gleamed unbroken, though it had already been tagged with spray paint. The sinks were clean. But across the shiny white-tiled floor lay a single track of a brownish-red viscous liquid, drying around the edges. It led into one of the stalls, ending at what looked like a massive lump—a lump with bare, cracked, swollen feet. The thing groaned, and the smell—a sour mix of feces, urine, sweat, alcohol, vomit, decay—seemed to grow worse.

I turned right around and walked out. Bladder be damned, I knew evil when I smelled it. Or I thought I did. But that didn't lessen my need to pee. Now on an urgent biological mission that was fast superseding my fear, I hustled toward an exit. In what I'd seen of New York in magazines and on TV, it looked like someone had dumped an ashtray over it. The city didn't disappoint in that regard. I could practically taste the filth when I stepped out into the night. Hookers and hustlers lined the streets under fitful neon signs advertising peep shows, sex shops, and strip clubs. Wrapped as I was in one of Kurt Junior's old hunting coat, a hoodie pulled over my head, I struck out east, looking for an establishment of any sort that didn't have the letter X or the word "adult" posted in its window. After skipping a couple of diners—they were too bright and as much as I wanted to pee, I just didn't want to see or be seen under such glare—I landed at an Irish pub.

On the dark side, with just a dash of dive, the place was doing a brisk business at the booths and tables, not so much at the bar itself. I pushed through the crowd and found the bathroom, down the stairs in the basement. A basement! We didn't have such things in Louisiana. Bladder relieved, I made my way back upstairs and found an empty stretch of bar, where I ordered a Bud Light from the bartender, who had a real live Irish accent.

Accent or no, he asked for an ID and told me to push back the hoodie. "Don't want the Broadway folk getting scared," he said. I pushed it back and shook out my hair as best I could. After the bus ride, it felt like greased rope; I had to resist the urge to scratch my scalp. "Well then," he said, taking me in. I don't know what he saw, but he returned with a Bud Light and a rocks glass with a few ice cubes covered in brown liquor. "Luck of the Irish," he said. "And you'll probably need it."

This was my first time in a bar alone, without a large group of drunk kids my age, without a lead to follow. "Am I supposed to shoot it or sip it?"

He offered me a crooked smile. "It don't care how you drink it," he said.

I wanted to shoot it. I wanted to prove how grown up I was—I was young enough to think grown-up people in grown-up bars shot their booze down, like cowboys. I wanted to shock my system, alert it to the fact that it was in a different world now. But I didn't want to puke. So I braced for the burn and took a sip. I wasn't disappointed. It lit a fire down my throat and into my stomach. It hurt, but in a good way.

"What is it?" I asked.

"Jameson," he said. "Like it?"

"Yessir," I said.

"That's my girl," he said and then shoved off to take care of other patrons.

I sipped the whiskey, then the beer, while puzzling out the crowd in the place. The people at the other end of the bar were old, grizzled men and women, drinking whiskey and draft beer and smoking cigarettes. They looked like Mama and Daddy. Those at the booths and tables were dressed better and were picking at fried-food platters, drinking wine and mixed drinks and light beer, which they'd pour from their bottles into tall glasses. Those must have been the Broadway people, having a night out after seeing a show. Most were older, but there were a couple of tables of people my age.

Before long, my drinks were gone and it began to occur to me that I had absolutely no idea what my next move was going to be. I pulled a wallet out of my bag, opened it and stared. Three hundred dollars. How long was that going to last me? How much was a hotel? How much were the drinks? While I was looking at my money, willing it to reproduce before my eyes, I felt a shadow fall over me. Without thinking about it, I snatched the wallet shut and pulled it close to my body.

"It's okay," he said, laughing. "I'm not going to take it."

I looked up. Midthirties, golden-blond feathered hair. He looked like Officer Jon Baker from CHiPs. A charming smile built with perfect white teeth. He smelled like English Leather and wore a navy blazer, white shirt, and khaki pants, the latter two of which were the uniforms of the kids who went to Opelousas Catholic back home, which, as silly as it seems, put me a little more at ease. Or maybe that was the Jameson.

"Let me get your next round," he said, taking the stool next to me and waving the bartender over. "Another round for her, and the same for me," he said.

The bartender looked at me. "You sure?" he asked in a tone that might have been a warning. If it was, I completely missed it. I was in no condition to land a man, but I was flattered and, just as important, wasn't going to pass up a free drink.

Drinks in hand, we talked. I can't remember what foolishness spilled out of my mouth. I didn't tell him everything, only the things

I shouldn't have. I was fresh off the bus. Had almost no money. No place to stay. I might as well have hung a sign around my neck that said victim. But it didn't matter. We were safe in the bar. The bartender was keeping an eye out for me and Prince Charming had driven into the city with friends from Long Island, so it wasn't like he was going to leave them. He flirted, I giggled, we had another drink and soon enough the drinks demanded to be released.

"I have to go to the ladies' room," I said.

"Gotta go powder your nose?" he asked.

"Yeah," I said, blushing, the comment going completely over my head.

I looked down at my duffel bag, all my earthly belongings. "Can you watch my stuff?"

"Sure," he said. "Why not?"

It was only when I climbed down from the stool that I realized how drunk I was. "Whoa," I said. "I think I might be tipsy."

"I bet," he said, laughing, grabbing my waist to steady me.

I made my way through the smoke, through the noise, down the stairs, holding onto the handrail. The basement was warm, damp, close. I pushed into the bathroom, into the stall and sat heavily down on the toilet and peed for what felt like half an hour. I'd been holding it, afraid I'd look like a child if I had to go to the bathroom after one drink.

I was blowing my nose when he came through the door.

"Aw, c'mon, baby," he said. "You finished without me?"

"What are you doing in here?" I said, backing into the corner, knocking over a garbage can full of paper towels.

"I thought you wanted to party?"

"Party?"

He reached into his jacket.

"Don't," I said, certain he was going to pull out a gun.

Instead he produced a little amber vial. "Nothing to worry about. I got my own. Lot more where this came from, too. If you play your cards right."

He was practically on top of me by that point, leaning over me, trying to kiss me.

"Get away from me," I said, pushing him back.

"Don't be silly." He leaned back in, pinning my arms against the wall. I squirmed while he nuzzled my ears, kissed my neck. *Fucking men.* The thought burned through my mind. When he planted his lips on mine, I opened my mouth just a little, then bit down hard and brought my knee into his crotch.

"What the fuck?" he roared, letting go of me.

I was free, but not for long. He grabbed me and threw me onto the floor. Having exhausted my other options, I screamed. Loud, long, piercing.

"Shut up," he said. "Shut the fuck up. I'll give you something to scream about."

He was undoing his belt buckle when the bartender burst in. "You piece of trash," he said, grabbing Prince Charming by the collar. I thought it was over at that point, that the bartender was going to drag him upstairs and out onto the street. Instead, he punched him twice in the head, hard enough to drop him to the ground, then started kicking him. Prince Charming tried to cover himself, but it didn't do much good. He covered his head and the bartender kicked him in the stomach. It sounded like a sack of wet flour hitting the floor. Prince Charming covered his stomach and for his efforts got a shoe in the teeth, a cracking sound, then blood. He flipped himself, showing his back to the bartender, who simply bent down, turned him back over and kicked him some more. Then Prince Charming's friends showed up.

"We're going to beat your ass, you mick piece of shit," one of them said, swelling himself up, moving toward the bartender.

Three against one, I didn't know how he'd get out of it. Until he produced a pistol from his waistband and waved it at them.

All three of them put their hands up.

"Get your friend and get the hell out of the bar," he said. "Do it now before I call the cops."

With the wolf pack gone, he turned to me. "You okay?"

I ran my hands over my body just to be sure. "Yeah, I think so."

"Let's get you off that floor. You look bad enough. You don't want to *smell* like a homeless person on your first night in the city."

"How could you tell?" A question only a twenty-year-old would be dumb enough to ask.

He took my hand and pulled me up with a grunt. "Girlie, everyone can. Though I'd expect a tear or two after an incident like that."

I shrugged.

"Guess you're running away from worse. Is that the story?"

I shrugged again, felt my stomach turn. I was in no condition to answer those questions.

As if having a second thought, he grabbed me by the shoulders and looked into my eyes. "You're not on anything, are you?"

"On anything?"

"Drugs. Shooting up in the bathroom. Lines off the sink. You're not on anything?"

"No sir. Other than what you poisoned me with upstairs, no." I offered him a smirk. But that little act fell apart after my stomach did another flip and everything came boiling out to the surface. I pushed into a stall and let it all up without even falling to my knees. Done, I went to the sink, rinsed off my face and dried up with paper towels.

"Bad waste of good whiskey," he said. "Let's get you upstairs."

When we emerged from the basement, all eyes turned toward us—the ones that were left. The incident had cleared out most of the Broadway crowd, who likely thought the violence would bubble up from below or simply saw an opportunity to dine and dash. He sat me in a booth and motioned to the girl he'd left guarding the bar. "Candy, can you bring her a menu and a ginger ale?"

"Sure thing, Charlie," she said.

"Thanks, Charlie," I said as he headed back to take the helm of his mahogany ship.

"You just try to stay out of trouble," he answered.

Trouble was doing a good job of finding me, if my first hour in New York was any indication. I may not have been crying, but under the table my hands were shaking violently. Left alone for a moment, I started replaying the attack in my head—the attack and the moments leading up to it. What had I done wrong? How had I led him on? I'd never been on the singles scene. It had been all Lawrence, all the time. A boy, really, one who'd grown up with me, who would never have hurt me. Until he did.

The thought of his name was what finally got me to crying. That and how stupid I'd been to come to New York. I should have run to Houston or Florida or someplace closer, warmer, less hostile. But I'd wanted to put maximum distance between Louisiana and me. I wasn't looking for trouble. I was looking for anonymity in a place that wouldn't carry any reminders of home.

The waitress placed the menu gently in front of me, then slid into the booth. She took my hand in hers, their long, graceful fingers tipped with perhaps the tackiest shade of green nail polish I'd ever seen. "It's not your fault, you know. You shouldn't think that."

"I didn't," I said. But I had, hadn't I? The minute I'd had a moment to reflect, I started wondering what I'd done to provoke Prince Charming. "I mean, I don't."

"It's okay," she said. "You're confused, maybe in shock. Just sit for a bit and collect yourself."

I looked at her, this skinny thing with disproportionately big boobs sitting across from me. She was my age but looked older, not from wrinkles or bad skin, but because she'd troweled on enough makeup to make Ronald McDonald jealous. Her hair was highlighted and teased, her bangs towering over the both of us. Hoop earrings completed the picture. She was a pretty girl, but, hypocrite that I was, I found something vaguely white-trashy about her look and carriage. In short, Candy was the sort of girl we'd never have let into the sorority.

"Hey, you got a place to stay tonight?" she asked. "Why don't you stay with me? My roommate just moved out."

Candy, I thought, might be the classiest, prettiest woman in the universe.

"I don't have any money," I said. "Well, probably not enough to pay the rent."

She waved a hand. "We'll worry about that later."

So I stayed. Five years with her. And thirty and counting in the city.

Two people in an apartment that size was far from ideal, but it worked. It worked because we needed one another. Candy needed a friend, another woman to help her break away from her own addiction to jerks as she completed her last year of school. I needed a guide to a city that wasted no time in proving how little regard it had for my vague intentions. My intention had been to run from a place. That's about as far as I'd gotten in thinking things through. So as accidental as it was, Candy gave me a place to run to.

▫ ▫ ▫

"That bad?" she texts back. Then: "You'll have to pick up a bottle. House is dry."

Maybe threatening to go to a bar alone was cheap. She'd kill me if she knew about my solo trips to the Brazen Head. Even if I explained to her that it was perfectly safe, that I knew everyone there, that the bathrooms were upstairs, that she'd been a barfly herself once. She's one of those people who crossed forty and somehow forgot that she was once a person who behaved irresponsibly. She calls it growing up. I call it a certain kind of amnesia. At least she hasn't found Jesus or anything.

Candy and I still meet for brunch every other Saturday. She cancels as often as she shows up—migraines, stress, anxiety, it's too hot, it's too cold, allergies, drizzle, snow, fog, humidity—but I let her off the hook. And when she does show up, it's a nonstop litany about men, a parade of rejections and bad decisions. Asshole coworkers. Asshole ex-boyfriends. Asshole current girlfriends of those ex-boyfriends. Asshole ex-girlfriends of current boyfriends. Asshole ex-boyfriends who were no longer assholes and deserved a second chance. Not that there have been many boyfriends of any stripe the last few years. Which is another thing entirely.

By the time I get to her apartment, I'm sort of regretting my decision to text her and wishing I'd just gone straight home to lobotomize myself with a few hours of reality TV.

But I need to vent or sit in silence with someone who doesn't need an hour to get up to speed. I can simply mention the names Kendra-Sue and Kane and she'll know what the issue is.

In fact, as she opens the door, I say to her: "It's Kane's birthday. And Kendra-Sue is posting shit all over Facebook." It's my signal that I'm here to talk about me, that we'll have to save the sob stories from her dating life for another time. I'll invite her to drinks to make up for it.

"Ohhhhh, Katherine," she says. "I'm sorry." She gives me a long hug, rubs my back. There's no denying that that little bit of human contact feels good and I melt just a little. "That's exactly why I stay off of Facebook," she adds.

I let the comment slide and step past her, through her Pottery Barn-decorated living room and into her Williams-Sonoma kitchen, really one large room separated by a kitchen island topped by approximately seven tons of marble. She's got enough counter space for one of those Rabbit wine openers and I make a beeline for it, but I stop short, just for a second, to look out of her view: the Upper East Side neighborhood giving way to the East River and bridges and Brooklyn and Queens, the rest of Long Island furling out behind them. Not quite my fourth-floor one bedroom in the hundred-year-old building with the stunning view of the CVS across the street. But she's got her version of New York and I've got mine.

As I open the first bottle of wine, I start in on Kendra-Sue and her many sins against me. Candy knows her role is to nod and agree and not actually push me. She's not my shrink, I'm not paying her to fix me—and besides, she does enough of that in her day job. I just want someone to talk at. So I do. By the time the first bottle of wine is gone, I'm done, slumped back on her ridiculously comfortable couch, breathing as if I've just run a couple of miles.

Candy squeezes my hand. "I'm going to open the other bottle of wine," she says.

"Sometimes, you know exactly the right thing to say, Candy."

"That's why I get paid the big bucks." The cork finds its freedom with a soft thwoop. "If we're going to polish this one off, too, you can sleep over. Should be some PJs or warm-ups in the second bedroom."

I briefly run the numbers on getting back to Brooklyn, half drunk, still angry, slightly sad. Cab or subway, it's going to take a while and my luck with trains and traffic lately hasn't been good.

"You don't mind?"

"Of course not," she says. "You go change. I'll go change. It'll be like old times."

In the second bedroom, I find a pair of old warm-ups and a T-shirt. After wrestling out of my work clothes, I lie back on the bed—a queen size! In the second bedroom!—and stare at the ceiling, then look out the window at the twinkling of Manhattan and Queens. For a moment, I briefly entertain a Golden Girls fantasy, Candy and me sharing an apartment in our sunset years, though I'm not sure who would be Dorothy and who would be Blanche. Neither of our mothers is alive, so that would throw off the Sophie situation. And we'd have to find a Rose.

The fantasy doesn't last long.

"I ran into Howie last week," Candy says when we're back in the living room.

"Is that right?"

For some reason, she can't help bringing up my ex-husband. They work in the same neighborhood and seem to run into one another quite a bit.

"He looks good. Seeing someone."

My stomach doesn't turn flips, my heart doesn't crack. I called the whole thing off. "Good for him," I say. "Maybe he'll stop being pissed at me."

"Yeah, well," she says, which means that they actually talk about his feelings about me. Or he does. Or she does. Either way, it annoys me more than a little.

"What? Are you kidding me? That was six, seven years ago. You'd think he'd let it go by now."

"You're talking about letting things go?" She laughs just enough that I don't get really pissed off. "When's the last time you went back to Louisiana?"

I pause. "Two years ago? Christmas?"

"No. Two years ago, you went to Cambodia for Christmas. It's been four years. I remember because you were so freaked out by the visit that you actually called me on an actual phone and wanted to talk."

"Whatever. That's completely different. Totally different. Worlds different." I go to the kitchen and pour another glass of wine. "Besides, I practically did him a favor. I released him from a lifetime of me. He's got no reason to hate me."

"He doesn't really hate you, Katherine. He was humiliated is all. You know how men are."

"Oh, that whole 'I took a vow in front of a judge and the state' business?"

"Yes. That. I think he's holding onto the anger on principle alone."

"That's so stupid."

"Says the pot to the kettle."

I put the glass down just hard enough on the marble countertop to make it clear I'm considering tossing on my clothes and heading back to Brooklyn. "If I wanted this kind of abuse, I could have called Kendra-Sue."

Candy puts her hands up. "Sorry." But I think she's secretly pleased that I compared her to one of my real sisters. "I was out of line."

"Can we just change the subject?"

"Sure. What do you want to talk about?"

"Nothing," I say. "I'm sort of exhausted by the world at the moment."

"Only one fix for that," she says. "Reality TV."

CHAPTER THREE

We're sitting in a meeting in the windowed conference room, the same one the bosses were in yesterday. Today, the shades aren't pulled down. Why? Because people are working, rather than plotting. Working on something called 40 Under 40. If I were my usual self, I'd point out that we cover advertising, so everyone is pretty much under 40, the little bastards. But all I can feel is heartburn and headache. And they're all quibbling over some guy who's 39 now but will turn 40 before the list comes out. Then, from the depths of my stomach—loud enough so that the room falls silent for just a moment and eyes turn my way—whale song. WORRNHH? A short burst. A question, maybe. Then REEERRNNNNNNNN, as if there are two of them in there, the second answering the first.

"Something I ate," I say, shrugging as if it's no big deal. After all, I've been here so long, we're like family, right? Still, I can feel my ears burn red. I can also feel the end product of that whale song working its way up my esophagus, where I reroute it through my nose and pray to God it doesn't smell like a hangover burp.

Katherine Fontenot, growing old gracefully, ladies and gentlemen.

The reporters and a few editors go back to arguing. The copy editors, designers and I go back to nodding, tossing in a word now and then to make it seem like we're invested or empowered or whatever business-management buzzword we're supposed to feel when asked to attend meetings we really have no interest in. We all have our phones out on the table. We all check them frequently. If anyone asks, we're checking work email—though 98% of the people who'd be sending important work emails are sitting in this room. What we're doing is texting, checking Gmail, posting to Twitter and Facebook.

When Patrick's eyes light up and his thumbs start working furiously, I know it won't be long before there's something worth reading on Facebook, something that will kill a minute or two. He's one of those savants who always seem to find the weirdest web wonders before everyone else. Celebrity sex videos. Top-secret corporate memos. Baby otters hugging each other. Talking goats. And, one I'll never forget no matter how hard I try, a young chimp orally raping a frog as a family at some unidentified zoo somewhere in America taped the entire assault.

So I pull up Facebook. His status reads, "Bad day at the office," five innocuous words perched above a headline stating, "One Hurt During Rhino Escape; Animal Shot and Killed by Locals." It doesn't occur to me to click the link. Instead, I read the comments below Patrick's status, which are often more amusing than whatever it is he's linking to.

"Oh me so horny!"

"Rampaging rhinos are the advance guard in the coming ape revolution." (Apes and monkeys are big with this crowd, though screaming goats are gaining ground.)

"Going to need more than a toilet donut after that one!"

"Chinese aphrodisiac. U doing it wong."

And then this one: "Figures it would be Louisiana. Black rhino can't catch a break. They wouldna done a white rhino that way."

The mention of my home state prompts me to click on the link to the news story and read the grisly tale written in a second-grade prose that will later be breathlessly exclaimed on the 5:30 local broadcast.

At approximately eleven o'clock that morning, at the Zoo of Acadiana in Broussard, Louisiana, something had set off Huey, the black rhino. After bowling over one zoo worker, he burst from his enclosure, ran through some weak outer fences and charged off in the general direction of Lafayette, disappearing into the woods and pastures. The zoo rallied, its staff members clambering into pickups with tranquilizer guns, but they'd lost so much time calling and waiting for the paramedics and shutting down the zoo, they had no choice but to call the Lafayette Parish Sheriff's Department and the Lafayette City Police, knowing full well that once word hit the police scanners, the chances of the animal surviving the day were slim to none. But better one dead rhino than trampled children. Sure enough, after an afternoon of sporadic sightings, the beast turned up on the outskirts of Lafayette, where it was brought down in a hail of bullets fired by a band of old Cajuns just doing their civic duty.

The last sentence of the story, almost a footnote to the action, read: "Zoo veterinarian Karen-Anne Castille, who was administering to the animal when it became enraged, was trampled and gored. She was taken to Lafayette General Hospital, where she is in critical but stable condition."

Karen-Anne Castille, formerly Karen-Anne Fontenot. My immediate younger sister, who works at the Zoo of Acadiana.

I pick up the phone, walk out of the room—Katherine shirking duties for the third time this week!—and call Kendra-Sue on her cell, getting her on the third ring. For one brief moment, I consider giving her grief for not calling and telling me, but manage to control myself.

I don't even say "Hi." Instead, I say, "Karen-Anne? I just found out." And Kendra-Sue gives me the report.

Karen-Anne, not surprisingly, is in bad shape—broken ribs, a broken femur, concussion. But the rhino's horn, miraculously, missed any vital organs.

"Couple inches in either direction and you'd be getting on a plane," Kendra-Sue says.

"So she's okay?" I ask.

"Well, okay is a strong word."

"You know what I'm saying."

"Sure. I know what you're saying, sis. No, Katie-Lee, you don't have to take time off of work and drag your ass to the swamp."

"God damn it, Kendra-Sue." But we both know that's exactly what I was getting at. For approximately the twentieth year in a row, I'd avoided Thanksgiving and was actually putting off the phone call to explain I'd be spending Christmas somewhere tropical. But now's not the time to bring that up.

"Sorry," she says, relenting. "Look, I got some other calls to make and I want to check in on Sonny and them. That man can't function without her around. I'll call if anything changes."

I go back to Patrick's Facebook status and type: "This isn't funny, assholes. Doesn't it even occur to you that there are real people involved in these stories? This is my sister!!!"

I email the boss man a link to the story, explain that my sister's been hurt and make for home, as if being there rather than at my computer will somehow hurry the healing. But one thing about being a woman and having a man for a boss, they do cut you some slack anytime something emotional happens. They'll take a little lost productivity over tears every time.

On the subway ride to Brooklyn, I try to conjure an image of Karen-Anne and am embarrassed I can't come up with much. Sure, she works at a zoo. Yes, she's married and has kids—well, offspring who are now adults. But her day-to-day life? What Karen-Anne does? I've got nothing. Instead, what I get is the Tooth Fairy. What I get is a humid night in 1967.

▫ ▫ ▫

We were still in the old house then, the one built of cypress planks and tar paper. Seven years old. I hadn't known anything beyond the world of sharecropping on sweet-potato farms in Grand Prairie, smack dab in the middle of nowhere Louisiana. Had you told that child she'd one day live in a one-bedroom apartment above a Lebanese music store in Brooklyn, she'd have asked first what a Brooklyn and a Lebanese were. The one-bedroom she could have grasped, crammed as we were into that house. But paying $1,200 a month for it? Such sums would have been beyond the understanding of that little girl's brain—or anyone else's in the family.

In fact, I lay awake that night, worn cotton shift sticking to my body in the heat, listening to Mama and Daddy argue about a dime. I shared a full-size bed with Karla-Jean, Kendra-Sue, and Karen-Anne, who were piled into a tangle of sweaty limbs to my left. Beyond them, Kurt Junior snored away on a cot under the window, a sweaty thing slightly beyond my comprehension. He'd changed recently. He smelled funny and had sad little patches of hair growing here and there, like the clumps of grass that struggled to survive in the chicken yard.

I'd claimed the edge of the bed closest to the wall separating our room from Mama and Daddy's so I could keep an eye on Joey. The baby of the family, he'd just turned two and I was as obsessed with him that night as the day he'd been born. What a weird and wonderful thing he was. Starting with his name. In order, we were Kurt Junior, Karla-Jean, Kendra-Sue, Katie-Lee, Karen-Anne and... Joseph. As if Mama had exhausted the letter K—or maybe thought that trying a biblical name would bring the family luck.

I'd decided early on that he was going to be mine, my chief ally. I hadn't been the baby of the family very long before Karen-Anne had come along. It wasn't only that Karen-Anne had nudged me closer to the middle. She also had a tendency to hog the spotlight. She was a fast developer; I, a late bloomer. At five, she was the same height as me. People at church took us for twins even though they damn well knew better. Just that day she'd lost her first baby tooth. My face was still crammed full, not a loose one among them.

And it was Karen-Anne's lost tooth Mama and Daddy were arguing about.

Somehow, Karen-Anne had learned of the existence of the Tooth Fairy. No one knew where she'd picked up this bit of mythology.

Maybe one of the chickens told her, out of spite for our taking their eggs, chopping off their heads. Maybe they were just jealous because they didn't have teeth. You never could understand a chicken.

Regardless, we were too poor for such visitations. None of the older children had received so much as a penny for their discards. Hell, we considered ourselves lucky if Santa showed up with one present for us to squabble over. And the Easter Bunny? He knew better than to come around a house full of Cajuns who might prefer to eat him than any chocolate he might be delivering. But Karen-Anne had learned of the Tooth Fairy from somewhere, and after that tooth fell out of her head, she cleaned it and placed it under a pillow, declaring to all that she expected a visitation. Mama had tried to dislodge this notion as nonsense, but it had already taken root.

"There's no such thing as a Tooth Fairy," Mama said bluntly.

"Prove it," Karen-Anne said.

"Have you ever seen one?" Mama asked.

"No."

"Well then."

"But I never seen Jesus, neither."

"Karen-Anne!" Mama shouted.

"What?" Karen-Anne said, shrugging.

What, indeed. The only thing Jesus ever did for Karen-Anne was give her nightmares about his mangled corpse strung up on the cross, reminding her not of salvation, but of hell. The Tooth Fairy, on the other hand—whatever it looked like—promised to bring cold, hard cash.

"Go outside," Mama said, her closing argument when she had nothing better to go on.

Daddy, of course, wanted to give Karen-Anne the damn dime. She was his favorite and he hers. He could be gruff, Daddy, driving us out of bed in the mornings and out into the fields to help with the crops, which took precedence over pretty much everything—even school. He had to pay the man who owned the place and if that meant us missing classes during harvest and falling behind for the first half of the school year, so be it. "No point learning to read if you just gonna die in the woods of starvation," he said once. Mama jumped him good for that one, and it was the last time we heard that particular theory. Daddy didn't like to argue with Mama. He didn't like two-way conversation in general, it sometimes seemed. He definitely didn't like explaining things more than once, and the back of his leathery hand thwacking across the back of our thick heads was usually enough to guarantee he didn't have to. He worked us hard, but took any chance to spoil us, even if it was just a penny candy here or a fresh orange there.

Mama, she was the real disciplinarian—for us and for Daddy. Where Daddy might knuckle one of us across the head every once in a while, it was Mama who'd break up a fight or administer justice with Henry, the switch she'd cut from a crape-myrtle tree. About four feet long, the whip-like branch whistled through the air before biting into bare legs hard enough to raise welts. We were fast learners. She had a harder time with Daddy, though, trying to rein in his gestures of generosity and more often than not failing, possibly because she couldn't, as she said, "beat some sense into his head."

She begrudged him pennies, so the thought of his placing a dime under Karen-Anne's pillow had brought out the claws.

"Well hell, Kurt, why don't you just take a sack of dollar bills out into the pasture and light 'em on fire," she hissed, her voice snaking through the wall.

"C'mon, now, Beverly. It's just a dime."

"Just a dime? Ten of 'em make a dollar. They add up. And we're this close—this close—to having enough saved to get off this dirt patch and move to Opelousas. And you want to start paying the kids for rotten teeth?"

I was shocked—shocked enough to start chewing on my hair in excitement. This was the first I'd heard of Mama's grand scheme. It hadn't even occurred to me that Mama could scheme. Cook, clean, help in the fields, whip the kids into line. That was about it. And here she was planning to move us to town. Paved roads. Traffic lights.

Bordelon Ford and St. Landry Bank and Abdalla's clothing store marching up Main Street toward the majesty of St. Landry Catholic Church. I'd been to Opelousas once in my life. Living there? The idea made my head spin.

"And if you start with Karen-Anne, you gonna have to give to Katie-Lee and then Joseph. How many teeth is that? How many dimes between the three of them? And then you'll feel guilty you didn't give to the older three, so you'll make up some kind of excuse to give something to them, too!"

"Fine, Beverly," Daddy said. "Fine. Have it your way. I just like to do something nice for the kids."

Her battle won, Mama now tried to console him. "I know, baby. I know. But you wanna do something nice, just keep saving and we'll move to town so they can go to school and get an education instead of working in them fields."

I don't know how I fell asleep that night. Moving to town was one thing. Going to school during the harvest—not having a harvest—that was crazy talk. I had a secret, knew something the other kids didn't know. Even better? Karen-Anne was going to get herself one rude awakening in the morning.

We were the ones rudely awakened, however. By Karen-Anne's bellowing cries from the front porch. I'd expected some hysterics, but this? It sounded like she was being attacked or grieving a death—or being attacked while grieving a death.

We all ran out to see what was the matter, Daddy with a shotgun in hand. We found her standing red-faced in her nightgown, tears trickling, snot streaming, pointing to a mangled pile of blood and fur on the steps leading up to the porch.

"Ruh-ruh-ruh-Rex kilt the Tooth Fairy," she hollered. "He kilt her and ate her!"

What had happened was this. Before first light, Karen-Anne, heeding that internal clock that wakes kids on Christmas morning, opened her eyes. Hand under pillow, she felt only a tooth. She lifted the pillow for confirmation and, sure enough, found not a dime, not even a nickel, but only the oddly shaped bit of enamel she'd placed there the night before. Unable to square her faith with reality, she climbed out of bed and went out to the porch, perhaps hoping to find, if not the Tooth Fairy, then a rational explanation. What she found was the mangled remains of a rabbit. And, with the sort of deductive reasoning only a five-year-old would be capable of, she quickly solved the mystery. There was no dime under her pillow. Thus, the Tooth Fairy had not come. Only death could stop the Tooth Fairy. Thus, the Tooth Fairy was dead. Here was a dead rabbit on the front steps. Thus, the Tooth Fairy was a rabbit—or vice versa—perhaps kin to the Easter Bunny.

And this rabbit, this Tooth Fairy, had been murdered by our old coonhound, Rex.

I guess Karen-Anne always had a scientist's mind. That girl could assemble a couple of plain facts into the most absurd theories you could imagine.

Never mind that Rex was still chained to the pecan tree, barking his head off at the commotion. Never mind that there wasn't a dime or a little bag of previously harvested teeth to be found anywhere near the corpse. Karen-Anne had reached a conclusion.

Kurt Junior laughed so hard, he fell off the edge of the porch. Even Mama had to turn away and hide her face behind her hands. Daddy knelt down, took Karen-Anne in his arms, sheltering her from our cruelty—and from the fact that he himself was laughing so hard he was crying. Five minutes later, we were still laughing, Karen-Anne still sobbing in his arms, when Baby Joey, whom we'd left in the crib, started wailing.

"All right," Daddy said. "That's enough."

He and Mama exchanged a glance and in that moment decided it would be easier—and cheaper—to let Karen-Anne think the Tooth Fairy was dead than explain to her that one of the yard cats had simply left us an offering.

This would have unforeseen consequences. She got into a number of schoolyard scrapes after some kid or another argued that the Tooth Fairy was damn well still alive and he or she had the dime to prove it. She never ate another bite of rabbit again—even years later when she was old enough to know fact from fiction. But other than that, she became the rationalist of the family, the scientist and, eventually, a vet.

▫ ▫ ▫

I climb out of the subway and stand on the corner of Court and Joralemon checking my phone. Nothing. No missed calls from a 337 area code. No texts. Just snowflakes landing on the screen, then melting, as if my phone is crying—poor thing hates being neglected for longer than half an hour. I look up into the sky. It's coming down now. The early-week storm left behind two inches, much of which has melted. This one is supposed to drop at least six, none of which is expected to melt anytime soon.

Thinking Kendra-Sue might call back with news, I skip the Brazen Head and head home. It wouldn't do to answer half drunk. Or even a little drunk.

I kill an hour with a P90X workout. I hate working out at home. Hate it. And I'm sure my downstairs neighbor doesn't appreciate it much either. But being at the gym might be a worse excuse for missing Kendra-Sue's call than being at a bar. Hell, who doesn't need a drink when your little sister is in the hospital? But going to the gym? So what if working out is a good way to deal with stress? So what if it clears my mind, makes me feel a little less guilty about other choices I've made in any given week? No, Kendra-Sue would simply see it as something a sad, self-absorbed, fifty-year-old single woman in New York is doing so she can desperately hold on to the idea that she can live like someone half her age.

Which is something she actually said to me when I told her I was thinking of taking mixed martial arts classes.

But Kendra-Sue does not call back. And I'm too chicken to call her. And I don't feel I know Karen-Anne's husband well enough to just up and call. What would I say? "Hi! Remember me? Your sister's sister? Last time we spoke was four or five years ago? So I heard

Karen-Anne got stomped by a rhino. How are things?" I know that Kendra-Sue would tell me I'm being ridiculous, that I should just pick up the phone, call Sonny and say, "Hi. Is everything okay? Can I do anything?" She'd tell me, "It's the thought that counts, Katie-Lee, and I know that's a cliché, but it's what decent people do. What grown-ups do. Just pick up the phone, say something nice and comforting, and it'll be over in five minutes."

I, on the other hand, tell myself that Sonny probably has enough on his mind already and doesn't need to deal with me at the moment.

So I turn to Facebook.

I might have noticed the prayers earlier today had I not developed the habit of skipping immediately past any status update containing the words Jesus, God, Our Holy Father, capitalized He and Him, or two sets of numbers separated by a colon and followed by thee and thou or any of the aforementioned words. A younger version of myself, a thirty-year-old Katherine, would have made some loud proclamation about religion being the opiate of the masses and then blocked most if not all of the offenders. But older Katherine is exhausted by the mere thought of arguing about religion.

Besides, the prayers and bible verses were one of the few surefire ways I had of identifying someone as family.

I scroll down through my feed and, sure enough, predating Patrick's link to the news story was a post from someone named Steve Gautreaux: "We ask for your prayers at this time. Keep us in your thoughts." It takes me five minutes of sleuthing to figure out exactly my relation to Steve Gautreaux, who turns out to be the husband of Leslie, Karen-Anne's middle child. Once I notice the first one, the others jumped out of the noise. Kendra-Sue. Abe, her youngest child. Kurt Junior's girls, Stacey, Stephanie, and Stella. Someone named Tammy, who turns out to be the wife of Brent Junior, Kendra-Sue's oldest boy, my godchild. All of them, at the outset, asking for prayers; all of them getting upwards of thirty comments from people offering them just that.

It strikes me as tacky at first—even worse than the people who swap out their own profile photos with pictures of their babies, the folks who offer status updates on baby's first smile, baby's first coo, baby's first poop. Or the people who take passive-aggressive swipes at coworkers and spouses.

How many of these people are drama parasites? I don't know what else to call them. People who circle tragedy like buzzards over a corpse. A celebrity dies and they post tributes, go on and on about what a loss it is. A school shooting happens somewhere on the other side of the country and they notify the world that they're thinking of pulling their children out of school for the next week. Your sister gets run over by a rhinoceros and they just come crawling out of the woodwork to attach themselves to your narrative.

I'm sure as hell not posting anything. The thought of Vanessa from work offering her prayers makes me want to gnash my teeth and rend my garments.

None of which is fair to the folks I'm reading on Facebook at this moment. I don't know who these people are expressing condolences on the prayer threads of my extended family. Hell, they probably all know Karen-Anne better than I do.

Like Blake, who writes: "Karen-Anne's too hardheaded to let something like this keep her down for long."

And Suzanne, who writes: "I know she will pull through. We sure are praying hard over here."

I mean, yeah, last I checked, Karen-Anne was an atheist, so maybe all this overheated prayerifying might be uncalled for, but people go with what they know.

Like Claudette, who writes: "Praying that Our Lord God and Savior will watch over Karen-Anne and your family at this time. She is a kind and caring person, and her faith will carry her through."

And, son of a bitch. There it is again. Lawrence Moore. "Praying for yall," he's written on one of Leslie's posts. That's all it says. But that means Karen-Anne's daughter has accepted a friendship request from Lawrence. What the holy hell?

I can't even look at his name. I close the laptop, wishing I could slam it shut. My need for a dramatic flourish unsatisfied, I yank the power cord from the wall. Or try to. It takes me three tries—old outlets—and by the time I get it out, I'm pissed off about that as well. I stomp three steps into the kitchen and grab a bottle of bourbon off of the rickety shelf that serves as my liquor cabinet. Two cubes of ice, one shot of bourbon. No, two shots of bourbon. Deep breath. Deep breath. Deep breath. As I settle, I hear the faint click of snow blowing against the window. I sit at my tiny kitchen café table and pull the curtain back. It's coming down now, the wind already constructing little piles on my side of Court Street. There's enough on the ground to show tire tracks of the cars passing by. How much longer before the plows come scraping down the street?

All these years later—and with the full knowledge that I'll be cursing my way through it tomorrow on the way to work—I'm still captivated by snow. It conjures up Sears Roebuck images of wood-paneled walls, a comfortable chair, a glass of whiskey, and a big yellow dog sleeping in front of a fireplace. Born and raised in Louisiana, it was the stuff of fairytales and legend. I know from Facebook and hysterically excited texts that it's snowed every year for the past three years down that way, but I only remember snow once growing up.

◘ ◘ ◘

It had to have been in '67 or '68. It was after the Tooth Fairy was murdered but before we moved to Opelousas, which happened in the summer of '68.

All six of us kids were cooped up in our bedroom, staring out the windows waiting. For what, we didn't know. We had no frame of reference other than a couple of picture books about Christmas. We'd never seen real snow. We didn't have a TV, so we hadn't seen TV snow. And between the five of us old enough to have seen a movie, we'd never seen one that had any snow in it. So we sat there, fogging up the windows, ready to pop out of our skins.

"What yall up to?" Mama shouted from the kitchen. "It's too quiet in there!"

As a group, we rolled our eyes.

"Dang, Mama," Kurt Junior called back. "You sent us in here cuz we were making too much noise, now we not making enough."

A spoon stopped stirring in a pot and we heard her footsteps crossing the floor, coming closer. The door opened.

"Mama," Baby Joey said.

She ignored him and pointed that big wooden spoon at Kurt Junior. "You better watch your mouth, Kurt Junior, or I'm gonna smack it right off your face." With that, she turned and closed the door behind her.

"You lucky she's in a good mood," Karla-Jean said, disappointed Kurt Junior hadn't caught a whipping. She was like that, always hoping somebody would get punished for doing wrong.

"Shut up," Kurt Junior told her. "Or *I'll* slap the freckles right off *your* face."

"I'ma tell," Karla-Jean said. Despite being second oldest, she was the biggest tattletale in the family.

"Go on and tell," he said, knowing Mama was just as likely to whip Karla-Jean for tattling as come after him.

But he knew too—we all did—Mama *was* in a good mood. If she hadn't been, no way she would have let Kurt Junior get away with sassing her like that. Truth was, she seemed as excited about the snow as we were. She'd had the radio on all the night before and all morning long listening to weather reports. Daddy'd come back from hunting that morning with eight squirrels, and she'd set to work immediately on a roux for gumbo, the smell of which had unleashed something crazy in us, sending us crashing about the house, chasing each other, tickling, giggling, rolling on the floor and in general threatening to shake the place apart. Aside from meals and sleeping, we were never all in the house at the same time. It wasn't allowed. If it wasn't raining, we were shoved out the door first thing in the morning and not let back in until suppertime. If it was raining, we were sequestered on the porch where we sat watching rain run off the roof and keeping a lookout for tornadoes that never came.

But it was too cold that day to just sit us out on the porch. We didn't have winter clothes sufficient enough to simply sit in the cold doing nothing. That's where Daddy was, sitting out there alone, smoking cigarettes and absentmindedly scratching Rex behind the ears. "Stupid dog," Karen-Anne said, still holding on to her grudge.

So we tore around the house until Mama shouted, "That's enough!" and sent us to our room.

When it finally started snowing, we weren't even paying attention. We'd grown bored with our vigil and set up a blanket tunnel between the bed and Kurt Junior's cot. Karla-Jean, Kendra-Sue, and Kurt Junior had found a deck of cards and were teaching Karen-Anne how to play bourré . I was trying to get Baby Joey to say my name. He had *mama* and *dada* down. If I was his third word, that'd be a small victory.

"Katie-Lee," I said in a singsong, while trying to lift him up and down, making him laugh. It looked ridiculous—he was already half my size and I wouldn't be able to carry him much longer. "Can you say Katie-Lee? Yes you can. Oh, yes you can. Katie-Lee, Katie-Lee, Katie-Lee."

"More like Smelly-Pee," Kendra-Sue said.

I stopped shaking him and shot her a look. "Go ahead, you. See what I do to you in your sleep. See if Red-Eye don't come get you."

Red-Eye was some bit of foolishness dreamed up by Kurt Junior to scare the rest of us. A demon who nested in the stovepipe, Red-Eye crept out at night and snatched up little girls to take them down to hell where they became the bride of Satan. The story didn't hold much power over Karla-Jean, Karen-Anne, or me. But for some inexplicable reason, it still gave Kendra-Sue nightmares.

"Shut your face," she told me and turned back to her cards, allowing me to focus again on Baby Joey.

"Katie-Lee," I said again. "Can you say Katie-Lee?"

He chirped and burbled and spit up a little before coming out with "Kay-Lee!"

That was good enough for me.

"Yall heard that? He said my name!"

"God," Kendra-Sue said, rolling her eyes.

It was starting to look like we weren't going to escape the day without a little hair-pulling and scratching and, most likely, a switching from Mama.

"Yall get out here," Daddy shouted from the front door, freezing us all in mid action, stopping our very thoughts. "C'mon. Yall missing the snow."

With that, we tried to get all six of our bodies through the bedroom door at once and stormed out onto the porch, where we stopped short. Breathing heavily in our excitement, we looked like overworked horses, steam puffing from our nostrils.

I don't know how long it had been snowing before he called us out, but the ground was covered and it was still coming down. Silence reigned, our breathing the only sound to be heard. The lighting was strange, a gray dusk in the middle of the day serving as backdrop to the white flakes falling from the sky. I stuck my hand out from under the porch's overhang, hoping to catch some of the magic, but it only melted.

"Can we go play in it?" Kurt Junior asked.

"Not enough to play in yet," Daddy said. "Let's give it a little time."

That seemed about like asking pigs to wait a few minutes before eating the slop right in front of them, but we all said, "Okay, Daddy," and deferred to his wisdom. Obviously he knew a thing or two about snow. Even if he knew only one thing about snow, it was one thing more than the rest of us.

"Come on," he said. "Let's go eat some gumbo."

We usually ate like a pack of wild animals, tearing through what food we had and hoping beyond the realm of all experience that there would somehow be more. But that day we were too nervous to eat, worrying that the snow would stop or that it would melt by the time we were allowed out to play.

An hour later, when we were let outside bundled up in what clothes we could find, there was a full inch on the ground. It wasn't much, but to us it might as well have been the North Pole. After working as a team to build a two-foot tall snowman that was as much dirt and sticks as it was snow, we declared war on each other, practically scraping every inch of snow off of the ground and fence rails and the truck and low-hanging tree limbs to arm ourselves.

Since Baby Joey was too small to stay out for long, the warring factions broke down as they often did, Kendra-Sue and me against the other three. Fight like cats and dogs as often as we did, together we were an unstoppable force. Or, an alternate reason, given by Kurt Junior: "Yall too hateful to separate." Meaning that if we were on opposing teams, the play fighting would at some point turn into real violence—and we'd all get a switching from Mama.

Still, Kurt Junior probably wished he could have both of us on his team. As Kendra-Sue and I worked silently to build our arsenal, we could hear Karla-Jean nagging him.

"We need a plan and we need to build a fort."

"Mais, what you gonna build a fort with? There's not that much snow. Just pack some snowballs before them two come get us."

I listened not so much to the words as to the way they carried in the cold air. Kurt Junior, Karla-Jean, and Karen-Anne were on the other side of the house, but sounded like they were in the same room. Karen-Anne whined that her fingers hurt from the cold.

Mine burned, too. Red and raw. It was the most disappointing thing about the reality of snow. I don't know what I'd expected. Something soft? Clouds that could be packed into solid form? It hadn't occurred to me that I'd basically be sticking my hands in cold water for an hour or more. But I held my tongue. For all I knew, this was a once-in-a-lifetime event.

I stuck my head around the side of the house to spy on the enemy.

"Kurt Junior's sneaking off behind the barn," I reported.

"Good. We'll get Karla-Jean first."

She didn't need to explain to me why. Swooping down on Karen-Anne might prompt Kurt Junior to counterattack with force. He'd do nothing to protect Karla-Jean. If we hit her hard enough, she'd give up immediately.

When we stormed around the house, Karen-Anne bolted away from Karla-Jean, who was bent over a bare patch of ground trying to coax a fort out of mud and what was left of the snow. It looked more like a snake. Whatever it was, the three-inch mound did nothing to protect her from the four snowballs we hurled at her face from point-blank range, knocking her onto her butt. In a second, she was back on her feet, red-faced, blood streaming from her nose. She was a sight. Tall for her age, topped with flaming red hair that apparently struck at least one Fontenot in every generation. And so mad she couldn't speak or make up her mind which one of us to kill first. Not that either of us was going to stick around to make her decision easier. We took off in separate directions and rendezvoused on the other side of the house.

Karla-Jean's voice split the air. "I quit! Yall hear me? I quit. I'm going inside. Stupid. That's what yall are. I hope yall freeze to death out here."

"That was probably the best thing ever in my life," Kendra-Sue said. She looked like a dog that had just eaten a week-old opossum.

"You think she's gonna tell?" I asked.

"Let her. The only person gonna listen to her crybabying is Jesus."

That was true. And Karla-Jean was smart enough not to ruin Mama's mood by tattling.

"Who's next?" I asked.

"I don't know. What do you think?"

We sat for a bit, mulling it over, sticking our tongues out to catch the snow. We made more snowballs. Kept an ear out for the approaching enemy. If past war experience—and we had plenty of it, waging pitched battles with chinaberries, rotten eggs, acorns, and yes, on occasion, hardened cow pies—was an indicator, Kurt Junior would lie in wait like a sniper. He could out-wait any of us. Sooner or later, we'd go looking for him and, from some tree limb or barn rafter, he'd rain death from above. And just like death, it didn't matter that we were expecting him, he always caught us by surprise. But what was he going to do with Karen-Anne?

We found out soon enough when she poked her head around the corner. He'd sent her to spy. Big mistake.

Without even discussing it, Kendra-Sue and I said at the same time, "Wanna be on our team?"

Not five minutes later, we'd completely turned her with a promise that she'd be the key to our first victory over that stupid, smelly boy we called our brother.

And she was. Our general plan amounted to little more than Kendra-Sue and me walking through the yard pretending to look for Kurt Junior, while also pretending not to see Karen-Anne, who'd be pretending to sneak up on us from ten yards back. That was all it took. Seeing this, Kurt Junior dropped from a tree and screamed, "Now, Karen-Anne," expecting her to form the bottom slice of bread on a Kendra-Sue and Katie-Lee sandwich. Instead, she ran forward and threw herself at his legs, wrapping her arms around his ankles and holding on for dear life while we first pelted him with snow and then tackled him.

"I surrender," he finally called, laughing at our treachery, before running off to the porch.

"We won! We won!" Karen-Anne shouted, hopping up and down in victory.

"Game ain't over yet," Kendra-Sue said.

It took all of three seconds for the meaning of her words to get through to Karen-Anne and perhaps another two seconds for our little sister to spin on her heels and make a dash for the house. But there was no escape. We hit her with so much snow, she looked more like a snowman than the actual snowman. Except she cried a good deal more than he did.

Mission complete, Kendra-Sue and I marched back into the house soaked and shivering happily—and hungry enough to destroy any hopes Mama had of gumbo leftovers the next day.

"Y'all should be ashamed of yourselves," Mama said.

"Nope," Kendra-Sue answered.

"I'd sure hate to run into you two in a dark alley," Daddy said.

"That's right, you would," Kendra-Sue said, beaming with pride in our ruthless teamwork.

At which point, Karla-Jean came in from the back room carrying Baby Joey. "Joey got something to say," she said. "Go on baby. Say it." She looked right at Kendra-Sue.

"Katie-Lee," he said, his voice loud, his pronunciation clear.

I darted from the table, scooped him in my arms and forgot all about our battlefield victory.

◘ ◘ ◘

The calls for prayers have tapered off by the time I get to work on Thursday morning, replaced by updates from Karen-Anne's kids—Lucy, Leslie, and Sonny Junior—and Leslie's husband, Steve.

"The doc says she's doing okay. Fingers crossed."

"Made it through the night. Feeling a little better this morning. Painkillers making her nauseated."

"She asked to see her grandbabies, so we brought in Lisa and my baby-bump. Lisa was afraid maw-maw would be smushed flat like in the cartoons."

There's a knock on the metal frame of my cubicle—a sound that never fails to make me cringe. I turn to find Patrick wearing a stricken look on his face.

"I'm sorry, Katherine. I had no idea." He stands there, hands jammed in his pockets.

"Don't worry about it."

"If there's anything I can do," he starts, then stops.

What could he do? Even less than offer Facebook prayers, I imagine. But that's the point. Someone saying, "I'm helpless to help you, but I see you are in pain and I understand it and wish I could do something about it." I'm just about to absolve him—and by extension, the rest of the office—when I notice a body moving in from the left. Patrick's presence at my cubicle—an oddity in an office that communicates mostly by IM and email—has alerted Vanessa.

"Oh my God, Katherine, I just heard," she says. "I'm so sorry."

Across the field of beige, waist-high cubicle walls, the tops of heads lift to reveal eyes, all now locked on me. I try to ignore them, focusing instead on Vanessa and her stupid highlighted hair and her ridiculous peasant blouse and hippie skirt—inappropriate for the office, inappropriate for the weather and inappropriate for her age. Not that I care about propriety. It's just her and her hand on her chest and her sad eyes and faux compassion.

I stand up. Vanessa takes this as a cue to hug me.

I stop her with a finger pointed at her chest. "Don't touch me," I say, perhaps a little too loudly, then stomp off to the bathroom.

I look awful. And that's fine. If I can just focus on the horror show of my reflection, I can avoid the real terror, that my sister is lying mangled in a hospital in south Louisiana. That maybe the final winnowing has begun. They—we—die young in Louisiana. And we're not young anymore. I guess I figured it would start with Kurt Junior, oldest first. Something pedestrian like cancer—the universe punishing him for surviving Vietnam. Then again, starting at the bottom makes a certain kind of sense—picking up where it left off.

The bathroom door opens and in waltzes this vision of beauty. Our newest reporter, twenty-five years old and bursting with motivation, earnestness, hope. And boobs, too. Christ, middle of winter and she doesn't have a bra on and they're standing straight out. And her hair is long and shiny, her teeth gleaming white. Her name is Britney. That's an actual thing her mother called her when she came into the world. For a brief moment, I hate her with the power of a thousand suns.

"Oh, hi," she says, stopping just inside the door, suddenly unsure of herself. "Is everything okay?"

We lock eyes in the mirror. I take one deep breath. Another. Do not be that bitchy old lady, Katherine. Do not begrudge this girl her youth.

"Just," I start. "It's just one of those days. One of those weeks."

"Oh," she says. I wonder if she knows. She might not. The contours of office gossip are strange that way. She's new enough not to be friends with anyone on Facebook. And the reporters—the younger ones especially—don't know what to make of the art and copy folks penned up in the back corner like slightly dangerous pets.

She moves to the sink and breaks out a makeup bag. "My boyfriend's taking me to a fancy lunch," she explains, almost embarrassed. "Celebrate my first cover story."

"That's right. Congrats," I say. Britney likely sees it as a stepping stone, the first bright spot on a long career that takes her to the most-influential magazines and newspapers in the world, but the little Grinch who lives in my head knows that in twenty years, she'll still be here, writing about the latest ad campaign for Pampers. "Try not to mind me. Just having a moment."

She closes up her bag. It took her all of two minutes to freshen up. "I heard. I'm sorry," she says.

"Oh." I don't know why, but this is enough to make we want to cry. "Thanks," I manage.

"Can I say something that might be inappropriate?" she asks.

"Might be the best thing to say," I respond and grasp the edge of the sink tight, steeling myself for whatever words of wisdom this kid is about to offer.

"This is going to sound silly, but I really, really love your hair," she says, and for one tiny moment, reaches out and touches it.

"Well, bless," I start and then stop myself, eyes wide with shock. "Oh my god."

"What?" she asks, suddenly frightened.

I'm laughing. Or crying. Or both. "I almost said 'Bless your heart'!"

She smiles nervously.

"It's just such an old lady thing to say. Old ladies say that. Jesus."

Britney backs slowly out the door. "I hope you feel better," she says.

"You and me both," I mutter to myself. "You and me both."

CHAPTER FOUR

Standing on the corner of Sullivan and West 3rd Street, I check the map on my phone, look for the sign. Shade Bar. Right place. Close enough to the right time. It's snowing again. Good for another couple of inches, it looks like. But not enough to keep the kids off the streets. It's Thursday night, the first night of the weekend for the unbridled youth of NYU, who, along with the tourists on Bleecker Street, are cruising for drink specials and cheap food in establishments that are, decades later, trying to milk the fact that Dylan and his ilk once played here. I wonder if Britney and her boyfriend are out here somewhere.

Shade's not a bad place, it turns out. Black curtains and tables, red cushions on the seats, and lights turned down low to let the candles do their work, it's a welcome change from the frigid, windblown streets. I unwrap the scarf from around my face and neck—no doubt I look like a puffy version of Lawrence of Arabia—and sweep the room for Danielle, who is tucked away in the back corner, halfway through her first drink and reading something on an e-reader. It slightly annoys me that I can no longer judge people by their books' covers.

"You find it okay?" she asks as I take my seat. No air kisses or hugs for us.

"C'mon," I say, patting my phone guiltily. "How long have I lived here?"

"You kidding? People wander into the West Village and never leave."

"Idiots." Truth is, the college scene isn't the only reason I'm not a fan of the Village. The grid that covers most of Manhattan speaks to a certain part of me. A neighborhood where 10th Street and 4th Street intersect, not so much. "Looks like you picked another good place," I say.

She rarely goes wrong, which is one of the reasons I leave my fate in her hands for our weekly meetings. I'd have settled on the first decent bar we discovered ten years ago and never changed venue. But our arrangement lets her explore and allows me some unpredictability in my life, even if it's scheduled between 7 and 10 every Thursday.

"It's a gift," she says. "Besides, if I left it up to you, we'd be at the Brazen Head every week."

"Nothing wrong with having a neighborhood bar."

Our conversation is predictable, a ritual—something I find comfort in.

"I still can't believe you go to bars alone." She shudders. "Girl could get in trouble that way."

I try to remember if I've ever told her that particular story and decide I haven't. "You don't know the half of it," is all I say. "Besides, I'm not a girl. And it's not some random bar. It's safe."

"Even so. Just as soon get married and drink with my husband every night."

"But it's like *Cheers*. Familiar faces, people who recognize you. They're glad to see you—or at least pretend they are."

"Sounds like family to me," she says. "How long before you know their business, before the drunk—sorry the *other* drunk—at your end of the bar is spilling his guts. And what happens when you see them in the street? Or they friend you on Facebook? Entanglement! Entrapment! I go drinking to forget my family, not find a new one."

This is why I keep Danielle in my life four years after she was cut from the magazine in the last round of layoffs. It also explains why I don't go to the Brazen Head as much as I used to.

"Besides, you wake up in the sack with one of these family members, it's almost as bad as incest."

My silence is a giveaway.

"Oh god. You didn't," she says, laughing. "Grayson?"

"Sometimes the body just assumes control."

She's on her second drink, so it remains to be seen whether she'll insist on details. She considers me for a moment, puts her glass down on the coaster, spins the coaster slowly around and then speaks. "If you start talking about biological clocks and getting pregnant, I'm walking out of here right now."

The truth is, she's doing it as much for herself as for me. Ranting about breeders is one of our favorite pastimes. We're like two Yankees fans cursing the Red Sox—or, to be more exact, two Yankees fans cursing a Yankee player who'd gone over to the Red Sox. All of our friends have switched sides. Marriage. Kids. Suburbs.

Married friends, I can handle. Everyone should try it at least once. And a girl needs to gripe just as much as the old man does. Suburban friends, I can take. I'm not completely opposed to leaving the city, and I'm certainly on board with scheduling drinks around train or bus schedules. But kids change everything. Plans are arranged. And then rearranged. And then canceled. And then rescheduled. Lather, rinse, repeat. And on those occasions when they are kept, chances are good the frazzled mother will show up an hour late—a close-to-unpardonable offense in my book. Everyone gets one chance. Things happen. But after the second time, Katherine will be making excuses for not getting together and will keep making them until you get the point and quit asking. And when mama-bear does show up, all she does is bitch about the kids or brag about the kids or show me all the damn photos I've seen already because they're cluttering up my Facebook stream. Or worse, she sits there looking exhausted, stunned, and jittery all at the same time, checking her watch, anxious to get back because—what, exactly?—Junior might spontaneously combust if mom's not around every second of the day to watch over him?

Danielle and I are galloping down this well-worn rut of a conversation, when she announces her new plan for us. "We win the lottery or sue the city for something," she says. "Then we open a pub in Brooklyn called 'Adult Swim.' "

"Beautiful," I said.

"But wait. Then we hang a sign out front that reads, 'No kids of any age allowed ever for any reason. Hire a fucking sitter.' "

We come close to cackling, which makes me a little sad.

"Christ," I say, "what's wrong with us?"

"Oh, you know, the usual. Bitter, dried-up crones, just hating on what we really want." Danielle's voice drips with sarcasm.

But I wonder. I don't stay awake at night thinking of imaginary husbands and clutching my womb in regret. But Danielle? She claims to be thirty-five, but is forty. Selfishly, I'd like to think she's passed into the safe zone, that she won't run off and get married and have babies and turn into one of those people, leaving me to find yet another single woman to hang out with. But you never know. She could meet a man online and move to Alaska. She could decide to adopt—or just get herself knocked up. She says she needs neither husband nor child. But she always picks the bar stool with the best view of the room or, like tonight, the chair that faces the door. She's listening, but she's looking as well, scanning the room for single guys. She might not drink alone, but if approached by the right guy after enough drinks, she wouldn't think twice before abandoning me. And she's worse than me with the phone, always glancing at it, touching the screen, as if one day she'll get one simple text message that changes everything.

I could push Danielle on these questions, dig deep, but I never do. I value the male quality of our relationship—the topsoil nature of it—too much to risk it, to reduce it to a therapist session that ends with us crying and too ashamed to look one another in the eye next time we meet. It's part of our unspoken contract.

But this week, she doesn't hold up her end of the bargain.

"So your sister was trampled by a rhinoceros?" she asks out of the blue.

"Facebook?"

"I saw your response to Patrick's status."

"Not one of my finer moments."

She waves it off. "So how's she doing?"

"Better. Apparently."

Danielle raises her glass. "Well, here's to . . . wait, what was her name?"

"Karen-Anne."

"Is that the mean one or the religious one?"

"The sane one, actually," I say. I look at my own phone. No text messages. No voice mails.

"Oh, the other one?"

"Probably the only one."

"Here's to Karen-Anne," she says. "To a speedy recovery."

We raise our glasses and drink.

"Listen," I say. "Don't tell Candy."

Danielle's face drops. "So she's gracing us with her presence tonight?"

"Sorry. Told her to show up at 8:30."

The disdain between Candy and Danielle is strong and mutual. I wish they'd get along better, but they don't. And I typically try to keep them apart. But sometimes I just get fed up, get it in my head that they can act like adults for an hour or two and we can all enjoy each other's company. Never mind that that's never actually happened.

"She complains about men, scowls at them, whines at them—and then wonders why no one asks her out. I mean, she literally sits at the bar with her arms crossed looking like she's going to bite or burst into tears. It's like a no-dick fly zone. You think with a name like Candy she'd be a little happier."

Danielle picks up her phone and pushes the unlock button repeatedly, causing the screen to light up, go dark, light up, go dark. "I'm going to remember this."

"Hey, I told her to come late. It's only an hour."

"If I wanted to spend an hour with a little dark cloud, I could have visited my mother." She drains her drink.

"C'mon," I plead.

"And you're the worst. You enable her."

"I know. I get it. Trust me. But you know how it is."

"Yeah, well, you owe me. You're paying for my drinks."

"Fine. But seriously, don't say anything about Karen-Anne. I can't deal with the hysterics and the concern. That's all she's going to want to talk about and I just want a couple hours of not thinking about it."

"How does she not know already?"

"I haven't told her."

Telling her about Kane and Kendra-Sue was one thing, nursing old wounds, so to speak, and turning to that one friend who's a bridge to the past. This is something else. I'm not mentally prepared to deal with Candy-flavored drama she would bring to this situation.

"Is she not on Facebook?"

"Nope."

Danielle looks at her phone as if pondering what life would be like without it. "Un-fucking-believable."

"I know. But that's Candy."

"But that's Candy. Sounds like a horrible '80s sitcom. But that's Candy."

A cold blast pushes through the heavy curtains blocking the door. Apparently saying her name three times in succession has conjured Candy. There she stands, blinking as if uncertain. I can tell by her long black coat and high heels that underneath the layers, she's dressed like she heard "wine bar" and thought we were going to one of those ridiculous cocktail lounges in a trendy hotel.

And she knows this.

"I'm so overdressed," she says by way of greeting. "I look like an asshole."

"You look fine," I say as she removes the coat to reveal a tight black dress. It actually does look pretty good on her.

"Sit down, have a couple of drinks and you'll forget all about it," Danielle adds.

"Oh, hi, Danielle," Candy says, with her best fake smile. "I didn't know you'd be here."

Which is complete bullshit. I'd told her as much.

"How's the job going?" Candy asks Danielle. She makes air quotes around the word job.

"It pays the bills," Danielle says.

"What is it that you do? Watch TV and then write summaries about the show that everyone watched already?"

"It's a little more complicated than that," Danielle says.

Actually, it's not. And she knows it. It's a bullshit job in a bullshit media world, but the fact that she was able to talk someone into paying her to do it—more power to her.

"Media blogger," Candy says, shaking her head. "I ran into another one the other night. She was going on and on about CNN like it was Shakespeare or something. Curly hair, huge rack—"

Danielle cuts her off. "And no brains. Yeah, I know her. She thinks she's doing a service for humanity with her blogging, thinks that cable news says something deeper about society than that we're all a bunch of easily amused and misinformed idiots. That's why I stick to reality shows."

They both laugh. They're having a moment. So I laugh, too, and wonder if I should take a picture.

"How's the dating life?" Danielle asks.

I tense up. I was so wrapped up in myself the other night, I hadn't even thought to ask. More surprising is that she didn't bring it up.

"Think it's about time to move to Alaska," Candy says, laughing.

Phew.

"Seriously, I take a two-year break from Match.com, go back on the other day, and it's the same guys! And they're all two years older and still looking for girls under thirty. Ridiculous."

Her chocolate martini arrives and she downs half of it in one go. "Went on a date last night. You'll appreciate this one, Katherine. He's from Louisiana—didn't know you, hadn't even heard of your town, I asked. He must be relatively fresh off the boat because he suggested Delta Grill. I tried to warn him off, but he insisted."

"Oh no," I say. I long ago gave up looking for Louisiana food in New York. The city that can do every cuisine can't do Cajun worth a damn. Popeyes is the only thing that comes remotely close to realistic.

"Yeah. He didn't make it past the seafood gumbo."

"What happened? Did he cry?"

"Nope. He picked it up, walked into the kitchen and started berating the chef. 'Where's the roux? Let me see the roux! Why are there tomatoes in this? Where is the fucking roux?' I could hear him from out in the restaurant."

Danielle's killing herself laughing. "Oh my god. What did you do?"

"I just grabbed my stuff and walked out the door."

"Wow," I say, teasing. "Sounds like the fiery kind of guy you're a sucker for."

"It *was* kind of a turn-on," she says. "But he had bad teeth and hairy knuckles, so I'd already written him off. But I can set you two up. You can cry over bad Cajun food together. Maybe you can try giving cooking another stab. He looked strong enough to yank out that black iron pot you have rusting in the back of that cabinet."

"Oh, I'm good, thank you very much."

We settle down some and order another round of drinks.

"Saw Howie again," Candy says.

I clench my jaw a little. Just for a moment, I wonder if they're dating, but I know he'd never go for her.

My phone jumps to life on the table, buzzing loudly once then falling silent. My heart drops and Danielle squeezes my hand under the table. I reach for it, gingerly almost, and unlock the screen to find an email notification from work.

"Christ."

"What is it?" Danielle asks.

"One of the reporters has an earth-shattering story that needs to be copy-edited and posted immediately."

"Really?" Candy asks.

"Yeah. The California Lottery picked a new ad agency. I'm off the clock. Somebody else's problem."

Still, the alert rattles me. My heart's racing and it takes effort to stop my hands from shaking. I was convinced it was Kendra-Sue with either bad news or a couple of words about me sitting in a bar laughing it up with my friends. After excusing myself, I take my phone to the bathroom and do a quick scroll through Facebook, where I'm relieved not to find anything new about Karen-Anne. So I go back to my friends and power through two more drinks while I pretend that I'm not worrying about my sister.

But in the cab on the way back to Brooklyn, I fire up the phone and find an update from Lucy, Karen-Anne's youngest:

"Mama has a fever. Getting higher. Doctor says it might be an infection."

I take a deep breath and call Kendra-Sue. No one answers. So what do I do? I go to the Brazen Head, looking for Jack Daniel and maybe Grayson. Instead, I get chatted up by a thirty-year-old who spends an hour telling me how hot he thinks older women are. I make out with him despite that.

■ ■ ■

On Friday, I find myself in the lowest part of the deepest valley of uselessness. I read a story over and over and can't remember what I've read well enough to write a headline. Chewing my hair, I return to Facebook repeatedly, hitting the refresh key as if it were pumping antibiotics and clean blood into Karen-Anne, waiting for a status update of hope. Writing headlines about advertising industry news, headlines that will both engage a reader *and* trick the Google gods into putting a story atop its search results—well, that just seems like the stupidest thing in the world to be doing, stupider than teeth on a chicken.

But not quite as stupid as spending one of the busiest days of the week with Facebook prominently displayed on my monitor.

There are whispers of layoffs. And that closed-door meeting the top editors held earlier in the week.

As if on cue, the boss man stands up from his cubicle, sighs deeply and walks into one of the conference rooms and says, "Hi," to someone already in there. Five minutes after he closes the door, two of the suits, in town from Detroit or Chicago, join them.

I finish typing the headline I'm working on and wander to the bathroom, stopping by the conference room to see if maybe, just maybe, I can hear something.

While I'm standing there, the door opens and the boss man, exiting the room with his head down, runs right into me.

"Shit," he says. "Sorry, Katherine. Sorry."

"It's fine," I say, hoping I don't look too guilty.

For some reason, he glances to either side of me, behind me, as if keeping an eye out for approaching enemies. He clears his throat and says, "I was just coming to look for you, as a matter of fact."

"That can't be good." I try my best to force a laugh, even as my stomach starts to crawl up into my chest.

He winces, then pushes the door all the way open and ushers me in. Lined up on one side of the table are the suits, including a woman from human resources.

"Come in. Have a seat," the human resources woman says, with some amount of concern in her voice. Then she looks down at a stack of folders and shuffles through them. "Katherine, right?"

For a moment, I plant my heels in the carpet and consider grabbing the doorframe and forcing them to drag me in.

"Katherine," the boss man whispers, putting his hand on the small of my back.

"Shit," I say.

What follows is a blur of corporate speak about the challenges facing the industry, tough decisions, moving forward and yadda, yadda, yadda. It's all very businesslike, nothing personal—almost as if it's designed to lull the victim into serenely accepting fate. Not that I could do anything about it anyway. The company is in a bind. I get it. And these people are just doing their jobs. I can't hold that against them.

But then the HR woman says, "Really, think of it as an opportunity. And we'll be giving you some material regarding other possibilities, continuing education, and professional development."

I swear I can feel blood vessels bursting in my brain.

"How old are you?" I ask her.

She looks up from her script.

"Excuse me?"

"How old are you?"

She stammers a bit before one of the suits cuts in. "That's not exactly relevant here."

"Really? Not relevant. A woman my age? I'll just be able to walk out onto Lexington and find a job. Or take some classes to land some exciting new opportunities? You look like you're getting up there. What if you're next?"

I'm building up a head of steam, ready to start shouting. I want to point at the HR woman, with her sensible suit and neat hair and stockings and pearl necklace, and scream, "SHAAAAAMMMME!"

In fact, I'm standing up to do just that, when it occurs to me that all three of them have been through this before. There's probably nothing I can say or do that they haven't heard.

I plop down in my seat. "You know, my sister is in the hospital right this minute. Could be dying. So thanks for rounding out a wonderful week."

The HR woman flinches, just a little bit.

The boss man says nothing.

I put my elbows on the table, my head in my hands, and start massaging my temples. "Look, let's just talk severance and get me out of here."

So they do. In exchange for my agreeing to not come back with a gun to shoot the place up or take to a blog and trash the company, I get a full twelve months. Which is nothing to sneeze at. I shake my head. I sign my papers.

On the way out, the HR woman asks me if I can send Vanessa in.

"Do your own dirty work," I tell her.

I return to my desk and fumble through my stuff. They've given me a box for my belongings, but even with thirteen years of crap accumulated on the desk, I come up with only enough items—a really old photo of Kendra-Sue and me as little girls, a black-and-white publicity still from the show "Sanford and Son," a copy of *Elements of Style,* postcards that I picked up in Thailand, Peru, Italy, Croatia, and beyond—to fill it halfway.

No one says anything to me. They see me packing up, Vanessa coming out of the conference room a hot mess of tears and hyperventilation, and all heads go down in prayer, *Please not me, please not me.* For the moment, we're tainted goods, filthy with layoff cooties that might rub off on them.

I head home and order three thousand calories of fried substances from The Chip Shop and stare at Facebook, hands hovering over the keyboard just ready to type out a rant against corporate America. But nothing comes out. It's not *just* the twelve months severance they bribed me with. I'm not really feeling anything. Maybe it will kick in later. Maybe I'll get dressed Monday morning and get halfway to Manhattan before I realize I don't have a place to go, then I'll be one of those people crying on the train. I consider texting Candy or Danielle, maybe walking over to the bar, but then I'd have to talk about it, then I might feel something—probably humiliation or shame, more than anything. And someone might ask me what I'm going to do next, a question for which I have no answer.

So I go back to Facebook and look for status updates from the family. While I was getting laid off, they've all fallen silent and I can't help but worry.

An update from Lucy confirms my fears: "They're putting her on dialysis. Please pray for her." Things are possibly getting too serious for Facebook. Or maybe everyone is gathered in one place.

I try Kendra-Sue again. Her cell. Her house. "Call me," is all I can say. Any more words than that, I might do something foolish like yell at her for not keeping me in the loop. I try Kurt Junior. Nothing. I consider other family members, but I can't bring myself to call them. I justify my cowardice by saying it would be an unnecessary intrusion. No one needs distant Aunt Katie-Lee calling at this horrible time with useless, awkward words.

I check Facebook again. In between all the check-ins at bars and photos of food, there's a new status update from Lucy.

"Doesn't look good. Doctor says if she can make it through the night, she has a chance. We need a miracle. Please pray for us."

CHAPTER FIVE

I don't need to look at the Caller ID to know that my cell phone is vibrating with bad news, an angry bee buzzing to life, the light of its screen breaking the pre-dawn darkness of the living room. I must have fallen asleep on the couch after taking an Ambien.

Area code: 337. South Louisiana.

Name: Kendra-Sue Andrepont.

Picture: One of Kendra-Sue's grandchildren or great-grandchildren, laughing, his face and blond hair smeared with strawberry jelly or, possibly, squirrel blood.

I don't want to answer, don't know if I can take the news, survive the heartbreak, the devastation in her voice. But I have no choice. I feel my heart clenching up as I press talk.

"Kendra-Sue," I say, my first words of the day hoarse, trying to will away the possibility of this call ever taking place.

Silence on the other side. Has the signal dropped?

"Hello?" I ask.

"Katie-Lee," she says. In her mouth, this morning, it's a hiccup almost, one moistened with the tears she's struggling to hold back—

or the few she has left after a night of crying. "Katie-Lee," she says again.

"Kendra-Sue." I wonder for a moment if we are now stuck, doomed to repeat one another's names for all eternity.

"It's—" Her voice drops to a whisper. "It's Karen-Anne." Another pause while she calls on some last reserve of strength. "She passed this morning. She's gone."

What she's saying makes no sense, the words rattling around in my chest, bruising my heart to a degree I thought no longer possible.

"Damn it, Katie-Lee, say something. Anything."

"Tooth Fairy," I say.

She's silent for a moment. Anyone else in the world would think I'm crazy—in shock, mumbling nonsense. I'm not even sure Kurt Junior or Karla-Jean would make the connection. But Kendra-Sue and I, even if we rarely talk anymore, share a common language, similar sensibilities.

"I haven't thought about that in years." I think I can hear a sad smile in her voice. "She never forgave that dog, did she?"

Quiet again. The only sound is a snowplow scraping down Court Street.

Finally Kendra-Sue speaks. "You don't have a choice on this one," she says.

I feel a hot flush of indignation, but swallow it down. Now is not the time. "Of course not," I say. "Have yall made any arrangements?"

"Nothing yet," she says. "Just try to get in as soon as possible."

"I will. I promise."

"Love you," she says, catching me completely off guard.

"Love you, too," I choke out, before hanging up the phone and crying.

▫ ▫ ▫

"So, what you're telling me is that a bereavement fare is actually more expensive than the regular fare?" I ask the Delta woman.

It's seven-thirty in the morning and I'm already on my second phone call of the day. Some kind of record. Too early for this, too early to be so close to screaming at a customer-service representative. And I'd forgotten to pin up my hair last night, which is now a tangled mess, a wilderness of knots, a jungle that little lice and baby bedbugs whisper about around campfires when trying to scare each other. On a good day, such a snarl makes me feel claustrophobic and defensive—an imagined chorus of "I told you so" and "A woman your age with that much hair. What did you expect?" echoing in my head.

This, obviously, is far from a good day.

"This makes absolutely no sense to me," I say.

"I know, ma'am. And I'm soooo sorry." She's got an accent, Georgian sorority girl, the sort that even the most studious Bangladeshi call-center operator could never duplicate, filled with sympathy, apology, and condescension all at once. This annoys me even more. "I guess it's maybe because the bereavement fare has flexible dates," she tells me.

"Or I guess maybe Delta Airlines likes to take advantage of people who are grieving. Maybe Delta can't pass up an opportunity to fuck someone over." I want to rattle her, feel a compulsive need to shake up her little world. "Bend 'em right over a barrel. Right up the ass! No lube!"

"Ma'am, I'm sure that's not the case."

"Yeah, I bet you're sure. My sister is dead and you're offering me a special rate of over six hundred dollars."

I punch the talk button as hard as I can, not for the first time in my life wishing I still had a landline and a proper phone, one with a cradle into which I could slam a handset.

I book the flight into Baton Rouge online, reserve a car without incident and then start to type an email to work requesting the days off, then I remember I have no job.

I've got to be at LaGuardia by 11 to catch the noon flight, which means I have to leave here at 10, in case of traffic. That gives me two hours to shower, pack and drop the mail keys off with Haleema, my neighbor and the building's super. I'd prefer to put them in an envelope and slide them under the door, but I can tell she's home by the cigarette smoke wafting its way from her bedroom window to mine, the cold morning air carrying her breath to me.

First things first, though. One Lexapro and half a bottle of hair conditioner later, I'm out of the shower, dressed and staring at a carry-on empty save for the Ziploc bag full of toiletries always ready to go. I consider myself a professional packer, but I'm momentarily stumped. What does one pack for a funeral in Louisiana? I've got plenty of black. I'm a New Yorker, after all. I toss in an extra pair of skinny jeans, sweatshirts, a few severe and age-appropriate dresses that will likely make me the most over-dressed person at the services, a couple of handfuls of undies and bras and deem the job done.

Now for Haleema. This is going to be difficult. To say she's emotional is like saying water is wet, the Pope Catholic. In fact, as I step into the hall between our apartments, I can hear her yelling. At the TV? Into the phone? In anger or anguish or delight? Who knows. She's speaking Arabic, a language that always sounds threatening to me. That she's a Lebanese Christian of strong opinions about many things only adds to the effect.

"Filthy Shia!" she yells in English. "Let Israel kill them if nobody else will!"

But when she opens the door, she's all smiles.

"Oh, Katherine! Come in, come in," she says. "You didn't go out last night? I hear you come back in early and not leave."

Anyone else spying on me like that, I might call the cops. But Haleema does it out of a neighborly concern that borders on mothering.

Haleema reminds me of Mama. Daddy. Creatures of smoke. I remember them sitting on the front porch of the old house in Grand Prairie just after the sun had set over the fields they'd never own, the two of them hidden in shadow, creaking back and forth in their rockers, the twin embers of those ever-present cigarettes glowing like dragon eyes in the darkness.

They'd both lived lives of deprivation and hard work and war that aged them beyond their years. To say they lived through the Great Depression would be a little inaccurate. Growing up sharecroppers in South Louisiana, their entire lives prior to World War II were a nonstop depression. Money was so rare as to be almost abstract. And Daddy never went to school enough as a boy to even think of taking advantage of the G.I. Bill. I imagine he was paid something for fighting in the war, but I suspect he might have blown it all on drinking the memories away when he returned to the States. Neither he nor Mama ever talked much about life before they met, but there was no escaping that they were extremely late starters for South Louisiana at that time. They met in '51, married in '52, and Kurt Junior came along in '53, when Daddy was twenty-seven and Mama, twenty-two. "Wasn't ready and nobody else was right," is all Daddy would ever say about why he waited so long to settle down. Whatever it was that happened to him in the South Pacific, it took him five years to get it out of his system—or enough of it out that he could consider starting a family.

The farming too, it aged them. Baking in the fields most of the year, sunup to sundown. I remember Mama being pretty. I do. But fact was, by the time she was forty, her hair had gone white and her skin was every bit as leathery as Daddy's. Her smoking didn't help either. By the time she finally got her house in town, the fields had permanently left their mark on her.

"You going on a trip?" Haleema asks me.

"I'm afraid so," I say.

Before I can explain, she's off.

"Give me your keys. I check your mail for you. Sit. Have a coffee. You have time for a coffee? Or some tea maybe?" She wanders into the kitchen, raising her voice. "I was on the phone with my friend Hasim. Men! Ridiculous, these men. He's divorced, you know, but his ex-wife, she take him to the doctor still. But he likes the nurse at the doctor's office, but don't know what to do. 'Hasim,' I tell him, 'ask her for coffee. Take her on a date.' But he worried she's going to divorce him, too, so he don't want to get involved. 'You're going to need a wife, Hasim,' I tell him. 'Your ex-wife is not going to always take you to the doctor.' "

I glance at my watch. Somehow, I have a little time before I need to leave for the airport. "So why did his first wife divorce him?"

"Who knows?" Haleema says, placing cup and saucer on the small coffee table before me. "Maybe he's too fat. Maybe he don't do the sex to her the way she likes. He ask me out, I said to him, 'Hasim, you a nice man, but I'm done with men. For good, done with them.' "

She may look like Mama, but it occurs to me she's more like me.

"So where are you going?" Haleema says, finally getting down to business.

"To Louisiana."

"Oh, where you're from, no?"

"Yes."

"Everything okay?" she asks, now suspecting something. It's unlike me to drop in an hour before leaving.

I pause, gather strength. I don't know how I'm going to react to voicing the words to someone else. I don't know how she's going to react.

"It's my sister. My little sister."

"Oh no," Haleema is saying already. "Oh, Katherine."

"She died. Last night."

I'm on the verge of crying, but Haleema, who gets weepy when talking about her own sisters in Lebanon, beats me to it. Tears streaming down her face, she stands up, fans herself with her hands.

"Oh no, Katherine. I am so sorry. So sorry." She's sobbing now. I wonder briefly if she's going to make that trilling, wailing sound that Middle Eastern women make. Or is that only a Muslim thing?

I stand up with her. "Haleema," I say, "it's okay." Of course it's not okay. And I don't know quite why I'm comforting her, but focusing on that allows me to regain my composure.

"No. It's not okay," Haleema says, sounding almost like a petulant child. "It's not okay." She starts walking the apartment. "Your sisters, they are like your best friends. I don't know what I'd do if one of my sisters died. I don't see them often. But I feel them. In my heart, I feel them. I talk to them all the time. Once a week at least. On the phone." Which is a lot more than I do. "If they were gone, I'd be alone. Completely alone. That's no way to go through life. No way. You have anyone else? Other sisters?"

"Yes, two other sisters," I tell her.

"Good, this is good." My answer seems to calm her down some. She doesn't even ask about brothers.

I stop her from pacing, grab her arm, pat her hand.

"We'll be okay," I tell her. "I promise. We're going to be okay."

CHAPTER SIX

After calling a car, I escape Haleema's apartment and head downstairs to stand in the cold air, watching the last flakes of last night's flurries melt in my hair, on my coat. So far it's only a dusting, just enough to cover the mounds plowed on either side of the road with a fresh coat of white, giving it all the appearance of a winter wonderland, a Southerner's idea of what snow might look like, a hushed world of fluffy drifts. It's a false front, an illusion shattered the moment a plow goes scraping down the street, adding another layer of black slush to the frozen heaps burying garbage bags, strollers, and bikes.

Also breaking the spell is one of the local crazies, standing out in front of the CVS, loudly declaring to the world, "She got a big ole dick and two big ole balls! Yessir! Big ole dick and two big ole balls!"

I hope he's not talking about me.

My phone buzzes once.

A text from Candy. "We still on for brunch this morning?"

"God damn it," I say, loud enough for the crazy across the street to notice me.

He points at me and screams, "She got a big ole dick and two big ole balls."

I step back inside my building and text Candy. "So sorry. Have to cancel. Something came up."

"That's too bad. I was really looking forward to it." Am I imagining a passive-aggressive sigh emanating from the phone?

I can tell her Karen-Anne died. But that would lead to a phone call. To details. Possibly to her saying it's just like that one time her uncle died from old age. She might then offer to come to Louisiana with me.

"Family emergency," I type back. "Getting on plane now. Will explain later."

Despite explaining that I'm getting on a plane, the phone rings and Candy's number pops up. I ignore it. She leaves a voicemail. "Hi Katherine. It's Candy. I hope everything is okay. I know you said you're getting on a plane, but I figured I'd try to call anyway. Do they let you use the phone on the plane anymore?" She's refused to step on a plane since 9/11, but the truth is she was terrified of them before then. "Anyway. I hope everything is okay. Call me when you land. Of if you need anything."

I reach up to the little window set into the building's front door and draw a frowny-face emoticon. The glass is cold against the tip of my finger. Frigid air swirls beneath the door and around my feet—I can feel it through my shoes.

The car shows up to whisk me off toward the airport, passing winter wastelands of filthy snow. Disgusting, sure, but one of the few times that 21st century New York resembles the wolves' den I moved to thirty years ago, back when even nice white girls living in Manhattan could end up on the wrong side of a knife if they weren't careful. Kids these days. They have it so easy when they get here. *Shut up, Katie-Lee,* I tell myself. I don't want to be that person, the one who thinks living in a cesspool is some badge of honor, something preferable to a clean, safe place. I came here for no other reason than to escape—escape home, escape pain, escape death.

And now I'm going back.

But first I have to endure something perhaps worse than all of that, LaGuardia on a Saturday, populated with frustrated families and the last of the angry, beat-down stragglers stranded by the previous snow. Finally able to make their escape, they don't know whether to laugh or cry. I don't either. But I make it through security in a timely fashion and, minor miracle piling upon minor miracle, the flight leaves on time, landing me in Atlanta, where I find a Popeyes in the terminal from which my BTR-bound flight is departing. Despite everything—my confusion, my heartache, my apprehension, my certainty that I'll be eating plenty of fried chicken in the oncoming days—I grab a seat and a two-piece dark, pull up Facebook, and check in. I just can't help myself.

And then the peculiar string of luck comes to an end when I feel a presence hovering over me. I look up, chicken leg still in my mouth, to see my ex-husband standing there.

He looks like he hasn't aged a day over thirty-five, the luck of the Asian. Especially galling since he'd let himself go to middle-aged chub during our brief marriage, the sort of man who'd wear a tropical shirt and solve cases on the beach in Hawaii. Now he's a rather strapping fellow, effortlessly stylish even on a Saturday, watching me shovel food into my face.

"Katherine," he says.

"Howie," I say.

"I'm sorry about your loss," he says.

How did he know? I don't have to look farther than the phone in my hand for my answer. Of course he'd know. We'd never taken the final step of unfriending one another on Facebook. He'd blocked me from his status stream immediately after the divorce—he'd told me as much during another of our chance encounters—but I guess he got over me enough to lift that particular ban.

I say got over me as if I had him wrapped in some sort of spell, as if I were the love of his life. That couldn't be farther from the truth—despite all the protestations he made when I left him. I wasn't any more the love of his life than he was of mine. What Howie had to get over, ultimately, was his wounded pride, his anger that I was the first one to recognize we were floating the sea of love not on a cruise ship or yacht or sailboat, but on a container vessel—a stable, dull thing built only to carry us safely to the end of our lives. Not even two years into the voyage, it was covered in barnacles and rust. I simply jumped ship first.

We'd eloped, Howie and me. No family invited. Truth is, even if I were the sort to return home frequently, I would have been terrified to bring him to Louisiana. In my imagination unspooled a dramatically racist blow-up from Kurt Junior, who'd fought in Vietnam and been scarred by it. His little sister turning up with an Asian man? Forget about it. I sent out the good word via email, with no photos. This was 2004. We weren't on Facebook yet.

And things were what they were until, one Tuesday morning, on my way to work, I walked out of the magazine shop without buying the Mega Millions and Powerball tickets I picked up twice a week. I realized that the thought of winning horrified me. If I won—if we won—we'd be stuck together forever. There'd be no escape, not without the sort of legal battle that would scorch our worlds completely. I tried to shake my head clear. I was being foolish. What were the chances of actually winning the lottery? But that was beside the point, wasn't it? It was that the thought of living with Howie for the rest of my life—even if I had $55 million dollars—filled me with dread.

And that's how it started, my midlife crisis. There I stood, on the sidewalk on 44th Street between Lexington and Third, staring off into the middle distance, mouth slightly open, looking for all the world like a mental defective. What was I doing with my life? None of this was meant to be. I'd been dealt my hand by fate and I'd tried to ditch it by marrying Howie. And this job? Why was I toiling away at this cubicle farm day in and day out? How much longer did I have left? Was I going to spend it toiling at a trade magazine, returning home to a dull marriage every day? Shouldn't I be doing something that mattered? Handing out medicine in the Amazon? Fighting for women's rights in Afghanistan? My chest tightened, my breath became shallow, the world went fuzzy and I had my very first panic attack. It wasn't to be my last. After the first, they came on more and more frequently. I couldn't hide them from Howie, of course, since he set them off as much as anything else. So I gave him the line about the job, about how my life lacked meaning. "So quit," he said. "We can afford it. Find something you like."

I went to a therapist and got from him what I wanted—a prescription. As for the therapy itself? It was doomed from the start. I was probably more honest with Howie than I ever was with Dr. Feinstein. And Dr. O'Hara. And Dr. Klowaski. I did some shopping until I found a therapist content just to leave me to talk and cry for an hour without prying. As an ex-Catholic, I expected to tell what I felt like telling, do my penance, and otherwise be left alone. It wasn't polite to go nosing around where you weren't wanted.

It didn't work. Ultimately, I gave Howie notice. We didn't own much together, but I lost quite a bit in the split, including a number of friends. I'll say this much for Howie: He engendered loyalty. I also lost the ability to trust myself not to hurt other people. I once fancied myself better than that, than to lead someone along, be so careless with a heart. But I guess I wasn't.

And now he sits here before me, his face full of concern for my family and me.

"How did you know?" I ask him, mostly for lack of anything better to say.

"Ah, you know," he says, sort of embarrassed. "Kendra-Sue and a couple of your cousins or nieces or something friended me. Saw it in their feeds."

Traitors.

"How are you holding up?" he asks.

"What are you doing here?" I counter.

"Business trip. Just blowing through," he says. "Long layover, saw your Facebook check-in. You okay?" He reaches across the table and takes one of my fries. The man could eat during a nuclear attack. He sits there like this is perfectly natural, like he belongs here checking up on me.

The scary thing? It almost feels right.

"Yeah, I'm fine," I say. "Well, I don't know. I haven't processed it yet. It doesn't make any sense. Get to be our age, going to the doctor, maintaining, trying to stave off thoughts of death. I mean, I guess it's going to start happening sooner or later, but I figured it would be Kurt Junior or Karla-Jean, cancer, heart attack. But this? Christ."

"When's the last time you went home?"

I look down at my food, lose my appetite in a hot flush of shame. "According to Candy, four years. Or five, maybe."

"Oof. That's going to be rough." He's not judging me. He joked sometimes that he wished his folks lived in a state other than Jersey so he'd have a valid excuse not to see them for years at a time. "I guess Kendra-Sue's probably not going to go easy on you."

"So, what, you two are best buds now?"

"Facebook's a funny thing. Besides, are you kidding me? Oh my god, she's hilarious."

I slap his hands out of my fries. "Fuck you," I say, laughing. "Speaking of traitors, Candy seems to run into you a lot. Tells me you're still mad."

He shrugs as if to signify that he can't help himself on that one, that I still have some penance to do.

"Admit it," I say, "if we'd stayed married, it'd be you leaving me at this point. You'd have gotten bored with my misery. Hell, you didn't even get the full brunt of my midlife crisis."

He chuckles, but looks down at his hands, seriously considering the question. One thing about Howie, he never liked to talk out of his ass. "Hard to say," he says. "I thought I was in it for the long haul. And, sometimes, I walk by some old place we used to hang out and—" He stops.

"Sad?" I ask. "Depressed?"

"Pissed, mostly."

I don't move, don't breathe.

He recovers. He was always good at that, Howie, pulling himself out of a tailspin—in public, at any rate. "But I got no complaints at the moment, I guess."

"You're looking good, at least," I say. "Lost some weight."

"See what you're missing out on?"

"Yeah, well, you weren't looking like that when we split."

"That's what marriage is about, richer or poorer, sickness and health, skinny or fat."

"You know damn well neither of us agreed to that last one." It's true. Even as old as we were, we were still shallow.

Our laughter fades away.

"Look, Katherine, I know this is going to be hard for you, going home. And I know how weird this sounds, but if you need some support, I'll change my flight right now and go back with you."

I look straight at him. "You're serious, aren't you?"

"As dirt," he says.

A flood of emotion washes over me and I have to bite my bottom lip, push the balls of my feet into the floor with all my might and look to the ceiling to stop myself from crying. If so much as a tear trickles down my cheek I'm going to lose it. Completely. A sobbing mess right here in the Popeyes in the airport.

"Hey," he says, "there's no crying in Popeyes."

I shake my head and wave at him to be quiet. "That's not helping," I manage.

Who the hell is he to make so generous an offer? He told me he'd hate me forever, laughed at my guilt-ridden suggestions that we could still be friends, spend holidays together if we were both extremely lonely. And now? Now he's offering to go to Louisiana with me, to a funeral, right into the fire.

I'm tempted, sorely tempted. To have at least one ally there, someone to stand as buffer between Kendra-Sue and me.

But who am I kidding? The thought of explaining to everyone who he is . . . "No, he's my ex-husband. We're just friends now." The quizzical looks. The sidelong glances. And Kurt Junior. God knows what he'd think.

"God, Howie," I say, finally finding my voice. "I want to. Really. Believe me. But I just don't think it's a good idea."

I expect him to slouch into a sulk, but he doesn't. "Hey," he says, putting up his hands. "Trust me. I understand." He grabs another fry. I don't know what he's on, but I want some of it.

"Seriously, Howie. Thanks even for the offer. I don't deserve it."

"Oh, we both know that," he says, smiling. "But look, Katie-Lee." He's the only person outside of Louisiana I allowed to use that name. "If you need anything, call, text, Facebook, tweet. Send smoke signals. Really."

"You're going to make me cry, god damn it," I say.

"Actually, you're going to miss your plane," he says, tapping his watch. "BTR outbound is boarding in five minutes."

No sooner does he say it than an announcement is made for the flight.

I stand. He stands.

"I'm not going to offer to hug you," he says.

"Thank you," I say, picking up my bag.

"Safe flying."

I walk off down the terminal, looking back over my shoulder only once. He's still there, standing, watching me go, eating my French fries.

And then I'm on a plane, winging my way back to Louisiana, not at all prepared for whatever it is I'm about to face.

CHAPTER SEVEN

The flight from Atlanta to Baton Rouge is a short hop on a small plane. I'd wanted the single seat on the left side of the pencil-thin jet, but no luck today. And when I get to my row, I find a broad-shouldered older woman sitting in my place. Her waist-length hair would mark her as a kindred spirit, but her long denim skirt and lack of makeup tell me she's a Pentecostal. Great. Just what I need. Someone preaching to me about the Holy Ghost for the length of the flight.

"I know I took your seat," she says, smiling at me. "But I was hoping you wouldn't mind the window. I get nervous looking at the wing on these tee-tiny little planes."

Shut up, shove over and close the shade, sister, is the first thought that comes to mind.

"That's fine," I say. There's enough misery floating around in the world at the moment. I'm not a fan of plane-talkers, unless they're single, attractive men interested in mature women. But the one thing worse than a plane-yakker, which she seems to be, is a plane-hysteric or a plane-clutching-the-armrest-hyperventilating-crying-and possibly-puking neurotic, which she'll turn into if she has to look at the stupid wing.

Besides, Harriet—as she introduces herself—will be a welcome distraction. Walking through the Jetway in Atlanta, my throat went dry, my mouth coppery—as good a sign as any that the anxiety about Louisiana was bubbling up, that I'd be stewing in it for the hour-and-a-half flight, possibly becoming a plane-crier myself before we landed.

Harriet and her husband had been up to Greenville, South Carolina, for a dog show. He was driving back to Melville, Louisiana, with the dog.

"These small planes make me nervous," she tells me, "but it's not nearly as bad as spending two days in a car with Ray."

"So how'd you do?" I ask, picturing Harriet or Ray shuffling around a convention-center floor behind an excitable coonhound.

"Best in show," she says nonchalantly. "No point traveling all that way just to come in second is what I say."

Well, excuse me. I've already written their story. Childless, they bought the dog to fill the void and lavished years of attention on her, raising her as a child, buying her clothes, feeding her steak and chicken, putting her in pageants. Somewhere in a scrapbook made originally for babies were photos of Harriet and Ray holding the puppy, walking it in a stroller. Maybe there was even a photo of Ray and the dog, standing on its hind legs and wearing a bow, dancing when she turned sixteen in dog years.

"Do you have any photos?"

Harriet starts riffling through her purse. "Ray kept the camera," she says. "He's working on this series of photos of people at rest areas. I thought he was crazy at first. It seems a little creepy. But they're real interesting. He already had one show at a gallery in Baton Rouge and he's got one lined up in New Orleans. At his age. Imagine that."

I'm trying to. But all I see is a ruddy-faced, white-haired, pot-bellied man in overalls standing outside a rest area with a Polaroid camera, lining strangers up. "Come on. Just one second. Yall smile."

"Here. Take one of these," she says, handing me a postcard from the Baton Rouge show. The photo is striking, taken from some vantage point to the side of a rest area in Mississippi, probably from a picnic table in the dog-walking area. The focus is on a trucker, head down, lighting a cigarette. But his eyes drag the viewer's over to a family, walking toward the main building, in the middle of a complete meltdown. Two teens sulking, a dad who looks like he's just blown his stack and a haggard mom dragging a screaming kid who's trying to plant her feet into the sidewalk.

I shudder at the sight of it.

"Oh, here we go," Harriet says, producing an iPhone.

The opening screen isn't the dog, as I'd been expecting, but Machu Picchu, Harriet and, I assume, Ray standing in front of a llama—or is it an alpaca? Ray is tall, skinny as a beanpole, wearing glasses and not a lick of hair on his head.

"Two years ago we did that," she says. "Beautiful. But goodness, that altitude like to kill me. And the potatoes! Those people sure like their potatoes. I've never seen so many. And I grew up on a sweet-potato farm. And those little guinea pigs some of them eat? Well, they just put them on a fire and cook them tough. Imagine cooking a squirrel like that. It would take you three days to eat the thing. Well, bless it if Ray didn't just get up, go in the kitchen and spend two hours showing them how to make a gravy."

I can't believe this, but I think I want Harriet to be my friend.

She slides the phone open, shuffles screens around and pokes up a photo of the dog, a ghost-gray Weimaraner. Beautiful dog, but they always put me in mind of a depressed Labrador Retriever. I keep that thought to myself as Harriet slides over to another photo of the dog on the show floor, marching slightly ahead of a matching man. There's no other way to describe it. Svelte, late thirties, trim gray suit, salon-styled hair, expensive shoes glistening under the auditorium lights.

"Who's that?"

Harriet laughs as if I'd said something funny. "Oh, that's Gavin, the handler. Handsome boy, but not exactly interested in women, if you know what I mean. Gretchen, our youngest daughter, was doing it for a bit, but she—" Harriet pauses, considers her words. "Well, I hate to say it, but dressing like a Pentecostal wasn't helping our chances. Besides, Gretchen just didn't have the winning touch. Ray wasn't too crazy about hiring a gay fella but I said to him, 'Ray, you want to win or you just want to drive around the country losing?' That made his mind up."

"So you have kids?"

"Three. All grown and out of our hair. I tell you, we were nervous. What were we going to do with all that time? But we fill it up. I'm fifty-five. Ray's sixty-five. We both got our health and some money saved up. So we don't sit still for long."

When I tell Harriet I live in New York, she says she'd never be able to live in such a place, but then proceeds to tell me every Broadway show they've ever been to. She's been to Top of the Rock, top of the Empire and even the top of the World Trade Center back when that was possible. She's been to Coney Island and the Guggenheim. She's been to the Natural History Museum and the Met—"the opera one and the art museum one," where Ray, typically, loved the medieval armor and she, despite herself, fell for all that Catholic and Byzantine Christian imagery.

"I know it's all idolatry and such, but it's so beautiful. Brother Martin, our preacher, would die if he heard me say it, but I could spend a month in Rome just walking around looking at all that Catholic stuff. But, hey, the Lord God gave us this world to see," she says, looking up at me and dropping the iPhone and its world of pictures into her lap. "Might as well git!" Here she pushes the palms of her hands together and then apart in motion that has the top one taking off like a plane. "Besides, I like to stay one step ahead of death. And when he does catch up to me and I get to them Pearly Gates and ol' St. Pete asks me what I done with my life, I hope I have an interesting story or two to tell him."

That makes me smile. I bet St. Pete's getting a good one from Karen-Anne right about now. "A rhino? In Louisiana? Get the hell out of here!" He then takes her by the arm and leads her off to a booth for a pitcher of beer. "Girl, you're gonna have to sit down and tell me this one."

"Anyway," continues Harriet, "if you don't keep moving at our age, you'll go out of your mind, just sitting there wondering what you've done with your time and how much you have left before your teeth fall out and the kids put you in a home."

What could she have been if she hadn't married at sixteen, hadn't been saddled with kids most of her adult life, if she'd had the benefit of college education and pop culture? I guess she could have been a single woman of fifty this close to getting a cat and looking into the mirror in the morning contemplating cosmetic surgery. Hell, I bet Harriet, shaped like a giant turnip as she is, doesn't even have body issues. It almost makes me hate her. Just a little bit.

"And what about you?" she asks.

"Me?" Where would I even start?

"What brings you to Louisiana?"

Oh. Is that all?

"Just going to visit family," I say.

"Really? Where from?"

"Ville Platte. Opelousas," remembering only now just how close those towns are to Melville, that this could lead to a guessing game called "Who's your mama and them?" and, before we know it, we're related and she's holding my hand and telling me how sorry she is about Karen-Anne.

But I'm saved by the bell—and the captain. "Folks, we are making our final approach," he says in that God-like voice they all have. Harriet's face goes white and she hustles to put the iPhone back in the purse and the purse back under the seat in front of her, as if by breaking the rules she'd personally bring down the plane.

"Shoot." She looks at me, her eyes pleading for understanding. "It's these small planes," she says. "Get me every time."

As if on cue, the plane drops and lurches through a crosswind or a downdraft or a gremlin attack. Whatever it is, Harriet grabs my hand.

"I'm sorry," she says, embarrassed now, her cheeks and neck

flushing bright red, no makeup there to hide it.

"It's okay. Why don't you tell me the worst ride you've been on?" I ask.

The tale that follows—involving an Alaskan bush plane, 800 gallons of gasoline, a remote mining outpost and Sarah Palin—is beyond belief, but it gets us to the gate without Harriet breaking my fingers. In the main lobby at BTR, we go our separate ways, she toward the parking garage, me to wherever it is they hide the rental counter. Before parting, I give Harriet my number.

"If you're ever in New York, give me a call."

"We get up that way a bit," she says. "Maybe we will."

"No maybe about it," I find myself insisting. "Promise."

"Okay," she laughs. "Promise."

With that, she's gone, and I'm standing alone in Louisiana, ferried there, I realize, by the sort of Christian conservative we make sport of in New York. BTR is no one's idea of heaven, I'll say that much. It's a small airport and at this time of day slow even for one of its size. The people getting off planes are wearing camo or purple-and-gold LSU gear—in some cases a mixture of both. Those waiting wear the same, as if they're afraid they might forget what state they're in. I can't remember what company I reserved the car with, but as the Enterprise counter is the only one with a person behind it—a bored woman buffing her nails—I don't have to wonder for long. Ten minutes later, I'm standing in a parking garage considering a Toyota Prius.

"Hell." Like I don't have enough of a reputation as a pain in the ass, East Coast, librul elite. When one of the talking heads on Fox News gets going on a good rant, I bet my family members automatically conjure up pictures of me. I peel off my coat—there's a warm breeze blowing—and dig for my sunglasses. It's dark here in the shelter of the garage, but the sun shines brightly beyond its borders. The smell of grass and trees drifts in, mingling with the motor oil and exhaust.

Ten minutes later, I'm still in the garage, sitting in the car. It took me five minutes to figure out what to do with the key—a plastic square thing with no actual key part. And now the car won't start, won't even turn over. The light's on, the radio's playing, but no engine. I'll have to drag my ass all the way back to the counter, swap out the car and—

There's a knock on the window. I scream. Loudly.

It's the counter woman. I roll down the window.

"Sorry," I say, "you scared me."

"It's okay, ma'am," she says in a tone that pretty much indicates it's not okay, that she's had it about up to here.

"I think the car's broken. It won't start."

"It ain't broke, ma'am," she says. "I forgot to tell you how to work it. It's already on."

"What do you mean?" I know what a car sounds like when it's running.

"It's on. Cain't hear it cuz it's electric when it's in park."

"But I don't hear it," I say stupidly, as if she didn't just tell me that it doesn't make any noise when it's in park.

She rolls her eyes, no doubt wondering if she's going to have to raise her voice to make me understand the words coming out of her mouth.

"Put it in reverse, ma'am."

"Okay." I reach down between the seats to find nothing.

"Shifter on the dash to the right of the steering wheel."

"Oh." Sure enough, the shifter is on the dash to the right of the steering wheel, a little knob really. Not a proper shifter at all.

"Okay. It's in reverse. Now what?"

"Now drive."

I can't help but notice she's dropped the *ma'am*. When I tentatively lift my foot off the brake, the car silently rolls backward a couple of inches.

"Weird," I say. "I'm sorry. Thanks."

"That's okay," she says. "Happens to everyone."

"Everyone who's a dumbass," I say, a weak joke offered as apology.

"Your words, not mine," she says, shaking her head and walking off.

Sitting in the garage, I consider my options. I've got five texts and a voicemail from Candy. No voicemail messages from Kendra-Sue with details for tonight or tomorrow or whenever this is supposed to happen.

"Any details yet?" I text and wait for a response. I'm in no hurry.

"Still working on it. Where u?"

"Just landed."

"U can stay hr 2nite."

Ugh. "Okay." A compulsion of mine. I always type out okay, even on phones, even though I've been trained at work by the AP Style Manual to always correct it to OK. To hell with the AP Style Manual. It doesn't like the Oxford comma and still insists on calling people black instead of African American.

"You taking 190 or I-10?"

She can't help herself. I wonder if other families in the area are as obsessed with the route a person takes from Baton Rouge to Opelousas. You could drive into town bleeding from both eyes and chased by flying zombies and one of my siblings would ask, "You took 190 or I-10?" And then fight with you about whatever choice you made—especially if that choice is I-10.

I ignore Kendra-Sue's text and drive. She knows damn well which road I'm taking. She just wants an opportunity to tell me I'm being an idiot. Beyond the darkness of the parking garage, the sun—even this late in the day—is nearly blinding. Not a cloud in the sky and there's still green. Lots of it. The trees, the shrubs, the green, green grass of home, the blades of which are practically jabbing my eyes, accustomed as I am to New York's winter palette of gray, brown and more gray. Don't these people know it's winter?

After making my way through what passes for traffic in Baton Rouge, I mount the Mississippi River Bridge, noticing the changes. Another nosebleed section has been grafted onto Tiger Stadium and a casino complex has sprouted along the riverfront next to the USS *Kidd*, a semifloating, tourist semi-attraction. But it's still the same brown river carrying the same tugs and push boats and barges loaded down with God only knows what kinds of caustic materials from the plants that ugly up the banks on either side.

To the west, on the horizon, I notice twin pillars of smoke rising impossibly high, thinning out at the top where the wind is catching the smoke, spreading it into the sky. My hands tighten on the wheel and I try to keep my eyes focused on the cars in front of me, squinting almost hard enough to give myself a headache. But it's no use. The highway unfurls in front of me, pointing directly at the smoke, sheering more now as the wind picks up, smudging the blue sky brown. By the time I've passed the Waffle House, Adult Video Superstore, and truck stops in Lobdell, I'm driving through a landscape that could pass for Mordor.

They're burning the cane fields. Perfectly rational explanation. It's part of Louisiana's life cycle. They do it every year.

But still.

The sight of acre upon acre of cane going up in smoke sets me off, unleashes something inside of me. Everything I've had tied down tightly since Kendra-Sue's phone call this morning—through willpower, distractions, and Lexapro—comes loose, clattering across the decks, breaking through hatches, tearing down carefully constructed bulkheads reinforced over the years by time and effort. I feel the tears dripping off my chin before I realize I've sprung a leak, that I'm silently crying, which in turn leads me to hyperventilating. Afraid I'll pass out, possibly taking a school bus full of kids with me, I exit at Grosse Tete and pull into the parking lot of the Tiger Truck Stop, where I try to catch my breath and calm myself, batten down the hatches, secure the decks. But the waves of memory and emotion wash over, drowning me.

▫ ▫ ▫

I was sitting in the shade of the carport, butt on the concrete slab, back to the wall, stunned into torpor by the midsummer heat. I hadn't moved for what seemed like hours, but sweat still beaded on my skin. When it gained enough mass and trickled down, it felt like bugs crawling across my body. Nothing moved—neither bird nor beast.

The air was thick with humidity, something to be swallowed rather than breathed. Baby Joey, five years old now, still young enough to be undeterred by heat, was drawing rockets and what he claimed were lunar orbiting modules on the pavement with a piece of chalk Mama had given him. They looked like turtles with spider legs.

I banged the back of my head softly, repeatedly against the house until Mama opened the kitchen door and shouted through the screen.

"I'm not gonna tell you again, Katie-Lee. Cut that out. It's driving me crazy."

"Can I come in the house?" I whined.

With Daddy working at the Lou-Ana plant and Kurt Junior working construction for the summer, they'd been able to scrape enough together to surprise Mama with a window unit for the kitchen. Now she could cook in chilly comfort.

"Yall stay outside. Don't need you under my feet."

"Why Karla-Jean gets to stay in the house?"

"Because Karla-Jean's been helping me all morning. If you want to come inside and shell peas or mop the floor or clean the bathroom, send Joey out to play with Kendra-Sue and Karen-Anne and come on then."

I considered this possibility for a moment or two, but Mama knew she had me.

"Crap," I mumbled to myself.

"What was that, Missy?"

"I said, 'No, ma'am.' I'll just stay out here with Joey."

"That's what I thought," she said. When she closed the door, a burst of cold kitchen air blew through the carport, carrying with it a complicated cloud of odors—Mama's round steak and gravy cooking on the stove, the earthy smell of peas being shelled, Pine-Sol from the bathroom cleaning, and if I wasn't mistaken, a Betty Crocker cake baking in the oven. Mama had never been a big baker back in Grand Prairie, never would have considered it during the summer. But between the twin marvels of air conditioning and boxed cake mixes, she baked at least three times a week after we moved to Opelousas.

Squeals of laughter came from behind the house, where Kendra-Sue and Karen-Anne were sitting under the mulberry trees growing along the fence line. In the two years we'd been living in town, the factions had become set: those two vs. Joey and me. That was the way I'd wanted it, that was the way I'd got it. But I didn't necessarily have to like it.

Living in town. It sounds like we'd moved into a proper city, when in fact we'd landed on the north side of Opelousas in a small house on a concrete slab sitting at the end of Linda Lane, a gravel road jutting from Washington Road into a field. It had probably been named after the daughter of whoever originally owned the big house across the lane, which was empty at the moment, as was the field between us and, in the distance, the projects being built up around North City Park. That empty field just about killed Daddy when he looked at it, all that land going to waste. He'd torn up half the backyard to plant a few rows of vegetables, but he'd stand under the carport after supper smoking cigarettes and looking out at that pasture.

Real town, where Washington Road turned into one-way Main Street just past the massive St. Landry Catholic Church, that was a five-minute car ride away. That's also where the black church—Holy Ghost—was, on Union Street. That's where the bank and Abdalla's and the Ford dealership and Burger Chef and the fire station and the courthouse and the Delta Grand movie house were. Not that we saw much of any of that, except the church. I couldn't have told you what went on during mass. I spent the hour in St. Landry staring into the high rafters, contemplating all the marble and gold, gawking at the other parishioners.

Still, it was town living to us. The house was small, but solid. It had a kitchen, a dining room and, after we'd moved in, three bedrooms. Mama and Daddy took over one bedroom, gave the other to Kurt Junior and Joey, and made what was meant to be the living room—the biggest room in the house—into a room for the girls. We each had our own bed, even if they were bunk beds, Karla-Jean and Kendra-Sue on the tops, Karen-Anne and I on the bottoms. Sleeping alone was weird, but most nights Joey crept out of his and Kurt Junior's room and climbed into bed with me.

Again, Kendra-Sue and Karen-Anne's laughter cut through the soupy air. I stood up and walked through the little breezeway at the back of the carport, between the house and the storeroom. Karen-Anne was hopping around the base of the big mulberry tree like a spastic.

Squinting into the sunlight, I shouted. "What's so funny back there?"

"Why don't you come over here and find out?" Kendra-Sue shouted back.

She was always trying to start something. I had half a mind to go back there, but just thinking about walking through the grass—Daddy hadn't had time to cut it—made my legs itch.

"I don't feel like it."

"Aw, come on," Karen-Anne said. She'd allied with Kendra-Sue, but was always trying to broker peace. That was Karen-Anne, always wanting one big happy family. Her favorite time of day was just after Daddy'd finished his postsupper cigarettes and we'd all sit around in the dining room listening to the radio or watching whatever station we could catch on the little black-and-white TV Mama had made Daddy buy for us. (To her thinking, that wasn't spoiling us, that was progress and education. She was going to drag the family into the 20th century if it bankrupted him.)

"Yall come over here," I countered.

Karen-Anne started to skip over toward the house, but Kendra-Sue grabbed her arm.

"No, yall come out here."

"It's too hot."

"Fine. Stay playing with the baby, you baby."

"Yeah? Well I hope them birds up in that tree shit all over your head!"

We all fell silent, shocked that I'd shouted "shit" so loudly. The kitchen window slid open.

"Katie-Lee! You want me to come out there and switch them legs until they bleed?"

"No ma'am."

"You want to come in here and eat a bar of soap?"

I thought about it. She'd sit me in the corner for at least ten minutes. Ten precious minutes of air conditioning.

"Well?"

But I could already taste the Lava soap on my tongue.

"No ma'am."

"Don't let me hear you again."

With that, the window slid shut. That's how hot it was—so hot Mama wouldn't even come outside to whip me.

I went back to my spot under the carport and plopped my butt down.

Joey stomped over to me.

"I'm not a baby," he said, his lip trembling. "Why yall keep calling me a baby?"

"It's okay, baby," I said without even thinking.

"Quit calling me baby, I said!" He stomped his foot again.

I wanted to laugh, but he looked so upset. I went to pull him onto my lap, but he slapped my hand away.

"Joey, it's just you're the youngest is all. It's just because we all love you so much."

"No," he said.

"No?"

"Look," he said, tears streaming now. He pointed to the spot on the carport where Karen-Anne had earlier written our names in her half-competent scrawl.

Kurt Junior.

Karla-Jean.

Kendra-Sue.

Katie-Lee.

Karen-Anne.

Joey.

Joey had underlined the first letter in each name.

"Yall all got Ks. I got a J. Kendra-Sue said that's because yall found me out in a sweet-potato patch."

He was crying real tears now and although I recognized how funny this was, what I really wanted to do was march back to that mulberry tree, snatch Kendra-Sue by the hair, drag her into the closest ditch, and hold her head down under the water. But the ditch was bone-dry.

"Joey, that's not true. Mama had you right there in that old house in Grand Prairie just like the rest of us."

"I don't remember it."

"Nobody remembers when they were born," I said.

"Then how you know where they got you?"

That was an excellent question. "Well, I don't know where they got me. I don't remember. But I was there when you were born, so I know they didn't find you in a potato patch."

"Hmph."

"Look, Mama gave you a J name because you were special."

"It don't feel special to me."

"But it is."

"No it isn't."

"So what we gonna do then, Joey?"

"I want a K name."

"We can't just change your name."

"Why not?"

I was ten years old at the time and that struck me as an excellent question. Why couldn't we change our names? The fact was I'd already tried. I'd taken a fair amount of ribbing when I started school in Opelousas. All the girls had. We were marked as country come to town—sun-darkened skin, out-of-fashion clothes, thicker Cajun accents, those hyphenated names. *Katie-Lee smells like pee, Kendra-Sue smells like poo, Karen-Anne trapped in the can.* Kendra-Sue reacted by fighting. Karen-Anne played the clown—it was she who provided "trapped in the can" when our tormenters struggled to find a bathroom-related rhyme for her, an ingratiating move, one that took some of the sting out of their taunts and resulted in their teasing her less. Me, I just kept my mouth shut and jumped at the first chance that presented itself. When the homeroom teacher, Ms. Darbonne, said, "Katie-Lee? That must be short for Katherine, right? Old as you are, how about we call you Katherine?" I nodded so hard I thought my head would pop off my neck. Had it been left to me, I would have become Katherine at age nine and stayed that way.

But on the playground that first week, Kendra-Sue cornered me, Karen-Anne in tow.

"What's this shit about you calling yourself Katherine?"

"Shit" was our favorite word. We'd picked it up from Kurt Junior and it made us both feel powerful, like boys.

Karen-Anne pranced around in the background like a princess. "Ooooohhh, hellooooooo. I'm Queen Katherine the Great. Ooooo-la-la."

"That's what Miss Darbonne called me," I said. "Besides, I can call myself whatever I want."

Kendra-Sue shoved me into the chain-link fence, just hard enough to let me know she meant business. "That's crap in a bucket, Katie-Lee."

"Yeah, Katie-Lee. Bucket crap," Karen-Anne said, giggling.

"What if she called you Gorilla Girl, huh? Mama and Daddy named you Katie-Lee. My sister's name is Katie-Lee. I ain't related to no Katherine."

"I'm *not* related to *any* Katherine," Karen-Anne corrected her. Karen-Anne's teacher had developed a novel approach to tackling the nonstandard English so many of her students were raised with. She taught the class to loudly correct—and humiliate—classmates, friends, even family members.

I smirked.

"Shut your face, Karen-Anne, or I'll shut it for you," Kendra-Sue said without taking her eyes off of me.

Even at that age, I understood—if only vaguely—that Kendra-Sue was trying to teach me something about loyalty. A sixth-grader, she was at the top of the pecking order at the elementary school and she protected her two younger sisters ferociously, even if it meant some of the other kids her age mocked her for it. We were family, her actions said on a daily basis. The least I could do was not turn my back on her.

So instead of pushing back, getting into a wrestling match that would grass-stain our clothes and set Karen-Anne to crying as she tried to separate us—how quickly that girl could go from laughing to crying—I apologized and went to Miss Darbonne the next morning and said I'd changed my mind on the whole Katherine thing.

And here was Joey, begging to change his name. Except he wasn't turning his back on us, he wanted to be more like the rest of us.

"I don't know if Mama and Daddy gonna let," I said weakly, already acquiescing.

"They might."

"Come here," I said, pulling him down onto my lap. His little body was hot and he smelled like, I don't know, boy. We were both wearing shorts and our legs stuck together with sweat, but neither of us cared.

"So what we gonna call you?"

"I don't know," he said, hanging his head now, wiping his sniffles with the heel of his palm.

"Kurly?"

"No."

"Kurt the Third?"

"No."

"Kringle?"

"No."

"King-Kong?"

"Katie-Lee!" He giggled and squirmed in my lap. "Noooo."

"Okay," I said. "Let's see."

"Karl?"

"No."

"Why not?"

"I don't know. I just don't like it."

He also didn't like Kenny or Kent or Kermit or Kevin or Keith or

Kris or Kirk or Kirby.

"You sure are picky," I said. "You have any bright ideas?"

"No," he said. "I want you to pick."

"Crap in a bucket," I whispered.

Looking around, hoping my surroundings would provide inspiration, my eyes settled on a row of yellow cans sitting on a shelf, paint brushes, screwdrivers, nails, bolts, screws, and other hardware bristling out of their tops. "Steen's 100% Pure Cane Syrup," the sides said. Steen's was thick and rich. It was as dark as the motor oil that Daddy took out from the truck when he changed the filter. We went through cases of the stuff. Put it on biscuits for breakfast. Put it on a slice of bread and you had dessert. Put it in pies and cakes. Sneak it right out of the can on the end of your finger. Years later, I'd trade in its overpowering tang for the simpler, cleaner joys of maple syrup, but as kids we had nothing to compare it to. Sugar was sugar was sugar.

"How about Kane?" I asked.

He didn't say no immediately.

"Joey?"

"I don't know. Maybe."

"Kane? Yeah? Say it with me."

"Kane," we said together.

"Sounds tough," I said. "Like a man's name." I almost told him it was in the Bible, one of Adam and Eve's kids, but then I'd have to explain why they were spelled differently. And I could never remember which one killed the other.

"Kane," he said.

"Kane," I said.

"I'm Kane," he said.

"Kane with a K," I added.

"With a K."

I pushed him off my lap and turned him around to face me.

"But it's our secret, okay? Just you and me, Joey?"

"Kane," he corrected me, stomping his foot again.

"Kane. Okay, Kane? Our secret. Just for now. Don't tell anyone else. You promise?"

"Why?"

"Because it's you and me, pal. I'm your best sister and your best friend and I don't know if the others are going to understand."

"Okay," he said.

"Okay? You promise?"

"I promise."

I was only ten, so I can be forgiven for thinking the word of a five-year-old was something that could be kept. He made it until supper.

"Joey, I'm not gonna tell you again," Mama said for the fourth time. "Eat them peas."

"Don't make me get my belt," Daddy bluffed.

Joey put his fork down and looked Mama square in the eyes.

"My name ain't Joey. It's Kane."

"My name is *not* Joey," Karen-Anne corrected.

I looked down at my plate.

"Excuse me?" Mama said.

"My name is Kane," Joey said.

"Since when?" Daddy asked.

"Since today," he said. "Katie-Lee named me."

"Oooooooohhhhh," Karen-Anne said. "Katie-Lee, you gonna get it now."

All eyes turned on me, amused mostly, except for Kendra-Sue, who hadn't yet decided if this was an offense.

"He wanted a K name. He was crying because he had a J name and *somebody* told him it was because he was adopted."

Everyone at the table laughed except Kendra-Sue, who was murdering me with her eyes, and Joey, who was getting indignant.

"It's not funny," he yelled.

"He just wanted to be more like the rest of us," I said, an offering to Kendra-Sue. The anger in her eyes died down some.

"So Cain like in the Bible?" Kurt Junior asked. "Don't that start with a C?"

"No," I said, before Joey could ask any questions. "Like sugarcane, but with a K."

"Huh," Kurt Junior grunted, then went back to shoveling food into his face.

"That's good," Mama said, messing Joey's hair and giving her blessing all at the same time, "Cuz my baby's sweet as sugarcane."

Joey smiled from ear to ear, now all but officially baptized as Kane. For whatever reason—partly because he was so adamant about it—it stuck, Kane becoming one of those nicknames that confounded teachers throughout his school years. Strangers, on the other hand, didn't even realize it was a nickname. This wasn't by any means a rare thing in Louisiana. You'd call a boy Tray for years before realizing it was actually Tres, for three, and he was actually Whatever the Third. I went to high school with a boy named Todd. That's how we knew him. But when I started college at USL and ran into him on campus, he'd turned into Brian, which was his real name. He didn't even know where Todd had come from.

I was twenty years old and 1,500 miles away before I could successfully rename myself. Joey did it at five years old. Kane, Kane, Sugar Kane, we'd say to him when we wanted to tease him. And he ate it up every time.

◘ ◘ ◘

"Kane," I whisper to myself.

I unwrap my fingers from the steering wheel of the Prius and brush the tears from my cheeks.

I look over at the cage that houses the tiger that gives the truck stop its name. The cat comes out of her ugly wooden box, climbs on top of it, and grooms herself a bit before her eyes fall on me or the car or some space beyond. There's no fire in those eyes. It was smothered long ago by gas fumes and captivity. Fifteen minutes back up I-10, Mike VI, a distant cousin of hers, lives in a million-dollar habitat on the side of Tiger Stadium, complete with swimming pool and toys and a dedicated staff of eager veterinary-science students. This girl gets iron bars, the smell of gasoline, cheap meat, an oversized dog house and about five hundred square feet in which to roam.

Which, it occurs to me, is the size of my apartment.

"I got half a mind to drive out there and shoot the owners and the tiger both," I remember Karen-Anne ranting. Was it this tiger? Or another one? How long do tigers live? "Put that thing out of its misery. That's no life for that kind of animal."

Oh, Karen-Anne, Karen-Anne, Karen-Anne.

I start crying again. I am in no way prepared for any of this. I need more time. Just a little.

I call Kendra-Sue's number.

"Hey, where are you?" she asks by way of greeting.

"At the Tiger Truck Stop."

"I knew you'd take I-10." Then: "That's all? Did you rent a tractor?"

"No," I say, unclear about how to proceed. "I'm just sitting here. Had a bit of a breakdown." I force out a fake laugh as if to say, "You know me, old crazy Katie-Lee."

"Christ," she says.

"I'm sorry, Kendra-Sue," I start.

"No," she cuts me off. "It's fine. Lots of that going around. Sonny Junior got stuck in Kuwait last night. He won't get back until tomorrow and his daddy's a mess, so we're still trying to get that squared away.

I thought for sure she'd tear into me. But since she's in an accepting mood, I push my luck. "Look, Kendra-Sue, don't be mad, but I think I'll just get a room in Lafayette tonight. Put myself together in the morning and head over."

Silence on the other end.

"Kendra-Sue?"

"Yeah. Okay," she says.

I can't get a read on her voice.

"Sorry," she apologizes. "I took a Valium about half an hour ago and it's just kicking in."

My older sister taking a pill? I can't even imagine. God knows if

I were in her position I'd wash down half a bottle of them with Jack Daniel's and call it a day.

"Look," she says, "just be at the funeral home for 10. It's on the highway just when you get into Ville Platte, on the right."

"Okay," I say.

"Love you, Katie-Lee," she says.

That was uncalled for. "Love you, too," I choke out and start crying again.

I'd drive to Ville Platte and do the Heimlich on Kendra-Sue if it meant I could get my hands on that Valium. The one thing my little pharmacy is lacking is something fast-acting. In an effort to calm myself, I focus again on the tiger.

Dull of eye, raggedy coat, I wonder if she'd like a goat.

I smile at my own silliness. Even in her diminished state, she inspires poetry. Gas-huffing burnout she might be, there's still something regal about her. And bad as things are at the moment, I've got it better than the Queen of Sheba there. I come and go as I please. I don't rely on a man to tell me when and what and how much to eat. I've got a fully functioning set of brain cells and my hair looks better than hers. Maybe I should rescue her, a tribute to Karen-Anne. Pull her out of that cage and stuff her into the back seat of the Prius, get her a leash, bring her to the funeral home and afterward, drive off, showing her the country.

"Oh no you don't," I say aloud. If she didn't eat me the minute I opened the cage, she'd get me sooner or later. And Karen-Anne would blame me for it. I remember her Facebook updates every time a domesticated wild animal attacked or killed a trainer or some other bystander. Hectoring tirades littered with all-caps and exclamation points. "This is what happens, people! These are WILD animals!!! They shouldn't be kept in homes or used in shows like circus FREAKS!!!" I wonder if she'd see the irony in her death.

"Sorry, tiger," I say and steer out of the truck stop, back onto I-10. The concrete carpet unfurls ahead of me, leading me through the wilds of the Atchafalaya Basin. The sun is setting now, an orange disc reflected in black water, the mossy heads and knobby knees of the cypress trees silhouetted against the violet sky. A blue heron wings down between the two spans of highway, looking for what? A night fishing spot? A place to sleep, safe from alligators? I reach for my phone, compelled to take a picture of this scene, to post it on Facebook and Twitter, as if it doesn't really exist until I share it with the world. "Stunning," I could caption it. Or, "I hope I don't run out of gas out here and get kidnapped by swamp people." Or, most honestly, "Tell me that at least one other person is taking in this scene of awe-inspiring beauty and that I am not alone in such a world."

But I don't. I'm driving. What really stops me, though, is the thought of my family seeing it on Facebook and wondering just why the hell Katie-Lee was driving around taking pictures and making smart-ass remarks for her city friends instead of helping with arrangements and consoling her siblings and nieces and nephews.

Besides, I'm not getting any service out here.

CHAPTER EIGHT

In Lafayette, I find a breed of standard American hotels has replaced the old crop of locally owned establishments that once catered to country couples honeymooning in the "city" and then oil-field workers on expense accounts and then, after the '80s crash, intransigents and dealers and hookers and, according to a *Daily Advertiser* clipping once sent to me by Kendra-Sue, the sort of couple who elevates domestic disputes to pouring gas on one another and lighting a match. "Hunka hunka burning love," she'd scribbled on the article.

Now? Quality, Comfort and Holiday Inns. A Super 8. A Fairfield by Marriot. I could be at any interstate exchange in the country. I find that more comforting than distressing. It takes some of the pressure off, makes it feel a little less like I'm in South Louisiana for my little sister's funeral.

Straight to the room and bar the door. Maybe I'll grab a bottle of wine later. If I need it. Truth is hotel rooms have an effect on me that's hard to describe. For some, they signify only work, business trips, being away from family. For me? Vacation, escape, relaxation, adventure. Anonymity and the possibility of reinvention. No one but the front desk knows who I really am. I could be anyone. And anyone could have been here. What's happened in this room? Family trips, high-school hookups, rekindled romances? Who knows?

Business travelers see a prison, I see a blank canvas.

"How can you travel all over the world and stay in a boring old hotel?" Vanessa at work asked me after my last trip. "Stay with a local family, in a hostel, a B & B. They're so charming."

They might be to someone who doesn't really have to work, to someone whose husband's banking salary allows them a Brooklyn carriage house renovated from top to bottom and featured in no fewer than three glossy home magazines.

"I've had enough charming to last a lifetime," I told her. If I wanted to spend my time in someone else's bedroom, hoping there'd be hot water in the morning and suffering through small talk in an accent I can barely understand, I'd just have a sleepover at Haleema's. "I only get so much vacation a year and I'd like to spend it relaxing. You and Philippe can go slumming with the poors and hippies and never let on that one of his paychecks would be enough for your host family to retire on."

That might have been uncalled for. She didn't speak to me for two weeks after that.

But the point remains. I could be anywhere in the world at this moment. On the other side of those curtains could be a snowcapped peak in the Rockies, that curve of beach leading up to Black Rock in Maui, the noise and heat and odors of Bangkok, the insanity-inducing light show of Tokyo, a street in Rome or Peru that winds its way to the ruins of an ancient civilization.

Or the Vine Street and Cane Street intersection outside the window of a room in The Ranch Motel in Opelousas in 1977.

◘ ◘ ◘

If Mama could have predicted what the move to Opelousas would have done to the family, we might all still be living in the woods in Grand Prairie, some third-generation albino child of ours playing banjo on the front porch. As it happened, Kurt Junior, Karla-Jean, Kendra-Sue, and Karen-Anne moved back to the country the first chance they got, as if city living was too much to bear.

And in 1976, it sure seemed that way.

Anyone walking through the side door of our house on Linda Lane on a late summer day that year might have been fooled into thinking he was witnessing a typical American family. Mama in the kitchen, fussing over the stove, a cigarette dangling from her mouth. Three kids in the back room—Karen-Ann, Kane, me—listening to records. Kurt Junior sleeping in the boys' room.

But spend a little more time and the cracks start to show. Sunday, and Daddy's not around. Middle of the day, Kurt Junior's still in bed and, at twenty-three, still living at home.

As it turns out, Daddy's dead, gone the year before. Kurt Junior's sleeping off another hangover, still trying to drink away whatever it was that happened to him in Vietnam. In six short months, he'll knock up Melinda, and in another nine she and that baby'll settle him down.

And speaking of knocked up, here comes Kendra-Sue—T-Brent on her right hip and Sally, squirming and squawlling, on her other—banging through the screen door.

"God damn it, Mama!" she screamed. "If Karla-Jean don't come get this child, I'm going to shake it to death."

The three of us come out of the back room just in time to see Mama point a spoon at her. "I'm not going to tell you again about that language in my house, Kendra-Sue. I mean it."

But the truth was, Mama had no control over Kendra-Sue anymore, her or Karla-Jean. They'd had babies. They were their own women now. Kendra-Sue might still be a dumb-as-dirt seventeen-year-old, but she was a woman.

Sort of.

"Language, my ass," Kendra-Sue said, thrusting the Sally-laden hip toward Mama. "Would you take your grandchild, please?" She took one of Mama's cigarettes and lit it up. "This is bullshit. I can't go out for a couple hours on a Saturday without catching the third degree, but she can go spend half Sunday at that Crazy Church."

Mama dried her hands and took Sally in her arms, cooed to her. "What's the matter, my baby? Mean ol' aunt Kendra-Sue wants to throw you in the thrash?" The baby quieted for a second, then started up again.

That was our cue to go back to the relative quiet of our room. I was getting to that age at which I wanted to be seen as a grown-up, one of the women, sit around talking about life and drinking coffee (even if mine was still mostly milk and sugar). But not so bad I wanted to put up with all that noise and commotion.

"Hey, Katie-Lee," Kendra-Sue called after me. "Yall don't want to take T-Brent back there with yall?"

"Nah. Kane got toys and junk all over the floor. That baby'd probably choke on something." The lie rolled off my tongue with no forethought, no extra effort. T-Brent might have been the quieter of the two kids, but that didn't mean we wanted him slobbering all over everything, crawling around and trying to stick his fingers in electric sockets. Kane almost hated them babies. He'd been the baby so long, now there he was, a ten-year-old boy surrounded by women who had two other infants to fuss over. And he with no daddy to take him hunting or fishing like the other kids his age were doing. His older brother might as well have been a vampire, sleeping most of the day, skulking around the house when awake and escaping after dark only to return just before dawn smelling like he'd rolled in something.

I shut the door to our room and we went back to our records. I'd like to brag that we were listening to the best of our times, soaking up the rock gods around us, but we were products of late '70s Louisiana, which meant we wanted to be part of wider America, wanted to gobble up the French fries from the new McDonald's over on Creswell, wanted to talk like the people on TV, and thought that Top 40 music on FM radio was about as cool as a person could get. Lots of unfortunate music on those lists, including one of our favorites, "Disco Duck."

We'd played that five or six times already. Kane's voice had gone ragged from doing his best duck: "Get down mama! Oh mama shake your tail feather!" So we'd switched to something a little more sophisticated, "December 1963." But even Kane and Karen-Anne caterwauling "Oh what a night" couldn't drown out the cacophony from the kitchen, where Kendra-Sue had dropped T-Brent into a playpen, prompting him to burst immediately into a screaming fit.

"Oh shut it, you," she said to him. "My arms are tired from carrying you around all morning."

"You need to put him down more often," Mama said. "I didn't carry yall around all the time like this. Spoils a kid. He's gonna be a titty-baby, you keep this up." Hypocrite. The words weren't even out of her mouth before she'd picked him up and was walking around with both grandkids bouncing on her hip.

"I know, Mama. But with them both going off at the same time like that, I can't stand it."

No kidding. I wanted to scream when they came over almost every night for supper. I swear I was developing an allergy to them, breaking out in hives at the dinner table. And I couldn't tolerate setting foot in the trailer she and Karla-Jean and the babies shared in the backyard. I never went in there unless absolutely forced to. Worse than the noise and the disorder and the size of the space was the feeling that Kendra-Sue was like a caged animal, prowling back and forth, just waiting to escape and tear up anything in her path.

She'd gone wild when she started high school, and it seemed nobody could control her. Daddy's lungs had given out on him and Kurt Junior was off shooting little Asian people. Karla-Jean always had her face in a Bible or was off with her Pentecostal boyfriend, praising Jesus and catching the Holy Ghost. Kendra-Sue tried to recruit me into her adventures, but I was a late bloomer—awkward, flat-chested, and scared of the world almost as much as I was scared by the wild look in her eyes (to say nothing of the older boys she ran around with). I was content to stay with Kane, thank you very much.

Hell, even Karen-Anne was afraid of the fire burning in Kendra-Sue. Fifteen years old and my older sister was going to swallow the world whole. "Fuck this place, man," she'd say, hanging out our bedroom window at night, blowing smoke into the humid air. "I'm getting out of here as soon as I can. Gonna go someplace big. New Orleans. Houston. Maybe even Hollywood."

Four months into her second year of high school, she was pregnant.

Mama and Daddy were disappointed, but they took it in stride. Circle of life and all. It may have embarrassed Mama some, but they weren't society people, had no reputation to lose. They were soon to have a grandbaby. There were worse things in the world.

But Karla-Jean? She practically threw a parade to celebrate the downfall.

"See what happens," she gloated. She was a senior in high school and therefore knew everything there was to know about anything. "Yall don't make her go to church. Yall let her do whatever she wants. Well, this is what you get. I told yall."

She had a point. She had told us—repeatedly. It was like living with a street preacher.

"You shut your Bible-thumping hole," Kendra-Sue had screamed. "I don't have to listen to this shit."

"Don't talk to me like that."

"Come on, then. Let's go outside. I might be pregnant but I'll whip your ass right there in the front yard."

"You'll have a lot to answer for before Jesus, Kendra-Sue."

"Oh, I got plenty of answers for him. Guess we'll see if he's got the right questions."

"You're going to burn in hell for talking like that!"

"That's it." Kendra-Sue marched right over to Karla-Jean, snatched her by the hair and headed for the door, Karla-Jean's hands a windmill of slaps.

"Son of a bitch! Yall stop it right now!" Daddy shouted, which, considering his condition, took a great deal of effort. More and more, he'd been reverting to Cajun French, his first language. His oldest boy off at war in Asia. A house full of fighting women. Lungs failing after a lifetime of cigarettes, pesticides, and whatever he'd been inhaling while scouring the holding tanks at the Lou-Ana plant. English just took too much energy.

So the fight stopped. Temporarily. Nothing but minor skirmishes occurred here and there for the next couple of weeks, but full-scale war broke out again when we found out Karla-Jean was pregnant.

"Well, well, well," Kendra-Sue said. "Did the Holy Virgin get a visitation from the Holy Ghost or did she do it the old-fashioned way, with Unholy Harold?"

It would have been funny if Karla-Jean weren't so ashamed, if she didn't have her face buried in Mama's shoulder. "Shut up," she cried, her voice muffled.

Okay. It was still a little funny.

"Of course she wants me to shut up. Judge ye not, lest ye be judged, Karla-Jean. How's that feel? You crying? You got something in your eye? Is that a mote or is that a whole damn beam?"

"Hush," Mama warned her.

"Oh, I'll hush. Soon as she apologizes, I'll hush."

Karla-Jean lifted her head, wiped her eyes and stood up. Her bottom lip still trembling, fists curled into balls, she crossed the room looking less like a woman ready to fight than a baby in the midst of a temper tantrum.

"I'm sorry, Kendra-Sue," she hissed. "I'm sorry you ruined your life and you're blaming everybody but your own self." Her voice started climbing. "You think I planned this? Huh? You think I wanted a baby at this age?" She was screaming now. "I had plans. I wanted to go to trade school. I was going to be a nurse." It was the first any of us had heard about these plans. "But I let down my guard one time—one time!—and, yeah, this is what happens. Punished for my sins, my whole life ruined. Ruined! And you just couldn't be happier!"

She'd backed Kendra-Sue into a corner, pinned her against the wall with her pointer finger and her rage.

"God, Karla-Jean," Kendra-Sue said. "It's just a baby."

Which, of course, was not a Zen-like understanding of the situation, but a fifteen-year-old girl's inability to grasp the reality of it.

And the reality was, Karla-Jean, for once, was right. A baby wasn't just a cute little person. A baby was like Charon taking you across the river Styx (something I'd looked up after hearing Styx's "Lady" on the radio). Instead of ferrying you from life to the underworld, a baby dragged you from girlhood to womanhood—fifteen, twenty-five, or thirty-five, it didn't matter.

Or put in less metaphorical terms, it was a screaming, moving, stinking thing that demanded your body, your time, your sleep and, of course, your money.

Not that they had any. And neither did Harold or Brent. To their credit, the boys stepped right up to the plate with no complaint and no show. They knew what was expected of them and didn't put on like they should be clapped on the back or given a trophy for it—not like some of these men today who spend more time telling you they're doing the right thing by their kids than actually raising them, blogging about fatherhood while the kid is eating bugs off the floor and maxing out his diaper. Whatever the case, Daddy didn't have to reach for his shotgun. But a Fort Knox full of honor and good intentions wasn't going to put food on the table or convince CLECO to keep the lights on. The boys needed money, and not the pennies they'd earn at McDonald's or some cushy retail job.

So, to the oil fields they went, rough-necking. The money would be good—more than good—if they didn't drink it away between setting foot on dry land and getting home, a common occurrence in South Louisiana. After seven, fourteen, twenty-one days out in the field, these young men would step off a boat or barge and be welcomed back to civilization and all its charms with a paycheck bigger than they'd ever seen. That probably ruined as many men as the dangerous working conditions.

Being gone that long complicated things for the girls. Pregnant or not, neither Karla-Jean nor Kendra-Sue had ever lived alone—

and for all her bluster, Kendra-Sue was less equipped for it than Karla-Jean, who'd been helping Mama run the house since she was thirteen. So the families put their heads and wallets together and moved a small two-bedroom trailer behind our house. A fragile peace held when Harold and Brent were home, but the minute they left, Karla-Jean and Kendra-Sue were like two tomcats scrapping over territory. Even when they weren't in our house—round-bellied, bloated, cranky, demanding Mama pick a side—we could hear them through the thin walls of the trailer. It was like living under high-tension wires, a sinister hum so persistent that when you were removed from its presence, you wondered if something had gone wrong before realizing, no, this is how other people lived.

Soon enough, Kurt Junior was back from the war and Karla-Jean had Sally and Kendra-Sue had Brent Junior—or T-Brent, as he was called.

Daddy got to hold his first two grandbabies. Weak as he was, he'd insist we prop them both in his lap. He'd sit there with this huge smile of contentment on his face. I didn't understand the fascination myself—those two squirming, messy, noisy things. Mama and Karen-Anne doted on them. But Daddy? Boy, those babies loved him. They'd go quiet in his lap. Daddy's big, dry, papery hands would rub their little bald heads and his eyes would light up and Mama would go find an onion to chop to hide the fact she was crying about it all. He was going, we all knew it. He did, too. Still, he seemed proud of what he was able to bring into this world. The only thing that made him brood was when Kurt Junior would head out drinking. He didn't get mad at Kurt Junior; he was worried was all. He never rustled him out of bed, never told him to get off his ass and get a job. I'd come home from school and find Daddy and Kurt Junior sitting in rocking chairs in the carport, looking out over the field. I don't know what they talked about—if they even talked. Talking didn't seem a crucial component of communication for men, as far as I could tell. They looked like two old coots in a retirement home keeping an eye on the horizon for the appearance of death. But their vigil couldn't save

Daddy. His lungs failed completely and he was, just like that, gone. He was so fragile and haggard by the end that it seemed only natural. He *looked* old. Other men his age, his generation, all did. Field work. War work. More field work. Heavy labor in dangerous heat. It wasn't until I was older and had moved out of Louisiana that I realized fifty was a ridiculous age for a man to die.

But life went on. Mama lost a little of her spirit. She missed him. We all did. But none of us had much time to mope. Another year blew by. Life—with its noise and demands and schedules—carried on. And Karla-Jean and Kendra-Sue and their two brats did as well, carrying on all hours of the day, screaming and crying and fighting, and now not even Daddy around to tell them to shut up.

It was into this maelstrom that Lawrence rode his white Ford Bronco.

Kendra-Sue was still screaming about the injustice of Karla-Jean's spending so much time at church when there was a knock on the door. The babies fell silent. Who could that be? We'd heard no car on the gravel lane, no doors slamming. Karen-Anne, Kane, and I darted from the back room just in time to see Kendra-Sue letting Lawrence in.

"Oh, hey," she said, "come in." As if someone like him just walked into our house every day.

"Hey, Kendra-Sue," he said.

He knew her name? That made sense. They were in the same grade before she dropped out.

"Hi Miss Beverly," he said to Mama. "Mama sent me over with your pie pan and said to tell you thanks."

"You're welcome," Mama said. "She should have come over herself," she added with a smile, a judgment hanging in the air. Had Lawrence's mother written us off as beneath her, the country people in the small house breeding like rabbits?

Lawrence's blush answered that question. "She, uh, she was late from church and was rushing to get supper ready. Some of Daddy's people coming over tonight."

"I understand," Mama said.

Lawrence looked around the house until his eyes settled on me. "Oh, hi Katie-Lee."

Oh my god. He knew my name.

A year older than me, he ran with Opelousas High's cool crowd. I ran with no one, sat with Kendra-Sue and some of her friends until she dropped out because of the baby, then fell in with some of the other country girls, the ones who still showed up with dirt under their nails, blisters on their palms, legs littered with scabs from their chores and adventures.

Skinny but not scrawny, Lawrence was a wide-receiver for the football team at OHS. He wore denim jackets and Rolling Stones and Led Zeppelin and Pink Floyd T-shirts. He had the longest eyelashes any of the girls had ever seen on a boy. Among the girls, that was his thing. There was no shortage of cute boys, so we focused on one feature of each of them, as if preparing for a quiz that would come one day: "What's so great about him?" Lance Thibodeaux had hair so curly it looked like a perm. Tommy Sebastian had fair blond hair that fell to his shoulders. Jake Soileau had shoulders so broad, he looked like Paul Bunyan. And Lawrence had long eyelashes.

Lawrence was a town boy, had lived in one of the big, old brick houses on the oak-lined streets between the courthouse and South City Park. Until they moved into the other house on Linda Lane, the big one across the way, closer to Washington Road, the one that had sat empty and wasting since we'd moved in, home only to the ghosts, deranged perverts, and homicidal maniacs of our grisly imaginations. When we walked the lane to get to the bus stop, Karen-Anne still ran the length of gravel in front of it, certain that something was going to fly out of there and snatch her up by the hair, drag her back in and feast on her soul.

But right now it was my soul up for grabs.

"Hi," I managed, venturing forth from the room, Kane following, Karen-Anne staying behind, no doubt convinced he'd come to murder us all.

"Joey, say hi," Mama said.

"Kane," he corrected her, then stepped between Lawrence and me. "My name's Kane." He stuck his hand out. With Daddy gone, Kurt Junior a phantom, Kane had gotten it into his head that he was the man of the house, as if Mama needed such a thing.

"A handshake?" Lawrence asked. "Give me five, my man." He held out his hand and Kane slapped it immediately, flipping his over to be slapped in return. "Now that's how dudes do it these days."

Kane smiled, fighting a blush, that one silly gesture transforming Lawrence from threat to a friend.

Lawrence left and Kane and I drifted back into the room in a dreamlike state, lost in our own thoughts. We didn't see Lawrence again for two weeks, not until the first day of the new school year. As we were walking down the lane to the bus stop, he rushed out onto their front porch.

"Hey, Katie-Lee, wait up."

He walked all the way out to the lane, dressed except for his bare feet.

Karen-Anne froze in place.

"You want a ride to school?" he asked.

I looked over at his Bronco, perhaps one of the ugliest vehicles I'd ever seen, as if I actually needed to think about my answer.

Kane tugged on my shirt. "What about us?"

Oh yeah, them. Kane and I shared a seat on the bus every morning until it dropped him at his school.

"They can come, too," Lawrence said, his enthusiasm waning a little.

"That's okay," Karen-Anne piped up, already shuffling toward the end of the lane. "I'm just going to take the bus."

Lawrence looked at her as if she'd sprouted a second head. Who wanted to take the bus to school?

I shrugged. "She likes to stick to herself." I figured that was a better explanation than "She thinks you are a family of demons."

And so it began with a ride to school, with me sitting there wondering if he was simply being neighborly or if he had—I hoped against hope—some other intention. I hoped so hard, I got ahead of myself. What if he asked me out? What would Mama say? Would she cordon me off in my room to prevent any further pregnancies? Would Lawrence's mom try to break us up because she saw me as white trash? How would Kane react? Would he get jealous? Would Lawrence get annoyed by this little kid tagging along? Would I be forced to choose?

I needn't have worried on the latter account.

That first day, I sat in stunned silence, not quite believing my luck, while Kane and Lawrence jabbered like monkeys about football and hunting and fishing, all the things Kane, as a South Louisiana boy, should have had in his life. But after we dropped Kane off, Lawrence, too, fell silent. I had sense enough to take this as a good sign. It meant he was nervous. It emboldened me enough to pop the glove box and dig through his eight-tracks. Stones. Eagles. Zeppelin.

"You have any Rick Dees or Frankie Valli?" I asked.

"Rick Dees?" he practically shouted. "I'm going to pretend you didn't say that."

"What? Why?" I stammered. Had I blown it already, said something so stupid and uncool he was going to pull over and chuck me out of the truck?

"That's not real music," he said.

"Says who?"

"Says everybody."

"News to me."

"My *mom* listens to Frankie Valli."

I couldn't think of anything less cool than his mom. "Oh."

"It's okay," he said, tentatively slapping my knee, sending an inexplicable jolt through my entire body. "I'll teach you what's what."

By the time we got to the school parking lot, I was already picking out a prom dress. I took my sweet time getting out of the Bronco, wanting to hold onto the moment a little longer. As I dismounted, I looked around for a friend or two so I could shout hello, call attention to myself. But all of my friends were on the front side of the school, stomping out of school buses.

Lawrence, though, was shouting left and right. "Chad!" "Toby!" "Chris, what's going on, man?"

And then to me, "Hey, I'm sorry, but I guess you'll have to take the bus home."

My heart tumbled into my stomach. I'd had us married with kids in the space of one car ride and he'd just been being nice. How could I have been so stupid? Who did I think I was?

I looked down at my feet, as if to watch my dignity fall into the dirt and gravel. "Yeah, that's cool." No. No it wasn't. It was definitely uncool.

"Yeah," he said. "I have football practice in the afternoons. That goes until five or six."

"Oh," I said. A small glimmer of hope rekindled in the ash heap of my little teenage heart.

"But I'll give you a ride tomorrow morning. If you want."

"Yeah, sure," I said, trying to stay calm but feeling a smile growing on my face, which of course made me blush.

"Who knows? Maybe the next day, too." He was teasing me!

"Who knows," I said, trying to hold my own. "I guess we'll see."

Once in the school hall, we went our separate ways and I didn't see him the rest of the school day. Maybe I'd imagined the whole thing. Maybe it had been a joke. Walking from the bus stop to the house that afternoon, I considered the spot in their drive where the Bronco should have been and became convinced it wouldn't be there in the morning, that a dirty yellow school bus would be my chariot for the rest of my entire life. That evening, when we sat down to supper—all of us: Karla-Jean and Sally, Kendra-Sue and T-Brent, Karen-Anne, Kane, Mama, even Kurt Junior had come out of his hole a little earlier than usual—I poked at the baked chicken and canned green beans and corn, my appetite gone off with my head.

There was a knock on the door. I tipped over my chair in a rush to answer, in that split second cursing myself for once again getting my hopes up. It couldn't be him. What would he be doing here? I hadn't left anything in the Bronco, though the thought had crossed my mind. Maybe it was his mama come to tell me she was sorry but Lawrence just couldn't be seen driving a girl of my sort to school.

But there he stood, on the other side of the screen door, the light of the carport gleaming off of his wet, black hair, plastered down and straight from being trapped in a football helmet all afternoon. He blinked and his eyelashes all but waved at me. He wore an orange mesh jersey that ended at his belly button and gray drawstring cotton shorts with "OHS TIGERS" wrapped around a football. In his hands he held a stack of records.

"Hey," he said. "Sorry for interrupting at supper."

"It's okay," I said.

"I just wanted to bring you some homework."

He held the albums out toward me, our fingers brushing as I took them.

"Thanks. You want to come in?"

"Nah. I gotta shower."

"Okay."

"See you tomorrow morning," he said before jogging off into the evening. I stared through the screen for a minute, oblivious to the June bugs and moths bouncing against it trying to get in.

"You letting all the damn cold air out," Kendra-Sue called.

I hurried to the bedroom and hid the records behind the dresser, not because they weren't allowed, but because I didn't want anyone else so much as looking at them until I finished with the dishes after supper.

"Who was that?" Mama asked, when I returned to the table.

"Just Lawrence," I said, looking down at my plate, fighting a blush as if my life depended on it. "He just dropped off a couple of records."

"He drove her and Kane to school this morning," Karen-Anne informed the table.

"Well, isn't that something," Karla-Jean said.

"You better slow down, Katie-Lee," Kendra-Sue chimed in, lighting a cigarette. "Karla-Jean and me don't have enough room back there for you and a baby."

"Kendra-Sue!" Mama said, trying to scold, but laughing too hard to mean it.

I felt my face burning.

"What's that mean?" Kane asked. "Why's your face so red, sissy?"

"My face isn't red," was all I could think to say.

"Yes it is."

"Kane, don't you worry yourself about that," Mama told him. "You'll understand when you're older."

"I'm plenty old enough," he informed her. "Besides, Lawrence is going to take me hunting when the season starts."

"Is that right?" Mama asked.

"Sure is," he said.

"Where you gonna get a gun? Who's gonna teach you how to use it?"

He looked shocked. It hadn't occurred to him that such preparation was needed.

"He can use the 20-gauge Daddy gave me when I was his age," Kurt Junior said.

We all looked at him as if he was speaking for the first time in years. He might as well have been for as little talking as he did.

"I'll get some shells and teach him out in the field."

"Yes!" Kane said before tucking back into his food.

After hurrying through the dishes, I hustled off to the bedroom, closed the door and pulled out the records. The rest of the family was gathered around the TV, all of them except Kurt Junior, who was knocking about in his room, no doubt getting ready for another drunk. I shuffled through the albums: Rolling Stones, Rolling Stones, The Beatles and more Beatles. Odd choices for someone who was telling me my music was uncool. How old were these? Our parents could have listened to these—if they'd grown up someplace else. A corner of loose-leaf paper stuck out of one of the sleeves, on it a note written in the kind of chicken scratch common to boys. "These might seem square, but you have to start at the beginning." Whatever that meant.

For no other reason than the cover, I picked the Stones' *Aftermath*. The boys in the band standing there, glittery and shimmery against a black background—it was kind of how I felt at the moment. I might have gotten stuck on the first track all night. There was just something about "Paint it Black" that hit me right in the stomach, rousing things in me that until then I hadn't been aware of, making me conscious of the confusion and chaos around me. I looked at the white walls of the bedroom. Maybe the Stones were going on about something else—they probably were, I figured—but why couldn't I just paint the walls black? Why couldn't I just do something to change my life? Was this cycle—go to school, get married, and have babies (or vice versa), grow old, die, all within a twenty-mile radius—mandatory? Was there a chance of escape?

But that was just a glimmer at the edges of realization. One thought of Lawrence, and the little girl that I was opened her arms wide to embrace tradition. Marriage, two kids and a dog. Give it to me and more.

Still, the song was captivating. I listened to it again. And again. I didn't notice Kurt Junior come into the room until he tapped me on the shoulder, scaring me so much that I screamed.

"Sorry," he said, before handing me his headphones, can-sized things that seemed they'd swallow my head.

"I can turn it down if it's too loud."

He picked up the record sleeve and looked at the cover, considering it as if it were some strange fossil he'd dug up in the backyard. "I just rather you use the headphones if you're gonna listen to the Stones."

A thought bubbled to the surface of my self-absorbed brain. "This what yall listened to over there?"

He looked away from the record and at me, through me almost. "Yeah, something like that."

"Oh," I said. "I'm sorry," I added.

"Not your fault, Katie-Lee," he said and bent down and kissed the top of my head and walked out.

Before I put the headphones on, I heard his own record player going, playing some old Cajun song. I listened all the way through that one and half of a swamp-pop number. It was the music Mama and Daddy used to listen to in the evenings before we had a TV. It was Kurt Junior trying to turn the clock back with each revolution of the record.

I was only interested in going forward.

Before I knew it, I had a boyfriend. A real, live boyfriend. My first. My first everything. First boyfriend. First date. First dance. But before the dancing was the first kiss.

It was long enough coming, that's for sure. The ride to school didn't exactly set the mood, what with Kane in the back seat. And when Lawrence came over to our house, there was Kane again, under foot. Lawrence was infinitely patient with him, often more so than I was. And while his house was so silent you could hear a mosquito walking across the floor, his mama had a rule. Well, she had many rules, that woman, but the one that rained on our parade was that Lawrence's bedroom door had to be open at all times. We could have snuck a kiss in there. Elevated like the house was, every step across its floors echoed, providing ample warning of approach. But he didn't have the courage to cross his mama, and the thought of her finding us kissing, reaffirming every assumption she'd made about me and my people—it just mortified me.

I had to do something, manufacture a way to stay after school long enough to catch an evening ride with him. I don't know why I didn't just wait until he took me on a proper date. In my mind, the hours after school were the only time something could happen. So I tried out for the cheerleading squad and was shocked when I actually made it.

"I don't see why you're so surprised," Lawrence told me on the way to school the next morning. "You're just about the prettiest girl in school."

"That's gross," Kane said from the back seat.

I said nothing, just blushed. It had been a while since I'd heard any such thing, since before Daddy had died. He always made sure to tell us girls how pretty we were. It wasn't the same thing as being told by a boy—or even one of the other girls at school—but it was something. Maybe Mama thought I was pretty, but she hadn't said anything about it. Maybe she wasn't the type. Maybe she was just exhausted from Karla-Jean and Kendra-Sue and all their nonsense, so exhausted she dreamed of the day Calgon would take her away. She kept boxes of it in the bathroom and would get cranky if she didn't get her long soak in. She believed in that soap commercial the way some people believed in God. It was her mantra. "Calgon, take me away," she'd start off. "Or take yall away. As long as I get one moment of peace around here."

Or maybe she thought if she started telling me and Karen-Anne we were pretty, she'd have another litter of grandbabies on the way.

That one little sentence from Lawrence altered the way I viewed myself. I spent extra time in the bathroom that night, posing in front of the mirror. Long, wavy black hair, brown eyes, brown skin from the Louisiana sun. I wasn't ugly. I didn't think that. But on my best day, I felt average, part of the background, just another body walking the halls at school. I'd finally grown a bit of a butt and had something resembling hips, but the boobs could have been bigger. They'd get there eventually, I thought, but they sure were taking their time. Knowing what I know now, I'd tell that little girl to be thankful. The large breasts gifted to her other siblings would just be something to sag and stretch and droop with age—which might be fine for married with children, but not something you wanted to deal with as an elder stateswoman on the singles scene. What do little girls know of such things? Funnier still, I thought I was too skinny. Different days, indeed. There's some young thing right this minute puking herself into a stupor, and there I was sneaking extra glasses of whole milk because I thought it would make me fill out faster. Maybe the cows back then didn't have enough hormones in them.

Looking into the mirror, I tried to see what Lawrence saw, but couldn't pull it off. I shrugged. Whatever the case, the kiss was going to happen and soon. I'd made cheerleaders. I had practice. He had practice. He'd give me a ride home from school soon and bing-bang-boom, it would happen.

The first day I had cheerleader practice, when we went our separate ways in the hall that morning, I took a deep breath and spoke.

"You can give me a ride this afternoon? After practice?"

"Of course," he said, suddenly shy.

At that moment, we both knew, which made it one of the longest school days ever. I didn't know how I was going to get through cheerleader practice, but that took care of itself. Working on a routine in the unairconditioned gym, it took everything in me to remember the cheers and the steps while trying not to vomit. I was a dripping mess by the time we were done, so disgusting I almost took Courtney Dupre up on her offer to drive me home. But I was going to see it through.

"No thanks," I told her. "Lawrence is giving me a ride."

"Oh my god, he's so cute," she said breathlessly. Courtney, the captain of the squad, jealous of me? The other girls agreed enthusiastically. It was a feeling akin to the one that surfaced after Lawrence told me I was pretty, except I felt a little less ambiguous about it.

That didn't make me any less sweaty when he pulled the Bronco around to the front of the school to collect me. Not that he was in better shape. After two hours of practice in that heat, he should have smelled like a moist gorilla, but if he did I didn't notice. Maybe at that age our bodies aren't a sack of toxins trying to force their way out.

All these years later, thinking about all that overheated, sticky flesh, I don't know how we kept our hands off each other for as long as we did, how we didn't rip into our ripe young bodies right there in the school parking lot. Maybe we were too young to know what we had, ignorant about what a blip in our lives days like that would be. Or maybe we were just nervous and stinky and too damn hot to do anything but sit still.

Lawrence took the Blow Pop out of his mouth—the other boys chewed tobacco during football season, smoked in the off-season; Lawrence ate Blow Pops year-round.

"Wanna go to Sonic? Get us each one of those giant cherry limeades?"

"That might be the best idea I ever heard," I said, unsticking the back of my thighs from the seat. The Bronco wasn't air-conditioned. "Wherever we're going, just drive."

"Yes, Boss Lady." He laughed, then put the Blow Pop back in his mouth before pulling out of the parking lot, spraying gravel all over the place.

The breeze cooled us some, and by the time we arrived at Sonic, the sun had taken mercy on us and slid from the sky. The place was hopping. We drove around twice before an empty slot opened up. Cherry limeades in hand, we drank greedily and let ourselves be distracted by those of our friends walking from car to car, joking, flirting, bumming cigarettes, offering booze from half-pint bottles, flitting around the Sonic parking lot in an imitation of the moths and June bugs circling the arc lights above us. It was no quieter than being at home, but it was a completely different vibe. Youth on parade, what little tension and worries we had far, far away. The economy may have been in the toilet, our families struggling to make ends meet, but with the war over, our worries were of pimples and gossip and boys and girls and getting laid. The biggest financial concern for anyone our age was keeping gas in our rides. Sure, we had chores and homework and tests and fighting parents and broken families and knocked-up sisters. Failing crops and mangled limbs from oil-field accidents. There were a few death-haunted, war-touched souls at school. But such things didn't make it through the brightly lit force field of Sonic. It was a safe harbor. Here, we weren't just some funny-talking Catholic kids in a Louisiana backwater, slipping weird snippets of French into our conversations. We were on an island in the United States of America.

But boy was it crowded.

"Let's go somewhere," I said, finally unable to take any more. As soon as I spoke, I was struck by the feeling that I'd been misreading the whole thing, that Lawrence might drive us straight home.

"Okay," was all he said.

He drove through the park and into a neighborhood I'd never been through—which said something about my limited experience of Opelousas. Past a dead-end sign that funneled us into an open gate marked by a sign that read, "Opelousas Tennis & Swimming Club: Members Only."

"It's closed on weekdays during the school year, so there won't be anyone here," he said.

It wasn't much. Four tennis courts, two at the bottom of a hill, two at the top. A massive swimming pool with a diving well and two diving boards sat behind a hurricane fence topped with barbed wire.

Lawrence killed the engine, turned off his headlights, and silence fell over us, the only sounds the ticks and tocks of the cooling engine and the occasional buzz of a mosquito.

No words were spoken. None were needed. We knew why we were there. I turned. He turned. We leaned in simultaneously. It started with a series of closed-mouthed kisses. Despite having two wanton hussies for sisters, I was an innocent. And he was patient. But soon enough, his tongue was in my mouth and the slight tingling that had started when our lips first touched blossomed into an electricity that raced the length of my body. I brought my hands up and threaded them into his hair. I smelled the trees and his sweat. And that damn Bronco. That ugly, beautiful white steed, that musty, dusty thing with the splitting seats, the close air, redolent with motor oil and boy. To this day, walking by an auto-body shop sends shivers down my spine.

I tasted the salt and the limeade and, yes, that damn Blow Pop. For a brief moment I felt like I was swallowing a circus, like I was eating cotton candy and peanuts and music and lights.

I opened my eyes. Pulled back a little. He did the same.

We both smiled. The pressure was off now. Then we kissed for another half an hour, kissed and nothing more, our hands never straying under clothes or below the belt. For months, it was all we needed. Making out in the Bronco, kissing each other good-bye before heading into school in the morning, holding hands in between.

"Gross," Kane said whenever our fingers intertwined across the empty space between the Bronco's front seats. But otherwise, he didn't complain. He liked Lawrence.

And Lawrence was good on his word to take Kane on his first hunting trip. In October, Lawrence pulled up to the house in the Bronco at 5 a.m. on the first day of squirrel season. Kane, who'd gone to bed in his camouflage the night before and slept all of two hours, was out of the house without even telling anyone good-bye, the screen door slamming behind him like a shot in the night. It woke me with a start, but I fell back to sleep with a smile, too young to contemplate the very real dangers of men and boys marching off into the woods with guns.

Mama, though, she fretted all morning. I woke to find her looking out of the window above the kitchen sink, as if it would give her a glimpse into the forest they were stalking instead of the view of Karla-Jean and Kendra-Sue's trailer.

"I shouldn't have let him go," she said. More than once.

"He'll be fine," Kurt Junior told her.

"How do you know?" she asked. "Anything could happen."

"Well, for one thing, the squirrels don't shoot back," he said.

She didn't answer, backing away as we always did from such talk.

Kurt Junior went on. "If anything, you should be worrying about Lawrence. Kane might get so excited he mistakes him for a squirrel and shoots him."

"That's not funny," she said. "I wish you'd gone with them."

"I taught him how to use the gun. About all I could take. Ain't ready to go walk in the woods with all that shooting going on."

"He's your brother," Mama said. "Do yall both good to spend some time together."

"Let Lawrence take him hunting. I'll take him fishing."

"Promise?" Mama said.

"Yes, Mama. I promise."

When Kane and Lawrence returned around noon, Kane practically bowled Mama over running toward her, one dead squirrel in hand.

"Mama, mama! Look!"

"Oh boy," she said, not exactly thrilled about the prospect of cooking one squirrel—something she needn't have worried about after Kane mangled it while trying to gut and skin it. "You'd think you killed an entire elephant," she said.

"Shoooo, Mama. I bet an elephant's a lot easier to shoot," he said, an expert on hunting now. "Those squirrels, they sneak around in them woods, hide behind them trees, come out of nowhere. You have to stay still-still or they'll see you."

At that, Kurt went back to his room.

"I bet," Mama said. "Now get that thing out of my house. Clean it and then go clean yourself. You stink."

▫ ▫ ▫

What passed for fall in Louisiana gave way to what passed for winter. No snow that year. Christmas, then New Year's went by and my relationship with Lawrence marched along as unstoppable as time. It was destined, fate. We said "I love you" to one another without hesitation or drama or the untold calculations adults run before letting that phrase pass between their lips. There were gifts and dates and dances and, for Lawrence, more hunting trips with Kane, the two becoming as close as brothers, satellites in my orbit, exerting their own pulls but never threatening to tear me apart.

But no sex. We hadn't progressed beyond some mild, above-the-clothes fondling. We were scared, the both of us. He of all the hectoring his mother had done, warning him about girls like me. I of turning into those other two girls like me, Karla-Jean and Kendra-Sue. Oh, and added to the mix, Kurt Junior. For months, he was a hermit, slinking between bars and his bedroom. We never asked where he went, what he did. Then one day he's rushing out into the front yard to calm down this tiny spark plug of a girl in nurse's scrubs who'd been pounding on his window. "Get out here, Kurt," she'd yelled. "No hiding from this one." We didn't even really get to know Melinda before they were married by a justice of the peace and living in the trailer park being developed in the field between our house and the gully and the projects. The field owned by Lawrence's daddy, who'd become a trailer-park baron and who'd offered Kurt Junior a job on one of his other developments. Mama wasn't crazy about that arrangement—struck her as too close to the life she'd tried to escape, working day to day and answering to the man in the big house, living on his property.

So it wasn't a surprise when, shortly after, she pulled Karen-Anne, Kane, and me into our room and closed and locked the door even though no one else was in the house at the moment.

"I want to talk to yall and I want yall to promise me you won't breathe a word of this to your sisters and brother. Lord knows I love them just as much as I love yall, but if either of you come home pregnant—or Kane, if you knock somebody up—so help me, I'm packing a bag and leaving for good. Calgon take me away."

"Mama!" I said, shocked and embarrassed.

She looked at me, her eyes searching for an answer.

"Kane's not old enough for this," I stammered, as if that was my real concern.

"I'm plenty old enough," he said. "It's when a man puts his thing in a woman's thing and it makes a baby. You're *supposed* to be married to do that." Eleven years old and expert on yet another facet of life.

Karen-Anne and I started to laugh, but Mama cut that off real quick. "That's exactly right, baby. And if I catch you putting your thing anywhere near a girl's thing." She made a snipping motion with her fingers. "I'ma cut it off."

I covered his ears with my hands. "Mama! I'm sure!"

"I'm serious, Katie-Lee. I can't take anymore. Your daddy and me scrimped and saved to get out of them woods and put yall somewhere civilized and look at what happened. Living in trailers on other people's property. Might as well be sharecropping."

"Mama," I started.

"And you especially, Katie-Lee."

My face caught fire.

"Lawrence is a nice boy, the kind it would be good to settle down with. But not now. Not yet. No need to rush anything. You could both go to college. Yall both smart. Don't go thinking you have to do whatever he wants. And don't think you have to trap him."

"Mama!" I said again, completely unable to formulate any other words.

"Promise me," she said.

"Promise what?"

"Promise me you gonna keep them legs closed."

"Mama!"

"Promise!"

"Fine! I promise."

"Karen-Anne?"

"That's gross, Mama," she said.

"You say that now. Promise me."

So Karen-Anne promised. Karen-Anne's copious reading of science books, her brief time as Kendra-Sue's confidant, and her own stew of emotions was apparently enough to put her off of sex for years to come. Breaking with family tradition, she married before getting pregnant.

My promise, I couldn't keep. Not completely. All I can say is that to my credit, I never got pregnant. I kept that part. But not the rest.

Lawrence was a gentleman as long as he could be. But as the weeks progressed, his declarations of "I love you so much" turned into pleas of "Baby, you drive me crazy."

I may have had something to do with that.

I'd been silent in our early make-out sessions, but I'd taken to moaning, breathing audibly, trying to give voice to those jolts of electricity coursing through my body.

Our hands discovered the territory under our shirts and began exploring what could be called the crotchular region—but only when either of us was wearing pants. We didn't talk about these things, didn't set rules. But if I had on a skirt or he had on shorts, our hands didn't go much above the knees—though his hand on the inside of my thigh in that fraction of allowable inch was almost enough to get me there. At first. For a while. I'd end the night with wet panties. And if his weren't sticky, he was practically doubled over in pain. We both wanted more but weren't exactly sure how to go about it, where to go about it. He half-jokingly suggested setting up a sleeping bag and pillow in the back of the Bronco, an idea I immediately shot down as unacceptable for our first time.

Which, of course, implied there was an acceptable place for our first time.

Which is how we ended up at The Ranch Motel after Junior-Senior prom, flush not only with the glow of young love and Boone's Farm Strawberry Hill, but also with pride. We'd been voted King and Queen of the dance, him a junior, me a sophomore. It was practically unheard of. If any of my coworkers knew I'd been a cheerleader or prom queen, that I was that girl, they'd fall out of their chairs in disbelief.

I was still wearing my crown when we pulled into the parking lot of The Ranch, having done my best queen's wave all the way from the gym to the corner of Cane and Vine. I walked through my "court," a bunch of high-school kids in tuxes and ugly dresses drinking beer outside of Roma's Place, the restaurant out in the parking lot, practically begging Roma to come out and shoot them. Lawrence and I were tipsy, but not drunk—certainly not as drunk as everyone else was that night. That changed soon enough. Lawrence had bought a bottle of champagne and kept it in a cooler in the back of the Bronco all night. When he popped the cork, I thought of the phrase popping the cherry and laughed so hard I almost wet myself. Who was that girl, who was so happy and saw the hilarity in things?

"What's so funny?" Lawrence asked, nervous that he'd already done something wrong and ruined his chances.

"Pop," I said, making my eyes big, losing it again.

"I don't get it," he said, starting to sulk. Boys and their fragile little egos.

"Just pour me some champagne," I said, kissing him on the ear and neck.

Half a bottle of André—and out-of-control hormones—powered us through the nerves and initial humiliation of getting the prom dress off me and a condom on him.

"Do I have to?" he asked.

"It's not even up for debate," I said, reaching for my dress, with absolutely no intention at that point of holding firm. Had he pushed, who knows how different life would have been?

But he didn't. He wasn't the type. Besides, he was in no position, mentally or physically, to argue. His face was red, his breathing heavy. I thought he might literally explode and I worried he might not even get the condom on without finishing.

He didn't last much longer than that. It was over as soon as it began. We made out. He kissed my boobs some and then there he was, there it was. It didn't hurt like I thought it would—I'd imagined stabbing pains shooting from there all the way to my neck. And, it goes without saying, no orgasm either. If I was capable of achieving one in that short span of time with so little stimulation, I'd probably have trouble putting on pants.

It didn't disappoint. We were too in love for that—had too much invested in building the mythology of our first time.

Still, he apologized, a good sign, a sign he was at least aware he could have lasted longer and that, love or not, I had needs that had gone unmet. Talking to the girls at school, I knew there were some two years into a sexual relationship and all they'd ever had were forty-five seconds of grunting. And I'd learn later, much later, about the guys who apologized the first time. And the second time. And the third time. Their words were cover for laziness, selfishness, or an underlying physical or mental issue that, sorry bub, wasn't my problem. They didn't get a fourth. Three strikes and you're out. But I was more forgiving back then, more optimistic, convinced Lawrence would learn. And he did. He got better. Much better.

That night, we fumbled around like kids do, tried a couple more times with mixed results. Like that first kiss, the first time was now out of the way. We were free to carry on with life. It put us at ease, made us different. We felt more mature. Whether we were or not is debatable. We felt we'd been together for always and knew we'd stay together forever. Which isn't exactly a sign of maturity. Or perhaps it was just a sign of faith and hope, the kind only attainable before life grabs you by the collar, laughs in your face, spits in your eye, and tosses you down into the dirt, giving you a swift kick in the stomach before walking off.

I woke up in that room at The Ranch Motel the next morning a little shocked by what we'd done, but happy. I looked over at Lawrence, sleeping still, face down and arm slung over the edge of the bed. I considered the room itself. No one would have given The Ranch five stars at that stage in its existence. It had seen better days. But to me, it was a magical place. We'd pulled into a parking lot the night before crowded with noisy kids, but when we closed the door behind us, they were gone. We had one bed, made up and turned down. One color TV, as promised by the sign outside. One air conditioner. A bathroom with a shower—the house on Linda Lane had only a tub. Wall-to-wall carpeting—it smelled of cigarettes, but everything did back then.

And it was quiet. Even the night before with all the hell-raising outside, it had felt like an oasis. And that morning? Peace. Solitude. The world itself had been turned off. No dead Daddy. No screaming sisters and their crying babies. No weird older brother. No brokenhearted Mama.

Was this the place to which she hoped Calgon would take her away?

It was a protective cocoon, an escape pod, a time machine.

Come in a girl, walk out a woman.

◘ ◘ ◘

And tonight? In Lafayette, all these years later? Is this room going to change me? Turn back time? Heal old wounds?

No. Of course not. Whatever the potential of a hotel room, I know what else occupies them. The ghosts of sad businessmen, sad crimes, sad affairs.

Frazzled women putting off the inevitable.

I open my carry-on, on the hunt for a little chemical comfort, and my heart drops into my stomach. The toiletries bag isn't nesting on top of my clothes.

"No," I say to myself.

Did I forget to pack it? No way. I've never set off for the airport without it. Ever.

"Fucking TSA."

That's it. I must have taken it out at security and simply left it behind. And the three women working security this morning were too busy to notice. My toiletries bag, with all the pills necessary to stop a crazy person like me from doing something rash. Like hijacking a plane with nothing but a plastic wine bottle.

"Calm down, Katie-Lee," I counsel myself. Just calm down. I look through the purse, starting slowly, methodically. Within a minute I'm holding it upside down above the taut comforter, shaking it as if were an enemy of the state unwilling to give up the location of an explosive device. Junk rains outs. Balled-up Kleenex. Band-Aids. A nail file—good job, TSA! Receipts. Hair clips. A brush. Mint. Gum. Pens and a No. 2 pencil.

But no happy brown bottles with child-proof caps.

I give it one more shake and two little purple-blue pills fall out.

Ambien.

"Shit."

It's better than nothing—and I can't even allow myself to think how I'm going to make it through the next few days without the rest of the medical arsenal. I'll have to figure something out.

The Ambien, at least, will get me to sleep. But it also means no bottle of wine for Katie-Lee tonight. Valium, Vicodin, Lexapro, Tylenol PM, Nyquil—I'll mix a lot of things with booze. But not Ambien. I'm convinced that if I mix booze and Ambien, I'll come to in the middle of the street, naked and eating a turkey club, mayo dripping onto my belly, my underwear hooked around one ankle.

So no booze. But it's only 7:30. If I take one now, I'll be awake by four.

I call up room service and order a $15 shrimp po'boy, overpriced and, when it shows up, flaccid. Right here in the capital of Cajun country and they can't get a damn shrimp po'boy right. Between grousing about the food and actually eating it I make it to 8 p.m. I watch a bit of "Joe Dirt" on cable, a movie I've seen snippets of ten thousand times but never watched all the way through. I cruise through Facebook and Twitter, but don't post, tweet, or check in. At this point, it will only raise questions I don't feel like answering.

There are more text messages.

The young guy from the bar: "You around tonight?" Perhaps if we had had sex—with the lights on—he wouldn't be so eager.

One from Danielle. "Thinking of you. Hope you're OK."

One from Howie: "Call if you need anything."

And six from Candy, all of which imply the same thing: "I'm a better friend than your other friends because I keep texting." I come *this close* to calling her, just to hear a voice in the night, but I know how the conversation will go. Five minutes about me, then a story about how her third cousin died from a bee sting, then an hour about how awesome it used to be when we lived together. Maybe I'll talk to her tomorrow, when she inevitably calls during the middle of the wake. It'll save me from something, I'm sure.

At 8:30 on the dot, I take one pill and chase it with a hot shower. I lie flat on my back staring at the ceiling. It occurs to me a hotel room can still be a time machine. I walk out of here in the morning, I'll be walking straight into my past.

My heart starts racing.

"Fuck it," I say and take the other blue pill.

CHAPTER NINE

The parking lot of the funeral home is three-quarters full when I pull into Ville Platte at 9:45 on Sunday morning. I steer the Prius between the mountain range of SUVs and minivans to a spot in the row farthest from the front doors, the one facing the road. Across the highway sits a field chock-full of rust-colored cows penned in by three strands of barbed wire.

Mirror check. Eyelids a little heavy still from the Ambien sleep, but otherwise not overly swollen or puffy from yesterday's crying. I expect that will change today. The hair is my hair, less something to be styled or controlled than managed—and just barely. The wrinkles I can't do much about. Mood-wise, I'm as good as I'm going to get, which isn't bad considering I'm pill free.

Cars whiz by, heading to church or Walmart. Not that there's much of a difference.

I'm quite pleased with the observation. Maybe I can share it on Twitter or Facebook.

Phone check.

"Oh dear God." I say this out loud. A prayer. A lamentation.

No bars. Not one. And the battery has already lost a quarter of its juice, meaning the phone's been overexerting itself in a valiant attempt to acquire a signal. My hand goes to my mouth. This is what I get for trying to save a few bucks a month by going with a third-rate carrier. Sure, it has excellent coverage in New York, other major cities. How would I know it wouldn't work out here? Maybe none of the carriers do.

As if in answer, a shaggy-bearded man, wearing torn jeans and layers of clothes, walks by on the shoulder on the highway, talking on a cell phone. He's carrying a cardboard sign that reads, "Vietnam vet. Will work for food." Has he wandered into the wrong decade?

"I'm gone out to the red light by the Walmart," he's saying. "Yeah. Okay, Mama. I'll be careful." Pause. "Yeah, I'll pick up some milk after I'm done. Yeah, and a box of wine. Okay, Mama. You want the purple or the pink?"

I look back at my phone. "Seriously?" I ask, but the bars don't light up in response. I've half a mind to throw it down onto the pavement and stomp it to death, but that would be like cutting off my arm. With it dead, I already feel I've lost a limb.

After a few deep breaths, I exit the car. Stay out here much longer and I'll hyperventilate myself right into a hissy fit. Just get on with it and hope for the best. All these cars. And kids everywhere. Already bored, they're weaving between the vehicles, playing in the parking lot unattended. What would the Brooklyn Mommies say about that?

This must be a double-parlor funeral home, like those wedding factories with movable walls and multiple dance floors. Except with death. Twice the mourning at half the price.

Worse comes to worse, I can seek refuge with the other family.

A voice shouts out. "Mais, look what the cat dragged in. What you so dressed up for?"

Kurt Junior. He's now about as round as he is tall. He could rest an open beer can on his stomach without it tipping it over—and he probably does.

And he's so old. Which shouldn't be a surprise. He looked no different four, five years ago. I see pictures of him online. But the Kurt Junior who lives in my head is the sepia-toned one, shirtless under the sun, in cut-off denim shorts, a bandana in his hair, leaning on a shovel in the gravel of Linda Lane. The picture was one I took with me when I left all those years ago. How old was he in that photo? He was just back from the war—his war—thin and ropy with muscle. His complexion had gone to shit. For a while we thought maybe he'd been exposed to Agent Orange. Instead, it was bad diet and worse grooming habits. He's wearing a smile in the photo. Undoubtedly, whoever snapped it had insisted on it, photos being a precious commodity in the days before a person could take hundreds of shots and delete at will. But the forced smile couldn't hide the distance in his eyes, the cloud that hovered over him at the time.

And now, he's standing with a gaggle of coots, off to the side of the building, laughing. They're all wearing camouflage jackets or shirts or both. And the sort of jeans made of denim so stiff they look like they could stand up on their own. They're enveloped in cigarette smoke. Occasionally, a brown stream of tobacco juice will shoot into the bushes or onto the foundation of the funeral home, stained from previous gatherings of a similar nature.

"Who dat, Kurt Junior?" one of the others asks, as if I'm not standing right there. The accent. I forgot how thick it is. Just last month I was mocking a cable channel show about Louisiana alligator hunters because it had chosen to subtitle the men as they boated around the swamps and bayous hollering, "Choot 'em. Choot dat ting, I said!" The subtitles helpfully explained: "Shoot him. Shoot that thing."

Now I wonder if I might have to hire a translator.

"Dat's Katie-Lee, you old fool," Kurt Junior says. "You don't recognize her?"

"Katie-Lee," the old man says, giving me a closer look. "Aw, yeah. Okay. You come down from New York City, hanh?" He gives me a quick hug, then pushes me back for further examination. "Why you all dressed up, girl? They must not have any good food up there, you so damn skinny." He touches my hair. "I bet your hair weigh more than you. Look at all dat! You not a Pentecostal, huh?"

"I'm wearing jeans," I stammer, as if this answers his questions. Jeans aren't dressed up. A Pentecostal woman would not be wearing jeans. Thank God I didn't wear a dress and heels. I still have no idea who he is.

"Frank, leave that girl alone," Kurt Junior says, then to me. "You remember your idiot cousin Frank?"

"Of course," I lie. Not really. Though now I vaguely remember someone who always had some smart-ass remark that he thought was much funnier than it ever actually was.

Kurt Junior and I exchange a half hug. One-armed, awkward, short—but long enough for me to catch the Kurt Junior smell of dirt and cigarette smoke and coffee and Dial soap. At least that much hasn't changed. I can practically see a brand-new, yellow-orange bar with the letters carved in.

"Can't believe you're smoking," I say.

"Only when I'm not drinking," he jokes, dropping the cigarette to the pavement, grinding it out. "You don't smoke no more?"

"No," I say. "I quit when it got to seven dollars a pack."

"Seven?" one of the men asks.

"In New York, it's thirteen a pack now."

"Keeee-yaaaaahhhhhhhhhh!" another exclaims. "You gotta be rich in New York just to have a bad habit. Thirteen damn dollars!"

"That's something else," one of the others says.

Yet another offers me an unopened pack. "Here. Bring dat back wichoo and sell dat. Send me back da profits."

This, his compatriots find hilarious. All except Cousin Frank, who's probably wishing he'd thought of the joke himself.

I turn my attention back to Kurt Junior. He's still got a head full of hair, all gone white now, shading to dark gray and black down in the beard regions.

"How are you doing?" I ask.

He shrugs, looks away. "Okay."

About what I expected. He may shed tears later—he's not embarrassed to cry, that much I know. What I didn't expect was to find him smack-dab in the middle of a clown break and him the ringleader. I can tell by the way the other men look at him that he's the Alpha Bozo. That, more than his physical appearance, unsettles me. Where's his dark cloud and far-away look? At some point I guess he sought refuge in humor. Better that than religion if you ask me. Would rather see him out here than on his knees praying and weeping. So what if they're smoking, taking nips from bottles, recharging with their old jokes and stories before they go back in?

"Everybody inside?"

"Mostly," he says. "Sonny Junior still not back yet from Afghanistan. But he's supposed to get in tonight."

"I can't imagine." But I can. Half a world away, serving in some mud-walled compound of huts, shitting in a hole, trying not to get killed. Then getting a call that your mama is dead. And then that flight home. Wanting nothing but to get back as fast as possible. But it takes hours and hours. Days, maybe. Alone with your thoughts waiting for a transfer in some airport lounge in Kuwait, millionaire sheiks walking by and giving you the stink eye although it's you and people like you keeping his neighbors—or his own people—from rising up and burning the place to the ground. "Poor thing."

"They all taking it pretty bad."

"I should go in."

"I'll go with you."

"There another service going on?" I ask.

"No," he says before opening the double doors to the lobby. "This is all Karen-Anne."

It's an awful lot. A sea of round, ruddy faces turns to see who's just walked through the door. The throng to my left looks only for a moment before going back to their hushed conversations about farm reports and football. I don't recognize any of them, but I know they're family. The hair. The eyes. The ears. The set of the mouth. Country cousins. They might not have been close to Karen-Anne—some probably hadn't seen her since Mama's funeral—but they're here. And they'll stay all day. Or until the food runs out.

To my right?

My breath stops in my chest. An informal receiving line of nieces and nephews that look so much like we did at that age that my head spins. At that age? Jesus. I think the youngest one is twenty. Twenty! Which means the smaller ones moving in and out like bees in a clover field are grandkids. How did we get so old? And where did all these kids come from? I knew these people existed, have seen proof of it littered all over Facebook, but that doesn't make it any easier to accept.

"Mawmaw," says one little voice. "Who's that?"

I locate the source—a little red-haired girl hiding behind Kendra-Sue's denim-clad legs.

"Hmmmm. I *think* that's your Aunt Katie-Lee," Kendra-Sue says. "It's been so long, I'm not sure. That you, Katie-Lee?"

Guess she left the Valium at home today. I don't take the bait. Instead, I take a deep breath and consider my sister. Short-haired, wide-hipped and big-assed, but still in pretty good shape for her age. Kendra-Sue refused to be frozen in my timeline, no matter how much I may have tried, what with her annoying insistence on communication, however fruitless those attempts may have been. The only difference I can spot between the version standing in front of me and the countless photos I've seen on Facebook is she's highlighted her hair. It's lighter than it's ever been. "Go say hi, Olive-Juice," she tells the girl.

The child buries her green eyes and freckled nose in her grandmother's mom jeans. Kendra-Sue was always so much like Mama, I half expect her to shove the child at me, tell her to quit being silly. Instead, she strokes Olivia's hair and gives me a shrug. Has she grown more accepting, patient in her old age? Or is that a shrug of condemnation. I don't know if such a thing exists, but Kendra-Sue could certainly invent it. "See, you're scaring the children," she could be saying.

"Olive?" I ask. "Are you the one I helped with the Flat Stanley project?" I'd carried the little cardboard guy around New York taking pictures of him in front of things for someone's school project.

"That's right," Kendra-Sue says. "Remember that, Olive? We sent Flat Stanley to New York City?"

The child shakes her head.

"You don't remember? That's probably because all his pictures were in front of pizza places and restaurants in Brooklyn. I guess Aunt Katie-Lee was too busy to get to the Statue of Liberty or Empire State building."

That's it. My ears burn, fists clench, and I'm just about to get the first blow-up out of the way, when a scarecrow-skinny woman, pale as a ghost, walks over and wraps her arms around me, squeezes tight and starts crying on my shoulder. Her hair makes my skin itch. Her long, sack-like dress smells of mothballs.

"Oh, Katie-Lee," she moans. "You're the baby girl, now. Oh, my sweet baby sister. Gone so long. But you're back. Praise Jesus."

I pull back and hold this apparition at arm's length. Red bristly hair in a rope down her back, curls fighting to escape. Frown lines around the mouth. Slightly upturned nose. Hazel eyes, which seem set too far back in her head. Freckles.

"Karla-Jean?"

I want to ask, "What the hell happened to you?" But I don't.

Kendra-Sue had told me she'd lost weight on some crazy diet, but I wasn't prepared for this. There was no way to. Her minister drove them all off Facebook—can't catch the Holy Ghost if you're raising fake cows and flirting with high-school boyfriends. And it sure looks like Karla-Jean's caught the Holy Ghost. Or maybe it's caught her and is feasting on her soul.

Either that or she has cancer. Or a tapeworm. Or both at the same time.

"My God, Karla-Jean," I say, forgetting myself. She physically flinches at the casual use of God. "You're so skinny!"

She used to be the biggest of us. Was always tall, hefty and, after the first baby, went immediately to fat.

"Yes," she says. "The Lord wouldn't have it any other way. You know, as I was telling Kendra-Sue earlier, if you just give yourself—"

Here, Kendra-Sue cuts in. "Not now, Karla-Jean," she says, as gently as Kendra-Sue can say anything.

To my right, Kurt Junior makes a sound that might as well be a literal "tee-hee." It reminds me of Roscoe P. Coltrane from the Dukes of Hazzard.

Karla-Jean smiles, undeterred, as if she's long grown accustomed to the doubts of the unfaithful, the machinations of those who'd stand between her and her God-assigned task of saving souls. "That's okay. But let's catch up, Katie-Lee," she says, patting my hand. "We have so much to talk about. There are things you need to hear."

Wow. She's a weird one.

"I'll be here the whole time, Karla-Jean. I'm sure we'll have plenty of time to catch up."

Kendra-Sue takes my arm and Karla-Jean's hand. "Come on, Kurt Junior. We're all here. Let's go see Karen-Anne."

The circle of nieces, nephews and grandkids opens around us, clearing a path to another set of double doors. Beyond, a room of chairs, all lined up, facing in one direction toward a wall of flowers. Set among the bouquets is a photo of Karen-Anne with Sonny and the kids, all smiling on the verge of laughing, as if the photographer had, for once in his life, said something that was actually funny.

And the casket. Shiny silver, the lower half covered in flowers. What kind? Did Karen-Anne even like flowers? Were these her favorites? Am I the world's worst sister because I don't know the answers to these questions?

The top half is open.

From the entrance of the room, I can't really make her out. Or I don't want to. Or both. What I want to do is plant both my heels into the carpet, stop dead, and pull back. I think of the kid in the postcard for Harriet's husband's art show, the child outside the rest area in Mississippi. Crying. Resisting the inevitable.

Kendra-Sue's grip remains firm.

A step closer. Another step. And there we are, the four of us standing over the body of our little sister.

I think I'm supposed to say something. But what? She looks peaceful? She looks pretty? They did a good job?

She's dead. My little sister is fucking dead. And she looks it. For a split second, anger flashes through me. She didn't die. She was murdered. God did it. Or the Holy Ghost. Or Nature in all Her Glory, through the Noble Rhinoceros. Or Science, via the nasty little microbes that invaded her blood. Someone should pay, I think, before the anger winks out like a candle.

Karla-Jean reaches out and touches her, but I can't. I'm afraid. If I touch her, death will rub off on me. How much time do any of us have left? I drop to the kneeler in front of the coffin, not out of an urge to pray, but because I can't stand any longer. Karla-Jean puts her death-tainted hand on my shoulder. Kurt Junior rubs my back. I lean my head on Kendra-Sue's thigh, much like Olivia did not five minutes earlier, afraid to look at the world.

She doesn't pull away.

Tears run down my cheeks. My brain races through past, present and future, so fast everything becomes a blur. If I don't say something, don't actually speak, I might start screaming.

"You guys put her in a Saints jersey?" I ask, feeling slightly guilty for skirting an opportunity for a deep moment, for catharsis. But I don't think we're ready for it. I'm not.

"Her idea," Kurt Junior says.

"It was in her will," Kendra-Sue says.

"In her will?"

"In the actual will," Kurt-Junior says. "That night they won the Super Bowl, she said, 'I'm gone see a lawyer tomorrow and change my will. Yall bury me in a Saints jersey.' "

"She said if we didn't," Karla-Jean starts, then stops.

Kendra-Sue comes to her rescue. "She said, 'Yall don't bury me in a Saints jersey, I'll haunt your sorry asses till you join me in hell.' "

I reach out and touch Karen-Anne now as we lapse into silence, trying to remember her sense of humor, her embrace of the strange and the weird, her willingness to take care of a sick hippopotamus or go bungee jumping or demand to be buried in a Drew Brees jersey. But it's hard. Her face is swollen under the thick makeup. How much is age? How much is weight gain? How much injury? I can't tell. People used to mistake us for twins, but she looks more like Kendra-Sue now than me. Short hair, extra pounds. They've lived the same life the last two decades.

"Come on," Kendra-Sue says finally. "You should say hi to Sonny and the kids."

In a small back room, one designed for immediate family to escape the suffocating intentions of the well-wishers, we find Sonny and the two older kids—Lucy and Leslie and Leslie's husband, Steve. Sonny and Lucy sit on a small sofa, Leslie and Steve on chairs facing them, forming a hunched-over circle, talking to a table top.

"Where you at?" Lucy asks in her flat Cajun accent.

"I'm here," a disjointed voice from far away answers.

"Where?"

"Just arrived."

"Okay."

"Okay."

"You okay?"

"It's cold."

It takes me longer than I'd like to admit to realize they're not having a séance, but are gathered around an iPhone, talking—or trying to talk—to someone on the other end.

"We love you," Lucy says.

"Love you, too," says the voice. "Be there tonight."

My second thought is more shameful than the first. The

question that comes to mind isn't, "Who are you talking to?" but rather, "Who's your service provider? And can I check Facebook?" Like my brain has been hardwired to immediately seek out the best phone and Internet connections in a new land. The very definition of addiction. At my age. I'm no different than a twelve-year-old boy sulking because his parents won't allow him to take his Nintendo DS into a restaurant.

The voice comes through again. "Daddy? You okay?"

Sonny swallows hard, forces himself to smile, as if his physical countenance will make his lie more believable.

"Yeah, buddy," he says, then pauses. "I'm fine." Another pause. "Hurry home." It seems two words are all he can manage before catching his breath, gathering his strength. One more word and the dam would burst. And not for the first time, it seems. Sonny, a broad-shouldered bearded guy, looks sort of like the Brawny Man—the old one, the one with the mustache, before they went and metrosexualized him. But now, he's a crumpled, wrinkled, red-eyed thing, two sizes two small.

"Love you," he manages.

The door behind me opens and a squat young woman wearing short hair and what looks like a man's business casual walks in. I figure she's the funeral director until she sits down next to Lucy and kisses her temple, strokes her hair out of her eyes and takes her hand.

"It's gonna be okay, baby," she says.

She then reaches across and takes Sonny's hand, too. He pats it. "Thanks, Tina," he says.

Leslie's husband fills Tina in on what she's missed. "Sonny Junior's in Atlanta. Looks like he'll get in this afternoon. Tonight at the latest."

"Where? Alexandria or Lafayette?" Tina asks.

"Don't know. Maybe even Baton Rouge or New Orleans. Depends on what he can get first."

"Shit," she says.

She's every bit the spouse that Steve is, it seems. They're doing their jobs, propping up their partners, taking care of the business end of things so the immediate family can grieve as needed.

Kendra-Sue interrupts. "Sonny?"

They all look up, as if they'd somehow not noticed the four people standing in the room listening to them. I can see Lucy and Leslie's processors crunching the data, trying to place a name to my face.

Sonny's eyes lock on mine and his lower lip starts to tremble. His head tilts. It's like watching a building implode. Don't do this, Sonny, is all I can think.

"Katie-Lee," he says, climbing out of the couch even as his face collapses. He stops in front of me. "You always did look the most like her," he says, sobbing now that he's exceeded his two-word maximum. He takes me into his arms.

"I'm so sorry," is all I can think to say.

"I'm so glad you came," he says after his crying tapers off to a manageable whimper. "Karen-Anne always said one of 'em would have to die to get you back here for something other than Christmas."

The comment stabs me, right in the gut. Suddenly, I'm horrified. With the horror comes panic, the room closing around me, my head swimming, lungs constricting.

"Excuse me," I try to say before darting out of the room.

CHAPTER TEN

I seek shelter in the Prius, a little bubble of solitude. Staring at the cows across the road, I briefly consider driving off. But I'm not a twenty-year-old girl. There's no running away from this one. I'll have to take my lumps. Maybe I can get a mulligan, walk back in and start over.

There's a knock on the passenger window.

Kurt Junior.

I unlock the door and he wedges his bulk into the passenger seat.

"Tight fit," I say.

"You should see me behind the wheel."

"You've driven one of these?"

"Own one. Or Melinda does. Gas prices like they are."

"Hmph," I say.

We sit for a while, considering the cows across the highway.

"It was just a joke," he says.

"What? You owning a Prius?"

"No, *couillon*!" he says, exasperated. "What Sonny said. He was joking. You know how him and Karen-Anne are. Some sick individuals."

"But it's true. What he said. It did take one of us dying."

To this, he doesn't respond.

"Say something, Kurt Junior."

He gives me a sly little smile. "Why don't we let Kendra-Sue jump your ass about that one?"

"Shit." I start hyperventilating all over again. "Like she hasn't already?"

"C'mon. She hasn't even started on you yet," he says.

I would kill for just half of one of my pills right now. If they juiced up cattle with anti-anxiety meds instead of hormones and antibiotics, I would walk across the pastures and suck the blood out of an entire cow. Kurt Junior reaches into his coat and pulls out a pint bottle of Jack Daniel's, hands it to me. When I fumble with the cap, he snatches it back.

"Look," he says, unscrewing the top. "We're all glad to see you. Even Sonny. Hell, that's the most words he said all day."

Bottle back in hand, I take a long pull, the burn racing down my throat, a punishment for my sins, a release from my sorrows. I feel better immediately. But not good enough to go back in.

"Kurt, I'm sorry I didn't invite any of you guys to my wedding." I feel like I need to apologize for a lot. Might as well start with that, with the easy stuff.

"I thought yall eloped," he says.

"Oh, we did. I mean I'm sorry for not telling you guys much. About him. Not bringing him down here to meet everyone."

"Not like yall stayed married that long anyway," he says.

"True. But still."

He takes the bottle from me. "Besides, we all met Howie anyway."

"What? What do you mean you met Howie?"

This was beyond belief. This was not a matter of some chance encounter in an airport. My family is not exactly one to rack up frequent-flier miles. Their trips to the airport usually involve meeting someone going to or coming from war.

"He come to New Orleans for Jazzfest, then saw Festival

International was going in Lafayette. So he drove there and I guess Kendra-Sue seen him on Facebook. She always on that damn thing. So she invited him to her house and called up the whole damn family."

Howie just happened to make a two-hour detour to Lafayette. Sounds like the man I met, the spontaneous one, always on the prowl for some adventure before marriage turned him into the sort of guy who considered switching beer brands a walk on the wild side. Was it marriage? Or was it me? Why do I care?

"Was he alone?"

"Yeah. He was by himself."

What a world. How easily, how casually we make connections. We may no longer speak to the neighbor across the hall or over the fence—hell, you didn't ask him to move in next door—but discover a like-minded soul online and you can find yourself on a cross-country flight for a one-night stand—or eating dinner with your ex-wife's family.

And no one—not one person—said anything.

"So somehow you all managed to keep it a secret?"

"He said you'd get mad."

"You think?"

"Don't see what the big deal is."

"You guys saw my ex-husband behind my back. Without asking me first or telling me after."

"It's not like he cheated on you or hurt you or nothing. Hell, both Harold and Brent are in that funeral home right now—and Karla-Jean's second ex, too—and them divorces were a lot uglier."

I wasn't around for the latter two. And as they happened in a time before Facebook or email, in a time when a long-distance phone call cost you a small fortune, I didn't get any first-hand accounts. All I knew was there was cheating and drinking and repeated separations and door-pounding and stalking and threats of violence.

"That's different," I say.

"Yeah, Howie probably never pushed you into a wall." He takes a pull from the bottle. "Though I mighta been tempted if I was him."

“That was a shitty thing to say,” I say.

▫ ▫ ▫

Of course, he wasn’t the first to imply that Howie would have been within his rights to give me a good throttling.

Howie and I weren’t exactly a Hollywood romance, not even at the start. The fact was, Howie and I were just tired. We’d both survived two decades in the cyclical hell that is the New York dating world. During the feasting cycle, it wasn’t uncommon to go on three dates in a week. And if I’m being honest, “dates”—during those times—meant dinner, drinks, and a roll in the sack. The famine side of the ledger needs no explanation other than those cold, winter nights alone, when you wondered how long it would be before anyone noticed if you died in your apartment.

Whatever the case, when we met in early 2002, we were both looking for something else, looking to get off the ride. We were also—all of us in New York, I think—still reeling from 9/11. Funny how the rest of the country still seems so caught up on it all these years later, while we’ve moved on. But at that point, we’d all been knocked for a loop. How many of us watched the world crumble, saw the ashes of the dead drifting down from the sky while cut off from the entire world, phone and internet severed, our only company the broken-hearted voice of CBS 2’s Pablo Guzman describing the terror?

So Howie and I met, saw something in one another, latched on. It was all very adult. No stalking. No jealousy. None of that panic common to the first few months of a relationship: *He didn’t call. Why didn’t he call? What does dating mean? Do we need a label? What are we doing?* None of that. And none of the passion, either. We had a first date. Then a second. Didn’t consummate anything until the third, as if we’d both decided, independently, that we were going to do this one by the rules.

I liked Howie. There was no denying that. He was straightforward, funny as hell, smart, and unlike so many New York men, he wasn’t a neurotic mess. He wasn’t a man-child—not in the same way a lot of New York men were. Maybe it was that Asian upbringing. Sure, he was spoiled and expected certain things from a woman in a relationship, but the trade off was adequate. He didn't cry or whine or mewl. He wasn't passive aggressive. He knew how to kill a mouse, change a light bulb, fix a running toilet, drive a car, tie a tie, and get his hair cut for under twenty bucks. I could do all of those things—except the last—but I didn't necessarily want to.

Within six months we'd exchanged the love word and moved in together. A year later, he was on his knees in the sand at Jones Beach, sticking an engagement ring in my face and mumbling out some confused attempt at a clever-but-not clichéd version of "Will you marry me?" It wasn't a surprise. The only surprise was that the immediate response from my inner voice was, "Don't do this, Katie-Lee. Say no." I should have known it was serious because it used my real name instead of Katherine. And it sounded like Kendra-Sue.

I ignored it. Of course I did. I wasn't that much different than my single friends—was getting afraid of the old dying-alone-and-eaten-by-your-cat scenario. Some of them, after passing up certifiable dreamboats in their twenties and early thirties, would happily settle, as Danielle put it, "for a guy with a job, some hair, and most of his teeth." And here was Howie, strong, handsome, stable, willing to give me the world.

He wasn't the love of my lifetime. But I said yes.

Candy liked Howie. Perhaps a little too much. She invited us over often. Invited herself over. Asked him for dating advice. Asked him if he had any single friends. And when I told her he'd proposed, she said, "Typical. You don't even *want* to get married and here's a husband just washing up at your door. Why don't you give him to me?" She meant it as a joke—or tried to pass it off as such. I wanted to tell her off but I swallowed my drink and kept my mouth shut.

I was mad because she was right, of course. I settled. As did Howie. In fact, Howie did a much better job of settling. He excelled at it. Talk about gender roles. "My wife" this and "the old lady" that. He'd escape on Sundays for football with the boys. "Honey, what's for dinner?" "Baby can you make lunch?" I played along. It was a challenge—to see if I could domesticate myself after all those years alone, to see if I could live up to his expectations.

We were man and woman, husband and wife. We got along. Had our flare-ups, but never really fought. Talked about children, but never seriously. Had sex twice a week, then once a week, then once every other week.

And that's what first set me off. One night, just a year and a half into the marriage, he's going down on me, I'm enjoying myself if for no other reason than it's been over two weeks. And it occurs to me I'm definitely not looking forward to the part where he climbs on top of me and I have to look at his face, watch him grimace, hear him grunt. It dawns on me that one of the reasons we're not having sex as frequently is because I'm not initiating it—ever. I was no longer sexually attracted to him. "It's just age, Katherine. You're getting older," I told myself. "Bullshit, Katie-Lee. You know better. You and the vibrator in your nightstand."

And then came the street-corner crisis, the therapy, and finally, Facebook. It seemed silly at first, a yearbook for grown-ups. But I signed up. As did Howie. And our immediate friends. And their friends. And more and more and more, until, finally, I went down the rabbit hole looking for, what? Lost loves, missed connections, second chances? I sat in front of a computer all day at work, so it was hard to resist. Howie practically had his laptop surgically attached due to his own work. He carried on in blissful ignorance for a while before my misery started to catch his attention.

But what really caught it were the comments from Paul, some ex of mine from back in the '90s, on every one of my status updates. Flirtatious, charming, almost always first to chime in. And funny. That was what finally set Howie off. Men have their limits. And even the most understanding, least jealous of men will not tolerate you saying—or typing—repeatedly to another man, "OMG. You're so funny." Like some teenage girl. I'd even say it aloud sometimes. "Howie, come read Paul's status. Oh my god, he's hilarious." It was a passive-aggressive, shitty thing to do. But not nearly as bad as leaving my laptop at home, logged into Facebook with a twenty-message private back-and-forth between Paul and me on the screen, a lurid reminiscence of our sexual escapades—and lord, did we have some—and dirty jokes, all of this *while* I was out having coffee with Paul.

Of course I wanted to get caught. I didn't need a therapist to tell me that. And none of them did because I conveniently left out my bad behavior from any of our sessions.

"You're fucking him, aren't you?" Howie asked when I got home. He was sitting on the couch, his head in his hands, unable to even look me in the eyes.

I don't think it was until that very moment that I realized two things. I had no choice but to leave him. And it was going to tear him to shreds.

But I couldn't lie. I should have. It might have made everything happen more quickly.

"No," I told him. "Nothing's happened." And it hadn't. Swear up and down as I might, I don't think he ever completely believed me. And I'm pretty sure a number of my friends didn't believe me either. But nothing had happened. Just the Facebook flirting and a cup of coffee. Would it have remained that innocent had I not been caught? Who knows.

What followed was two months of excruciating negotiations on Howie's part. I heard him out. I consoled him. I cried. He cried. We had hate sex and make-up sex and sorry sex. A bit of false hope, that, but we had our needs. He offered to go to couples counseling. I said I'd think about it, but decided against it. I told him, "It's not you, it's me." I said, "I love you, but I'm not in love with you." He thought he deserved better than that. "I took vows," he said. "Vows. Till death. And you're going to give me these lines that anyone over the age of eighteen would be embarrassed to say with a straight face."

But what was wrong with them? I did still love him. In many ways, he was still my best friend. My tears were real. What was I going to do when we split? Who was going to fill my hours? Put up with me? Why can't there be a happy medium for those of us who don't want husbands or children, but who don't want to die alone?

And it *was* me—more than him at any rate. These trite lines are overused for a reason, is what I think. They protect both parties. What was I going to tell him? That I wasn't sexually attracted to him anymore? That the sound of him slurping up pad thai made me want to cover his disproportionately large head in fish sauce and hold it down in a fire-ant hill? That even if he had ever had a burning spark for me, he'd gotten lazy in his love? And that none of that mattered at all because I'd never love him with my whole heart?

What would that have accomplished? Not a damn thing. So I kept my mouth shut. Apologized as much as I could and in the summer of 2006 packed my stuff and moved out. Divorced. End of story.

And when I told Candy this was happening? There was no joking that time.

She was disgusted by the way I'd tossed away a year-and-a-half marriage like it was just another relationship. Something she wanted so badly, and I crumpled it up like a piece of garbage. I thought Candy, who'd spent years trying to be the version of a sister she felt I needed, would have taken my side in anything. I pegged her for the sort who, if I served a plate full of kittens at a dinner party, would have not only rationalized it, she would have asked for seconds and taken home leftovers. But everyone has a line, that one thing, and I'd crossed hers.

"I knew you'd do this," she said to me. "You didn't deserve him."

"You are the world's shittiest sister," I said and walked out of the bar.

▫ ▫ ▫

"The point is," I tell Kurt Junior, "you're supposed to be on my side. Even if I'm the world's shittiest sister."

"Calm down. We hardly even talked about you."

"I bet." I take the bottle back from him. I should stop. At this rate I'll be drunk before noon. "So? What did you think of him?"

"Nice guy. Funny. Ate like a starved dog."

"Sounds like him."

"You never told me he was Thai."

I feel my face turn red.

"What?" he asks.

"I didn't know how you'd react if I brought an Asian home."

"Mais, what you thought I was gonna do?"

"I don't know. You know. The war and all."

"Give me my whiskey back," he says, grabbing the bottle. "Just for that, you can't have no more." He's trying to joke about it, but I can tell I've hurt him.

"I'm sorry. I just remember how Daddy felt about the Japanese."

"Katie-Lee, Daddy fought against the Japanese. I didn't fight against the Thais. Hell, that's where we went for R and R. Bangkok. Pattaya. We had staging bases in Thailand."

"Really? I had no idea."

I can't imagine my brother—heavy and round, white-haired, and gray-bearded—sweating in Bangkok, the noise of a million tuk-tuks buzzing around him, the wire-laden utility poles threatening to tip over, the smells of roti and mangosteen and fish sauce mixing with the reek of durian. And all those people jabbering away. Of course, Kurt Junior wasn't fat or old back then. He was an attractive, fit young man in a uniform prowling the streets of Bangkok, which itself—well, I have no idea what Bangkok was like back in the late '60s, early '70s. My vision of it as a 21st century madhouse can't be reconciled with history. I wonder if in another forty years, Americans will be vacationing in a Kabul or Peshawar or Baghdad unrecognizable to the young men who once fought there.

"You never asked," he says.

"I didn't think you wanted to talk about it. Any of it."

"Maybe I didn't. Maybe I did. Shit. I don't even remember. But I know none of yall asked. And it wasn't like I could just start talking about it at supper."

"I'm sorry," I say.

"It's okay. Mama had her hands full with Karla-Jean and Kendra-Sue. And you and Karen-Anne. And—" He stops himself. "Well, yall were just kids, really. At least I had Daddy there for a bit. That helped. A lot."

"I always wondered if you two actually talked while sitting out on that carport."

"Some. Yeah. It was enough he understood. Had seen it. And when Karen-Anne was in college, she did a paper or had a phase or something and couldn't get enough."

Karen-Anne always was full of crazy ideas—like asking people questions to get answers.

"Shit," I say, putting my head down on the steering wheel. "Karen-Anne." Kurt Junior puts his hand on my back and it's about the most soothing, nonpharmaceutical thing I've experienced since I was a kid. It feels like Daddy's hand on my back. I breathe. In. Out. In. Out. "I guess we should go back in."

"No rush," he says. "Gonna be a long day."

Which is the understatement of the century.

CHAPTER ELEVEN

When we return to the funeral home, it seems there are somehow more people. They all want to say hi, to touch us, to comfort and be comforted.

The kids—well, the nieces and nephews, who can hardly be considered kids anymore—seem fascinated with me, Aunt Katie-Lee, the glamorous aunt who lives way up in New York. Boy, would those illusions be easy to shatter. They talk of visiting. The world is smaller for their generation—if you have the money for a cheap ticket, hop on a plane and go. Hell, even some of the more countrified ones have done a fare bit of traveling, working for oil companies or contracting firms that have projects in Trinidad or California, Norway or New York. The world will be smaller by half for the next generation, I'm sure. And then what? Will there be anyone left in places like this? The answer, of course, is yes. For most of them, it will always be a round trip. Get out, see a little bit of the world and return to the comforts of home. For them, home *is* a comfort. All the ink spilled about the rebirth of the city and the death of the suburbs and rural America? Those books are written with at least a sprinkle of revenge, a dash of smug "I told you so" by people who, for some reason or other, ran from home. The hurt—the drug-addled screwups or brokenhearted cheerleaders escaping the past. And the bullied—nerds, band geeks, poets, gays.

Though I wonder if gays are still running off to the city in huge numbers.

I look at Lucy and Tina, watch them closely.

That Lucy is gay isn't exactly a surprise. At thirty years old, she's never been engaged or knocked up—which is normal in New York, but downright strange in South Louisiana. She's short and thick and square, almost. She could wear a sweater with a letter on it and go as an alphabet block for Halloween.

What has surprised me, though, is the interaction between Lucy and Tina and the rest of the family. The scene in the private room with Sonny and the others. The way Kendra-Sue and Kurt Junior—even Karla-Jean—comfort Tina, kid with her, try to make her feel at home. The nieces and nephews don't even notice. No one's pretending they're just roommates or best buds. Though, in the other room, among the extended family and friends, they keep a little distance from one another, don't hold hands or betray themselves with any other physical contact. Pick your battles, I suppose.

"They got married last month."

This is Catherine. Sixteen years old. T-Brent's oldest daughter, Kendra-Sue's first grandchild. She's a beautiful girl. In fact, another glance at the offspring of this generation confirms that the Fontenots have spawned a veritable Abercrombie & Fitch catalog. Or maybe once you hit my age, everyone that age seems like a model. Hell, she's likely considered on the heavy side by her peers, the little idiots. So she's hiding behind Goth-light. Hair dyed a deep black, too much mascara and eyeliner. Three piercings in each ear. A long black dress instead of jeans. But she'd be run out of a New York Goth group in a hot minute. You can tell it doesn't run deep. She smiles. Doesn't have cut marks on her forearms. Instead of a vial of blood, she wears a class ring, undoubtedly her boyfriend's, on a chain around her neck.

I bet she secretly listens to Justin Bieber still.

"They ran off to Iowa or Illinois or one of those 'I' states where it's legal."

She's attached herself to my hip, has been within my orbit since Kurt Junior and I came back in. I don't mind. It's good for the ego. She's also proving to be an excellent translator and tour guide to a country that's insisted on changing in my absence. And it helps me ignore the fact that Kendra-Sue and I are avoiding each other, circling the funeral home like fighters warily sizing up an opponent. Her first jab stung, so I'm not quite ready to close the gap again.

"How did that go over?"

She shrugs. "They didn't make too big a deal about it. All us kids knew. We could tell."

"And your Mawmaw?"

"Shit. She didn't care." I'm struck by how much Catherine sounds like Kendra-Sue in that instant. "Half her friends are twice as gay. She hangs out with some weirdoes, her. She bought me this skull ring and this dress."

Kendra-Sue, making one of her passes, chimes in. "I like to encourage this ugly-ass look she's got going on. Trying to keep the boys away, see if she can finish high school without getting pregnant."

Catherine rolls her eyes. "Just because yall couldn't keep your legs closed doesn't mean I can't."

"We'll see," Kendra-Sue says before moving off.

Was that encounter a peace offering or a trap?

"Uncle Sonny seemed cool with it. But then again, they said he went nuts when Leslie started dating, so maybe he was just happy not to have to worry about boys." Sixteen years old and she's already absorbing the family lore. "Aunt Karen-Anne, though, wasn't too thrilled about it. But she came around."

I wonder if she has any inkling at all what kind of shift has occurred in the world if gay people are openly conducting relationships in places like South Louisiana.

"Maybe she was just worried about how people would react," I say. "Worried people would treat them different."

"Yeah. Maybe."

"Do they?"

"Do who?"

"Do people treat them different?"

She shrugs. "Maybe? I don't know. They live in Lafayette. People there more open-minded. They got a couple of gay bars there."

"Sounds like the big time," I say.

"Please," she says, rolling her eyes. She's at that age where eye rolling is as involuntary as breathing. "So what's New York like?" she asks. "I bet it's awesome."

There's something touching about the way she says "awesome." And it's not just because of her Cajun accent. It's that she means it—not a hint of irony or sarcasm in her voice. It's the way a six-year-old would describe Disney World.

So I lie. Well, not lie, but skillfully edit. I don't tell her about my mind-numbing routine. Wake up, squeeze in a workout at the Y, board a crowded subway car, go to work, and sit in front of a computer all day. Train back to Brooklyn, order take out or eat a bowl of Special K. Watch TV.

But with twenty years in New York, I've got plenty of stories, some of which are even clean enough to tell someone her age. A handful of celebrity run-ins. And, always a crowd pleaser, crazy subway incidents.

I relate the story of the sandwich and the diaper. "O. M. G." Catherine says. She actually says the letters. "I totally saw that on YouTube."

Of course she did.

I want to cringe all over again thinking about the way I actually do cringe in the video, hand protecting my head as I turned my face toward the door. Instead of jumping in, doing something, breaking it up, I cowered in the corner as the fight stormed around me, exceeding my chaos threshold. It was a horrible, humiliating moment for all involved, which makes for great video.

Everyone had seen the damn thing.

Catherine whips out her smartphone, its sleek black casing and fingertip-smudged screen reminding me that I'm cut off from the rest of the world. A sudden urge strikes me. Snatch the phone and run to the corner. I see myself hunched over it, poking at it like a chimp trying to open a stolen coconut. Grunting in pleasure as the Twitter stream washes over me, not a Fail Whale in sight.

The screams from the phone attract a crowd of people, who stand over Catherine and me.

"Look at 'em go," someone says.

"Mais, Katie-Lee, you shoulda jumped in there and whipped that girl's ass, yeah."

Digital junkie that I might be, it strikes me as a little off that we're watching a YouTube video at a wake. Twenty years ago, we'd have been sitting around listening to some old fart tell a story we'd all heard a hundred times before, made newly relevant by the death of a loved one. Now they're watching a video they'd all seen before and it's made newly relevant because they know the identity of the one person in the background who isn't hooting and hollering and cheering on the combatants.

And it's just the sort of thing outsiders expect go on in the city every single day. It reaffirms assumptions about what it means to live there. No day-to-day grind, but a nonstop rotation of crazies and excitement. Danger. People like danger.

As if on cue, someone from outside the gathered circle speaks over the noise. "Yall know Katie-Lee was there for nine-eleven."

Kendra-Sue.

Son of a bitch. There she is, standing across the kitchen, drawing a cup of Community Coffee from its branded urn.

Why? I want to ask. Why do this to me? This is not a good story. Not from my point of view. Not as told by Katie-Lee. It lacks drama. All the action is out of the frame. But now I have to tell it. Tell, once again, how I was sleeping when it happened, that I'd decided the night before to call in sick, having had too many beers on a bad first date that involved watching the Giants lose to someone. Funny, I remember the Giants lost, but couldn't pick the guy I was with out of a lineup. So that morning, the phone starts ringing. And ringing. I ignored it. Figured it was work. Or a telemarketer. Until I heard Kendra-Sue's voice on the answering machine. "Katie-Lee. Just calling to see if you're okay." A strange message for a Tuesday. So I picked up. She told me to turn on the TV. "What channel?" I asked, forgetting for a moment that I didn't have cable so only had four to choose from. "Any of them," she said. And there they were, two towers smoldering, people jumping, workers fleeing, panicked reports of planes raining death from above across the entire country. Then static. Just like that. Transmission literally cut. "Oh my god," Kendra-Sue said. I stabbed at the remote. Fox Five: static. ABC Seven: static. CBS Two: an image that made no sense. "It fell," she said. And so it had, taking the broadcasting towers of three of the four networks with it. We stayed on the phone until the second tower fell, crying, not saying much. "I'm gonna go," I said finally. "We're tying up the phone lines," I explained, thinking of all those frightened families desperately trying to make contact. "You better not go down there," Kendra-Sue said. "Of course not," I said. But I tried. I walked from Park Slope, the Brooklyn neighborhood I was living in at the time, to the Brooklyn Heights promenade, walked against the flow of people escaping Manhattan, covered in the ash of the dead, looking like zombies themselves. I took pictures. I even had one taken of me. A beautiful sunny day, I'm wearing a skirt and sandals. Sunglasses. I'm leaning against the rail on the promenade, the East River behind me. And a massive cloud of smoke covering the remains of lower Manhattan. Why? To prove I was there? That I hadn't seen the whole thing on TV even though I lived only three miles away? One of the most documented tragedies in human history and I needed my own proof. How much worse would it have been if we all had Facebook and video phones? I was a terrified mess for months after—especially in the subway. Even a decade later, video of it reduces me immediately to scary, shuddering crying. But I wasn't there. Not really. I wasn't on the way to work. Didn't make a mad dash up a narrow downtown street as the towers came down. Wasn't among the ash-covered exodus walking across the bridges. Didn't even know anyone who died.

A weak story.

"That's when Sonny Junior decided he was going to join the army," Lucy says. Then there's that. "I remember that. Him being sixteen. He had to wait another two years because Mama wouldn't sign the waiver for him to join at seventeen."

At this, everyone chuckles.

"Your mama always was the only one of us who had any damn sense," I say, and the chuckle dies in its crib as those in the room parse this phrase. "I wanted to kill those bastards with my own bare hands. But if I had a son I wouldn't want him over there getting shot at."

I shake my head. How long has it been now? What tour is Sonny Junior on? They didn't even send him to Afghanistan—not the first time around. His first two tours were spent in Iraq. After they finished there, he re-upped. And then he got his bonus trips to Afghanistan. "All those boys lost."

"I'm sure it just keeps you up at night," Kendra-Sue says.

Every man, woman, and child in the room stops breathing. I'm not even sure how to respond to that one.

"Kendra-Sue," Kurt Junior says flatly.

"What?" she asks, hands up. "I'm just saying the rest of us have kids, some who've actually been over there."

Her eyes dart around the room. Realizing they all think she's crossed a line, she's going to have to apologize. And if I know my sister, that only pisses her off even more.

"Sorry," she says. "That was uncalled for."

Well, maybe she's changed.

"Besides, it's not like staying around here ever stopped a kid from getting—"

"Don't you even finish that sentence, Kendra-Sue," I say, finding my voice.

She looks right at me. "Shot."

"Kendra-Sue!"

I don't know who said it, but Kendra-Sue does. Her eyes sweep the room, lock on the woman, and this cousin or aunt or in-law bows her head and says nothing else. The other adults develop a sudden interest in studying the contours of their laps. Lucy and Catherine, though, I can feel them watching us. Catherine's fingers might even be itching to grab the cell phone, hit the record button.

"You don't own that grief, Katie-Lee," Kendra-Sue says. "Kane wasn't something that happened to just you. What about the rest of us?"

"You know it was different for me," I say, standing now, fists clenched. "You know it. God damn it, you know it."

My voice is inching up. I sound like an idiot, I'm sure. I can't think of anything coherent to say. There's so much there needing to come out that it all jams in my windpipe.

I feel a scream building inside me. That much is going to get through, I think. The back of my throat is just starting to loosen when the door opens and a gaggle of cousins barge in with six pounds of boudin, four boxes of Popeyes, two deli platters, and what looks like a birthday cake from Walmart.

Kurt Junior grabs me by the arm and escorts me toward the door. "Smoke break," he says loudly, kicking Kendra-Sue's shoe on the way out. He turns to the room. "Yall eat. Like Karen-Anne always said, 'Eat till yall shit!' "

No one laughs.

We're through the door and outside. The bottle of Jack is in my hand, to my lips. A lit cigarette is in my face, butt toward me.

"No," I manage.

"Take it," Kurt Junior says. "Gonna help more than hurt at this point."

The long drag makes my head swim, but the feeling goes away and I feel just half an ounce calmer.

"Why's she picking on me?"

"Who?"

"Who? Kendra-Sue, that's who."

He smiles. "You sound like Dr. Seuss." He's trying to distract me, take on a little of the anger himself.

"Kurt."

"She's under a lot of stress. She just forgets, that's all. You're right. It wasn't the same for her. But this? She and Karen-Anne were close."

"Even so," I say, then pause, shift course. "And she knows I don't like telling that damn nine-eleven story." I finish the cigarette in silence, holding the smoke in longer than I should.

"You might not like it, but that's what we're here to do."

"What? Remember national tragedy."

"No. Tell stories."

"But why that one? Why not talk about Mama or Daddy? All them damn kids running around?"

"We'll get to that. But we haven't heard your stories yet. It's been forever since we've seen you. Some of them kids have never seen you outside of Facebook." He blows a couple of smoke rings into the sky. The birds in the bushes are singing. They don't know that a funeral is going on, only that it's a bright sunny day in December. "Besides, Mama and Daddy, that's just going to lead to . . ." He trails off.

"Shit." I walk down to the back end of the building and back.

Karla-Jean comes around the corner talking on her cell phone, almost runs into Kurt Junior. She sees the smoke, the bottle of Jack Daniel's and shakes her head, pitying our damned souls before walking away without a word.

"Lord," Kurt Junior says, "she's gonna wear out her knees praying for us tonight."

A side door opens and Catherine drifts out, a little black dot of doom.

"Can I have a cigarette?" she asks me.

"What? No!"

Kurt Junior shakes one out and hands it to her.

"Kurt Junior!"

"What? She just gonna go get one from Kendra-Sue anyway."

"Mama and Mawmaw know I smoke."

"And if they said dealing crack was okay?"

This, she finds hilarious. "Aunt Katie-Lee! As if!" It wasn't really a funny joke. She puts me in mind of a desperate woman on a first date laughing overly hard at everything the man says. Not that I'd know anything about that.

"As if," I echo. "Filthy habit. You shouldn't start."

She gets shy all of a sudden. "Where you staying tonight?" Before I answer, she continues. "You can stay at Mawmaw's. That's where we all staying."

"At Kendra-Sue's?" The child must be angling for her own viral-video hit—her grandmother and I fighting to the death on Kendra-Sue's living room floor. "Cajun Cat Fight," she can call it.

"Mawmaw said to ask if you would."

"Kendra-Sue asked?"

"Yeah," she says, shrugging.

"See," Kurt Junior says as if reading my mind.

This is the closest I'm going to get to an apology for what just happened. I guess I can't say no. "Fine. What time we leaving?"

"Oh, I don't know," she says, stubbing out her cigarette. "It's only noon." With that, she goes back inside.

"Noon?"

Kurt hands me the bottle. "I told you it's going to be a long one."

◘ ◘ ◘

In Louisiana, one of the first stages of grief is eating your weight in Popeyes fried chicken. The second stage is doing the same with boudin. People have been known to swap the order. Or to do both at the same time.

The third stage is surviving wave upon wave of distant relatives trying to place you and, having succeeded only after you clue them in, embarking on a futile attempt to remember exactly when it was the last time you've seen one another. Variations on this exist. At some point during the day, an old man with a battered John Deere cap resting on his gigantic ears shuffles up to me and by way of introduction says, "Who you belong to?" But before we even delve into my lineage, he spots Kurt Junior across the room. "Kurt Junior!" he hollers, loud as you please. Kurt Junior flinches, but instead of looking up, puts down his plate of chicken and walks right out of the room.

Karen-Anne's coworkers make an appearance, easy to pick out because they're overdressed. Comparatively that is. Academics and scientists they may be in Lafayette, but in their tweedy sports jackets and navy blazers, they might as well be walking the red carpet at the Oscars.

A flock of brightly dressed black women—coreligionists of Karla-Jean—drift through, grandchildren in tow, terrified of being in such close quarters with this many white adults outside of their church.

My slightly creepy sister waves me over for an introduction, the little sister from New York.

"Ohhh, the big city," says one of the women.

"Ain't that something," says the other. "Yes indeed."

"We're sorry for your loss," says the first.

And that's about the extent of the conversation. What were we supposed to do? Talk about Harlem? Should I tell them I have a black friend in New York—well, a black coworker at any rate? I could tell them that New York is just as segregated as Louisiana—perhaps more so. But that would be rude. You don't talk about such things in mixed company in Louisiana.

"We gonna go pay our respects," says one of them, no doubt eager to get out of here. We might have a black president, but they're betting none of the people in this room voted for him.

Left alone with Karla-Jean, I'm tempted to run off and find that idiot cousin of mine.

"Come," she says, grabbing me by the wrist with her bony fingers. "I want you to meet Gene."

Gene. Karla-Jean and Gene. How weird is that? Not as weird as the man himself, it turns out.

"Oh, hiiiiiii," he says when I'm presented to him, his voice dripping with concern. He's a pasty, balding thing, thick around the middle, the elastic in his waistband stretched tight around his protruding gut. He's got a bulbous butt, a womanly one I'd say. "I am *so* sorry for yall's loss," he says, taking my hand between his. They're cool and dry and for some reason this makes me wonder if he has no soul. "So, so sorry. Karen-Anne was such a loving mother."

"What could you possibly know about Karen-Anne?" I'm tempted to ask him. But it occurs to me he might know more about her than I do, so I keep my mouth shut.

"We had her out to the church a few times," he says.

See, that I didn't know.

"Kind, kind woman. Smart, too." He pauses. "It's hard, I know. Must be. Sometimes, I think it's harder on the living." He pauses to let this sink in, as if he'd come up with that particular conceit all by himself. "But Karen-Anne, she's with Jesus now." He squeezes my hand just a little, as if daring me, the big-city girl, to challenge him on that particular statement.

"Thank you," I say. I don't know if that even makes sense, but it's the only polite thing I can think of.

"Gene, honey, can you let us be for a few minutes?" asks Karla-Jean. "We got some catching up to do."

"Sure thing," he says, with a smile. He releases my hand and kisses Karla-Jean on the lips—a squishy, wet kiss—before waddling off toward the coffee pots.

She pulls me down to a bench along the wall, where we watch as the other guests and family members make their appointed rounds. A group of little kids burst into the main lobby like a flock of birds and just as quickly fly out into the parking lot. One kid—I don't know who he belongs to—sits alone on the next bench poking intently at a handheld game of some sort. No one bothers us. It's as if Karla-Jean has a magic force field that keeps others at bay. Being weird has its advantages, I guess.

"I know what yall think of me," she says.

"What?" I say, perhaps louder than necessary. Truth be told, she spooked me. Has she been looking into my mind this whole time? Has she become some kind of clairvoyant?

"I know," she says, looking down at her lap, straightening a pleat on her dress, before looking back at me. "I'm the weird one. The Jesus freak. The Bible-thumper."

"Karla-Jean," I start.

She puts a hand up. "No need to say anything. It is what it is. I've got my faith to keep me strong. And Gene to get me by. I got no regrets. I just wish sometimes yall would let me in. Treat me like a sister instead of like some crazy cousin."

She states it matter-of-factly, without a hint of self-pity, which I find weird in itself. Why is she coming to me with this? If anyone is the distant, crazy cousin in this immediate family, it's me. But the truth of it is, I can't imagine sitting down at a table with this woman and having a cup of coffee and a conversation. My own sister. And this makes me feel like a small person. She's always been the odd one out, Karla-Jean. As the oldest girl, she wasn't so much a sibling as she was Mama's understudy. We thought she was spoiled, Mama's favorite, lucky to be in the house instead of outside. Now that I think about it, maybe she wanted to be outside playing with us, spending time with kids her own age, rather than cleaning house and cooking our food, for which we'd thank Mama if we thanked anyone at all. So she glommed onto religion, then the first boy she met. Then along came the war and the baby and Kendra-Sue's baby and Kane. The idea of a reward in the afterlife in exchange for all the suffering here may have been the only way to keep her sanity. Not that she looks particularly sane sitting next to me.

She taps my leg. "You let me know when you're done psychoanalyzing me," she says, smirking. "I'll wait."

"What?" The comment catches me so off guard I can't think of anything else to say. I feel my face turn red, betraying me.

"Sorry," she says. "That was unkind of me. I know it's got to be hard for you. All this commotion."

"Well," I start.

"You must not be used to it. Living all alone up there in New York. No family and children. Lord. I don't know how you do it. Sometimes I lay awake at night trying to imagine it and it scares me. And I say to myself, 'I sure hope Katie-Lee at least has a church to go to and some good people around her. Even a Catholic church, just so she's not completely alone.' Do you go to church, Katie-Lee?"

Just when I was starting to feel sorry for her, she does this. It wasn't that she was Mama's little helper—that's not why we shunned her. It was because she was a tattletale, a snitch, a do-gooder, a brown-noser.

"No," I say. "I don't. And I'm not alone. I have friends. I have work."

Well, I had work.

"Work can't keep you warm at night, Katie-Lee. It won't be there forever." She pauses. "And in this economy. And at our age. And journalism? Not exactly a secure field."

What? Is she a professional in media studies now? Maybe without TV and Facebook, she just reads all day—the *Economist*, *The New York Times*, Poynter Institute, *Columbia Journalism Review*, and just to keep tabs on the enemy, *Modern Atheist*. But these things are hard to consider now that she's smashed the work-related panic button in my brain. Almost of its own accord, my hand snakes into my purse and pulls out the phone. To do what? Start hitting the network? Look for a job, a freelancing assignment? But the phone's dead. Completely.

"Important phone call?" Karla-Jean asks.

I come this close to saying, "I wish"—or, better yet, answering a fake call and walking off. But I'm too flustered to lie. "No," I say. "It's dead. Phantom vibration."

I fully expect a lecture about the ills of technology and addiction. Instead, she says, "I get that all the time. I think it's ringing. Or I'm getting an email." She begins prattling, excited almost that we have some sort of common ground. "I pull it out of my pocket book and nothing! I told Brother Paul about it and he said it was probably a sign, that maybe I'm using it too much. But it's harmless. Mostly. I mean, I understood his point about Facebook. Lot of temptation there—breaking up a lot of marriages. 'The past is the past for a reason,' he likes to say. He knows best, so I closed my account. But I thought it was nice to catch up with old friends, keep up with you and the rest of the family."

The stream of her babble calms me some, makes me forget work just a little as I try to picture her staring at a Facebook stream, posting bible quotes and asking old friends if they've taken the Lord Jesus Christ as their personal savior.

"Hey, do you ever talk to Lawrence on Facebook?" she asks.

The question is like a kick in the gut. Worries about work, pictures of her surfing the web fly from my mind like startled birds. "What?" I ask. "No." I say. "Why? Why would I?"

"Well, Katie-Lee, yall were high-school sweethearts," she says.

Was this an elaborate set-up? Is she trying to get back at me for something I did to her? Is she stupid, clueless, or just plain-old mean?

"Jesus Christ," I spit, making her flinch. "Why in God's name would I talk to him? After what happened?"

She inches away from me on the bench. "Well, what about forgiveness, Katie-Lee? The greatest power is to—"

I stand up to leave. "There's no forgiving what he did. And you should damn well know that."

"But he's—"

I can't even begin to imagine where that's statement is going to go. "I don't care. What is it your Brother Paul said? The past is the past for a reason? Well, there you go."

"Now, Katie-Lee."

"Drop it," I say, trying to keep the tremor from my voice. "One more word about it and . . ." And what? What am I going to do? "Another peep and I'm going to tell Kendra-Sue."

Her eyes get big for a second. I recognize the look from childhood, that surprised, wounded look she'd get when Kendra-Sue would put her in her place or give her a good hard shove as the prelude to a fight. Maybe Kendra-Sue was picking on me today, but I'm pretty sure that if it came down to a choice between me and Karla-Jean, she'd side with me. The look on Karla-Jean's face tells me as much. For one moment I wish I could shoot lasers out of my eyes and set the end of her ridiculous braid on fire. In my mind it would burn like a fuse right up to her scalp, then her whole head would explode.

I feel a tug at my arm. "Aunt Katie-Lee." It's Catherine. "Mawmaw says come get some food. You haven't eaten all day."

I look to the glass door separating the kitchen from the lobby. Kendra-Sue offers me a shrug, then walks off, busying herself with other duties.

I look back to Karla-Jean, half expecting her to start up her lecture again, but she's up and off, heading toward Gene, tail between her legs. He looks over his shoulder at me and shakes his head a little. It's all I can do not to flip him off.

"Come on," Catherine says, taking my hand and pulling. "Before you kill one of them."

She drags me into the kitchen, where people are working on their third or fourth meals of the day. The smell of fried chicken and boudin is overwhelming—overwhelming and soothing. Pork and chicken grease, the aromatics of choice for the Cajun. Catherine sits me down—between Kurt Junior and a baby sleeping in a carriage, despite all the noise in the kitchen—and proceeds to pile food on a plate for me. I can't imagine eating, but somehow I do, one plate, then two, prodded on by those around me.

"Looks like they haven't been feeding you too good up in New York," someone says.

I consider going for a third plate. I don't know what the grease and salt and fat is doing to my brain chemistry, but it seems today that fried-chicken is a half decent substitute for anti-anxiety drugs.

Kurt Junior laughs and takes my plate from me. "You don't have to literally eat till you shit, Katie-Lee."

The rest of the family laughs with him. I blush a little, but I don't mind. They're laughing with me. Not at me. It says I'm part of the clan, that for 364 days a year I may be the black sheep, but today I'm one of them.

Besides, there will be plenty more time to eat today. Seven, eight, nine hours more of it, it turns out. On and on it goes, feeding and crying and hugging—and, yes, a delicate dance of avoidance as I keep out of Karla-Jean's orbit and Kendra-Sue keeps out of mine.

Then the sun is gone, and the food and coffee and people, too. And somehow we're back at Kendra-Sue's place, a massive two-story house two miles down a gravel road in Plaisance. We're too stunned, too exhausted to consider talking.

"Another long day tomorrow," Kendra-Sue says before going to her bedroom and not coming out again.

Catherine and I are sequestered in one of the bedrooms, best buds now. But no all-night slumber party ensues. Between the food and the whiskey and the grief and the stress—or despite all of that—I fall asleep almost immediately.

CHAPTER TWELVE

An island of warmth in a cold room. Cold and quiet. I wake up snug under a down comforter, Catherine snoring next to me, her body blazing like a lump of coal. It's nice to be able to actually use a down comforter, even if I had to come to Louisiana to do so. Like many New Yorkers who live in old buildings, I don't control the thermostat. The temperature drops below 40 and the old steam radiators come to life, spitting and hissing and clanging and banging for the duration of the season. As far as I can tell, the steam systems have two settings: "Off" and "Fiery Pits of Hell." Even when it's 20 degrees and snowing, I've got windows open and little more than a sheet to cover me.

Kendra-Sue, though, she keeps her house cold. Whether she's cheap or still battling hot flashes, I don't much care. It's a luxury to wake up under covers, rather than tangled up and sweaty. Nice, too, to wake up to a warm body sleeping next to me, to wake up to a human presence without feelings of regret, shame, nausea, headache, dry mouth, and the panicky realization that there isn't a used condom wrapper anywhere in sight.

Catherine rolls over and throws an arm over me. Without the

makeup and black clothes, fresh-faced and wearing a T-shirt and boxers, she looks like a little girl. But she isn't. She's already got one foot in the adult world. And God knows the adult world doesn't abide by the developmental guidelines used by the makers of toys, junior apparel, and tween makeup. All it takes is one clarifying event to snatch even the most innocent of us out of the fantasyland of childhood once and for all. Some people—thousands, maybe millions of them—live their entire lives without ever making that painful transition. We don't have any of those people in our family.

Will she make it? That's the question that floats through my mind. Of course she will. People do. Like it or not. But how will she make it? Happy? Sad? Angry? Bitter? Broken by her trials or forged by them? Will she get pregnant in high school? Or go to college? Or both? Will she stay in Louisiana her entire life or travel the world or set out on adventure and make it as far as Panama City and get stuck there?

She's so young. So young it frightens me.

This is not a metaphorical statement, but rather one of fact. Consider it the latest addition to the catalog of neuroses. Page 26, 2012: Panic Set Off By Presence of Youth. Free Shipping.

Summer is the worst. The interns ride out of the wastes of academia, storming corporate America in sundresses and tank tops and low-waisted jeans and open-toed shoes, armed with curves and perky boobs and peek-a-boo thongs and pedicured nails on toes that don't yet look like a dog's chew toy. Oh, and giggles and innocence, too.

But it's not just fresh-faced nineteen-year-olds. Even Danielle, my old reliable drinking buddy, who at forty is no one's idea of a spring chicken. Two months ago, she went from sober to drunk in the space of an hour. Turned out she'd had her first, second, and third gray hairs.

Pfft. Gray hairs. She still has milestones ahead of her: Sagging boobs. Droopy butt. Imaginary hot flashes. Real hot flashes. I don't even have those anymore. What do I have to look forward to? The final mile markers on the road to death—that's what. High blood pressure? Heart disease? My first tumor? The first tremble of Parkinson's? I'd actually quit running with the Leukemia & Lymphoma Society group because I became convinced I'd catch either leukemia or lymphoma.

There's a sick, blackened place inside of me that is thankful for the shitty economy, the company's dire straits. We will not be able to afford interns this summer.

We? Jesus. Was I that tied to the job? Am I one of those people?

I take a deep breath.

I want to wake up Catherine. Tell her these things, unburden myself. Ask her to be kind to her elders when she gets into the work force. Maybe wear sacks or bags to work. And to enjoy her first gray hair.

I guess that would frighten her.

Christ. I don't know how people do it—have kids. All that responsibility. The burden of knowing. The delusion that we can guide another human through life when we're all such hot messes to begin with. Our own tangled traps of neuroses and bad decisions. Here there be dragons—heartbreak, despair, death—and the map you'll be passing on is this barely legible collection of notes and half thoughts you've jotted down on the back of a Walmart receipt. And as jumbled and contradictory as such a map would be, the child would always be able to sniff out the bullshit, wouldn't she, to see through your words and find the actions. Love yourself, stand tall, don't take crap, I might tell a kid, but if she judged me by the example I set, one word would come shining through: "Run."

But run where?

▫ ▫ ▫

I remember that cab ride back to Candy's place the night she rescued me at the bar. My first night in the city, cutting through Times Square and heading down into the East Village. What a war zone it looked like back then. Runaways, cults, hardcore drug dealers, corrupt cops. And the junkies drifting through the streets and sidewalks, landing on stoops or piled against building facades like so much tumbleweed. I saw a pair of feet and a pool of blood reflecting the blue lights of the police cars that were, thankfully, hiding the rest of the scene. Two blocks later, we saw cops and firemen dragging out what looked like a tribe of hippies from a four-story building. "Squatters," Candy explained. "They don't hurt anyone—until their electrical work goes wrong. Look." She pointed to the top floor of the building being evacuated and, sure enough, smoke was seeping through a window—a window that had four bright orange extension cords snaking from it to the building next door.

The wiring in Candy's apartment didn't strike me as much better. Bare bulbs with pull strings; I felt almost like I was back in Grand Prairie. Except Candy had an indoor toilet. In fact, it was practically in the kitchen. Whoever had broken the place up into apartments had put the bathroom and kitchen doors in such a manner that it was a hassle to open one or the other. So someone had taken the bathroom door off. If you wanted privacy, you simply closed the kitchen door. It worked, but it wasn't ideal—which was pretty much the story of that apartment.

Stumbling into it that night, I was too exhausted to care. Not even a rat living inside the toilet bowl would have convinced me to head back into the streets. The plastic shower curtain was moldy, rust rivulets ran down from faucet to drain, and the towel Candy gave me smelled just a little bit musty. But to this day, I remember that as the best shower of my life. The attack at the bar, the homeless thing in the Port Authority bathroom, forty-eight hours of Greyhound and all the things that had preceded it in Louisiana were washed away. I don't know how long I stayed in there, unmoving, even when someone in an adjacent apartment flushed a toilet and the water scalded my head and back.

"Hey, you didn't go kill yourself in my bathroom?" Candy called through the kitchen door, only half joking.

"No," I called, trying to half laugh. "I just really needed that."

Drying off, I took in more of the cramped space. There was a can of Barbasol and a man's razor in the medicine cabinet. I lifted the toilet seat and found pee stains there.

"You have a boyfriend?" I asked, when I walked into the living room where she was setting up the couch for me to sleep on. "I don't want to get in the way."

The question made her flinch. She stopped moving for a full five seconds before shaking out the sheet as if scaring off a ghost. "No," she said. "I'm off men at the moment. Crazy as that might sound."

"Hunh," I said. "Sounds perfectly sane to me."

After she had the sheet situated to her liking, she plopped down on the couch. I wanted her to go to bed, to leave me alone, but figured that might not make me the most gracious guest in the world. I sat and we started talking. Or she started talking, intent perhaps on telling me everything even as I said nothing. She was from Ohio, had been in New York three years, had come with one bad boyfriend only to be abandoned and picked up by another and then another and then . . . and then I was down for the count. I woke once, briefly, to find my head in Candy's lap, her own head thrown back as she gently snored. It struck me as weird, too intimate. Who was this person? I didn't even know her. She could be a Satanist. She could be a lesbian pimp for all I knew. But her lap was comfortable and, besides, I felt as if I had a fifty-pound block of concrete on my chest. Short of a fire in the apartment, I wasn't moving. When I woke again, a gray winter light was seeping in from the kitchen window that faced onto the shaftway and Candy was gone. She'd left a note.

Sister from another mister,

Make yourself comfortable. Feels like we've known each other for years! My place is yours. I'm at class all day and have another shift tonight. Be back late. Extra set of keys for you—you'll probably need to go out for coffee, food or, well, anything. Sorry! We'll figure things out later.

Sister? I had enough of those, didn't I? Then again, she was an only child and had no standards, no sisterly expectations. Even if I had enough sisters, what I lacked was options. So I made myself comfortable—or tried to. The place was filthy. Overflowing ashtrays, dishes piled up in the sink, lumps of decay in the fridge, bills piled up on the coffee table, dust bunnies one evolutionary step from turning into dust wolves. Later, I'd learn that these were signs of depression brought on by a broken heart. But that morning I worried that she might be a spoiled and clueless only child of questionable moral character. A person's home said things and this chaos wasn't singing sweet songs to me. After rooting around for cleaning supplies and finding none, I showered again, bundled up, and headed out into the cold. The sky was a solid gray ceiling, flat and featureless. The wind was something I'd never experienced, an ice-edged blade that sawed at my ears, nose, and fingers. I ducked into the nearest corner shop, bought a box of Pop-Tarts, two cans of Chef Boyardee ravioli, a six-pack of Tab, a cup of steaming coffee—and Pine-Sol, Comet, paper towels, Brillo pads, and sponges. It cost me so much of my meager stash that I asked the guy behind the counter to repeat himself twice. As I made my way back to the apartment, the first snowflakes began to fall.

I scrubbed, I cleaned, I scoured, I swept. Then ran back into the snow and to the store because this supposedly adult woman did not own a mop.

I was watching Johnny Carson when Candy's keys rattled in the lock.

"What did you do?" she asked, dropping her knapsack onto the floor with a thud.

I shrugged. "Figured I'd earn my keep."

"Oh my god! Is that the color of the floor? I don't think I've ever seen it!"

"I really wish you hadn't told me that," I said, but laughed all the same, pleased that she was pleased.

She opened the fridge. "My pets! You've thrown them all away."

"Sorry."

"I'll get over it," she said, running a hand along the small counter, looking into her cabinets.

"Oh no," she said. "Okay. Now we *do* have to talk about this." She turned around, waving the can of Chef Boyardee at me, the one that

I hadn't eaten. "Not acceptable, Katherine. Uncool."

"What? Why? I wanted Italian." Despite it all, I was still a girl—a new girl in a new land. And that word, "uncool," held an almost magical power over me.

"You're in New York now. You want Italian, we'll get you real Italian. We don't eat pasta and sauce out of a can. Okay?"

"I didn't know."

"Don't sweat it," she said. "That's what I'm here for. To guide you. You keep the place this clean and promise to at least look for work, I'll show you the ropes. I'll be just like your big sister."

That word again. "You aren't mean or crazy enough to be one of my sisters," I said.

▫ ▫ ▫

There's a knock on the door and Clovis, Kendra-Sue's second husband, sticks his head in. It's something else, that head. Looks like something carved out of a cypress stump. It's got heft and is a dark, rich brown creased by wrinkles. Capped as it is by moss-gray hair and perched on top of his wiry body, he could pass for a little, walking tree.

"About time to get moving," he says.

"Okay."

"You doing okay, Katie-Lee?"

Maybe it's because he reminds me of Daddy, this little Cajun man who seemed to stumble into my sister's life from a previous generation, who gave her two more kids and an opportunity to go back to school and become a nurse. Or maybe it's Catherine's little-girl germs are seeping into me. Or maybe I'm just crazy.

But I shake my head, say, "No," and start crying. Again. How many tears can the human head hold?

Clovis comes in, sits on the side of the bed, and without hesitation, puts his gnarled hand, dry and smooth, upon my head, brushing the hair back, just like Daddy used to.

"I'm sorry," I whimper.

"Nothing to be sorry for."

"I'm such a mess."

"Mais, what you expect, Katie-Lee?" For a moment I'm convinced he's seen deep into my heart and will judge me. "Your little sister just died."

That's just the tip of the iceberg, I want to tell him, but I resist.

He looks out through the window. "My brother, he died two years ago. I cried like a little baby, me." He pauses, as if choosing his words carefully, looks over to make sure Catherine is still sleeping. "But it wasn't just because I was sad. We getting old. It scared me. A lot. How much time I got left? What if them preachers are right and I go to hell? What if Kendra-Sue goes before me?"

He trails off, swallows a lump in his throat, as if the mere thought of her going first is enough to make him cry.

"Kendra-Sue's lucky to have you," I say and start crying all over again because I don't have anyone like Clovis to cry over me. Closest I came was Howie and I kicked him to the curb.

Clovis looks down at me, smiling now. "Maybe you should tell her how lucky she is, because she sure don't listen to me when I do."

"Yeah, I'm sure she'll listen to me. She's probably in the next room, thinking I'm just one big crybaby."

His smile fades for a second. "Yall two are hardheaded and just alike. Don't let her fool you. She's hanging on by a thread. If you wasn't here for her to pick at, she'd be curled up under the bed crying."

So she *was* picking at me. I knew it. "I'm sure," I say.

"It's true," he says. "Whatever else happens, whatever she says or you do, that's your sister. Remember that. Now, *allons.* Yall get up. Get outta bed. All you gotta do is make it through the day."

"Is that all?"

"That's all," he says. "Take a deep breath. Take another one. Soldier through. And if you need to cry, don't be ashamed. Go ahead and cry. Even if it's about something else. Cry about it all. If you got some crying to do, today's the day to do it."

With that, he's off. Just like a man, to make it sound like

something out of an instruction manual. Step 1: Stop crying. Step 2: Get it together. Step 3: Carry on. Oddly enough, now that he's given me permission, I don't feel like crying. Not as much.

Catherine's arm squeezes around me.

"You were awake for all of that?"

"Yall making so much damn noise, how was I supposed to sleep?"

"Watch your language, young lady."

She giggles. "Grown-ups are messed up," she says.

"You don't know the half of it," I say. "Just you wait."

CHAPTER THIRTEEN

The funeral home crowd on this Monday morning is more subdued in attitude and attire. Jeans have been replaced by Dockers in khaki, black and navy, hunting and work shirts swapped for button-downs from L.L. Bean or Eddie Bauer. The women, too, are in slacks, topped off with somber blouses and jackets that don't bear the emblem of a college or NFL team.

Sonny is wearing a dark gray suit going shiny at the elbows. Lucy and Tina, now wearing pantsuits, look more like twins than lovers. Leslie, the middle child, wears a dress and her husband Steve a navy blazer that, miraculously, looks freshly pressed and properly fitted. And standing in Army dress blues, a full head taller than his daddy, is Sonny Junior.

They're lined up just outside the door to the viewing parlor. Hugs are exchanged. Sonny Junior remains stiff in my arms. Undoubtedly, he's seen plenty of death in the last decade—a decade! He's been at war twice as long as Daddy or Kurt Junior was. I wonder what's bothering him most of all, the grief or the sense of betrayal. This wasn't part of the deal. He'd gone off to visit death upon those who'd do his people harm and, while he was there, death crossed the ocean and paid a visit to his mom.

Poor child. I could have warned him about our family's relationship with death.

I follow three generations of Kendra-Sue's family into the parlor where the service will be held. Kurt Junior and Melinda, Karla-Jean and Gene are holding spots in the first row for Kendra-Sue, Clovis and me. The nieces, nephews and grandkids peel off to fill the second, third and fourth rows. I grab hold of Catherine and take her to the front with me.

Karla-Jean leans across Gene and says to Kendra-Sue, as if gloating, "Brother Paul will be here in half an hour."

"That's fine," is all the answer she gets.

"Brother?" I ask. "You got a Pentecostal to do the service?"

"Don't start," Kendra-Sue says.

"But Kendra-Sue."

"Look, Karen-Anne didn't go to church. Just as bad as you. Maybe worse. And we couldn't get a priest out of Ville Platte. I don't even know where to start with the one in Grand Prairie—if he's even a priest anymore. And the ones in Opelousas all but demanded a thousand- dollar donation."

"But a Pentecostal?"

Big-toothed, doughy, wispy-haired Gene leans over, the light of the Lord—or low-grade hysteria—burning in his eyes. "Oh, he isn't Pentecostal, Katie-Lee. Not at all."

"Then what is he?"

"He's non-denominational," he says and sits back as if this were a satisfactory response.

"Non-denominational?" I look to Catherine. "What does that even mean?"

She shrugs.

I turn to her grandmother. "Kendra-Sue, what does that mean?"

"I said don't start," she begins, but before she gets any further, there's a loud braying from the lobby, as if a hound has been loosed in the funeral home.

In fact, a hound *has* been loosed in the funeral home. A ropey, mottled coonhound comes bounding between the seats, barking and yipping and extremely delighted with so much attention from so many people.

His owner hobbles into the viewing parlor on crutches and shouts, "Mais, got dammit, Ghost. I'ma take you out back and choot you."

The dog barks, then runs up to the casket and starts sniffing at the open end. I cover my mouth, unsure if it'll be a laugh or a scream that comes out, convinced Karen-Anne's not going to even make it to her grave before she starts spinning. A dog! A Tooth Fairy-murdering dog.

"O. M. G." Catherine says.

"Son of a bitch," says her grandmother, before turning to the younger kids sitting behind us. "Yall stop laughing. It's not funny."

Try convincing a bunch of bored-out-of-their-head kids that a dog tearing ass inside a funeral home isn't funny. For them, this is the height of hilarity. A troop of farting clowns would pale in comparison.

Before Ghost can get into the casket or tip it over, Kurt Junior snatches him by the collar and yanks hard, producing a surprised yelp.

"Dog don't need to be shot, Ned Landry. It's you. How the hell you let a dog in the funeral home?"

"I let him out the truck cuz one of them lil kids out front wanted to pet him," Ned says.

"Let me rephrase my question," Kurt Junior says. "Why the hell you brought a dog to the funeral home in the first place?"

"Well, Kurt Junior!" Ned exclaims as if he were the one talking to an idiot. "Betty was working today and I didn't want to leave him at home by hisself." To Ned, this is an adequate answer.

"Tres," Kurt Junior says to his son. "Come get this dog out of here before I have to kick Ned's ass."

"Okay, Daddy," he says and grabs the dog. Kurt the Third—or Tres, as he's called—is 24 and old enough to know better than to laugh right now, but I can tell by the way he keeps his head down, his eyes on the floor, he's about to pop. If he makes eye contact with anyone wearing even a hint of a smile, he's going to lose it.

The dog is dragged out and the room is just returning to funeral-appropriate levels of chatter when an old man shuffles in on the arm of a slightly younger woman, his daughter, maybe. Ancient relations in from the woods. He's wearing a suit that looks like it's been stitched out of the hides of freshly killed Wranglers. His cowboy hat sports a long brown turkey feather, his belt buckle is the size of professional wrestling award. He's wearing a black eye patch.

"Who's that?" Catherine asks me.

"Who's that?" I ask Kendra-Sue.

"Uncle Caca," she says to me.

"Uncle Caca," I say to Catherine, who snorts at the sound of the word.

"Caca means poop," she says, stating the obvious.

"Katie-Lee," Kendra-Sue says.

"What? I didn't do anything."

"I was talking to my granddaughter," she says.

That's interesting. But not as interesting as Uncle Caca, who wobbles over to the casket and leans over. He grunts, then straightens up and speaks.

"Camille, turn me around."

"Okay, Daddy."

Satisfactorily turned around, Uncle Caca leans over again. Clears his throat. Leans over a little more. Then a little more. Catherine squeezes my hand. Hard. I bite my lower lip. Uncle Caca's head is, quite literally, in the casket.

"Daddy," Camille whispers.

"What?" he says loudly, practically shouting in Karen-Anne's face, his inside-voice no doubt a dim memory for him.

"Daddy, what are you doing?" She might be 65, but she sounds like a teenage daughter mortified by her father.

"Oh shut up, Camille," he says. "I'm just trying to get a look at her with my good eye."

Kendra-Sue whips her head around, fixing her own eyes on the kids. "Not. A. Peep," she says. "Notapeep."

No way am I turning around. I can practically see their little faces swelling from choked-back laughter, cartoon balloons with bulging eyes. Hell, Kurt Junior and Melinda are turning purple. When Kendra-Sue turns around, she puts a hand over her mouth and bows her head.

Clovis slaps her thigh. "Not a peep," he whispers.

As silently as possible, the entire front row loses it. I wonder why the kids behind us don't take this cue and run with it. Then it occurs to me they might think we're crying. They've seen a lot of mood swings in the last couple of days, seen the adults breaking down in public. Our heads are down, our shoulders shuddering, hands over our mouths. From behind, laughing and crying are indistinguishable.

Thank God.

By the time Brother Paul makes his entrance and instructs us to call him BP, we've regained our composure. BP's a mountain of a man, with a big belly, a twinkle in his eye and over-familiar sincerity in his voice.

"I sure am sorry for yall's loss," he says, as if he has any idea what any of it means for us.

Karen-Anne's family comes in behind him and takes their seats in chairs next to the casket, facing the mourners. Sonny, Sonny Junior, Leslie and Steve, Lucy, the grandchildren. They're all there except Tina. BP walks over to them and whispers something. What, I can't tell, but as one they look to Karen-Anne then back to the floor. Sonny takes a deep breath and stands up. The others follow suit and they make their way to the casket, laying their hands on Karen-Anne, wife, mother and grandmother. There's no mistaking this crying for laughter. They clasp onto one another, heads on shoulders, sobbing, wailing. Lucy lets out a low-pitched moan—heartbreak distilled. What was left unsaid between oldest daughter and mother? What petty squabbles is she remembering? She cries louder now. I look to Tina, standing against the wall alone, tears streaming down her face, unable to comfort her partner at this, her time of greatest need. Richer or poorer, sickness or in health, for better or worse—and there she is, isolated and useless.

"Mama," Lucy cries out. The gathered crowd gasps at her pain. Tina steps from the wall, but remembers where she is, steps back.

Sensing something, Sonny and Sonny Junior turn, at the exact same time, to Tina. They wave her over. She looks at the room, then to BP, who's trying to hide his disapproval—but not trying too hard. Tina shakes her head. "Come on," Sonny says. The circle opens. They take her in and let her arms wrap around Lucy, who wails loudly one last time before calming down.

Clovis said this was a day to cry, so I do. I cry. For no reason and every reason. For Karen-Anne. For her family. For Lucy and Tina and for all the people behind me and for myself. For the hurt in my life. For the hurts I've caused. For my selfishness, above all. I try to remember Karen-Anne. Try to remember Mama and Daddy. And it all gets jumbled in my head. We're sitting on the porch of the Grand Prairie house, all the wrong ages, together again, Mama, Daddy, Kurt Junior, Karla-Jean, Kendra-Sue, me, Karen-Anne and Kane. Oh, sweet, sweet Kane. And I lose myself again in a torrent of tears.

But BP's voice intrudes upon my reverie, insists its way into my head, pulls me back into the room. He's started in on his sermon—or whatever it's called. Heaven and Jesus and the Holy Ghost and Karen-Anne, as if he knew anything about her at all. Jackass.

Let it go, I counsel myself. He's just doing his job.

But then *he* doesn't let it go.

He's just finished telling us all about Karen-Anne being in heaven when his voice shifts. I don't know if anyone else senses it, but I do.

"Now, Karen-Anne's up in heaven where she belongs. And one day, God willing, you'll all be able to meet her up there in the great beyond. But."

But. Nothing good ever follows that word. But. It has no place here today. None.

But he continues.

"But it's important yall know something. Look, I'm not here to talk about religion today. There's a bunch of different ones in the room. Baptist, Methodist, Pentecostal." He pauses to make it damn well clear he's here to talk about religion—one in particular. "And Catholic. I know a lot of yall are Catholic."

I'd venture that 95% of the room is Catholic.

"What you call yourself isn't the point," he continues. "No Christian religion is better than the other as long as you do one thing. Personally accept our Lord and Savior Jesus Christ into your hearts and souls and minds. With no man standing between you and him."

By no man, he means no priest. I haven't set foot in a church in years, barely consider myself Catholic. But I'm livid. I cut a glance to Kendra-Sue and see her jaw working, a sure sign she's as pissed as I am.

"I did a funeral not too long ago. Room was empty. Young woman had lived a life of sin, spurned her family, turned her back on society. No one in the room. Not this room right here, but one just like it. Me and her. But don't feel bad for her. In her final days, she opened her heart to Jesus, gave herself over. She. Was. Saved."

Someone in the audience says "Amen," and it's all I can do not to stand up, turn around and demand a confession.

"Let me tell yall something, folks. You can go to church every day of the week. You can do all the good works on earth—feed the hungry, clothe the naked, teach the ignorant. You can be the richest man in the world and give away all your money to charity. But if you don't have a personal—and I do mean personal—relationship with Jesus, it don't matter one lick."

"Praise Jesus," the voice says and I'm convinced it's one of the old black ladies from Karla-Jean's church. I want to stand up and scream, "Just for that I'm not voting for Obama again!"

In case anyone's not following, he drives the point home. "And what's that mean? It means if you don't have that relationship with Jesus, you won't see Karen-Anne in heaven. I'm sorry folks, but that's the truth right there."

He pauses, his voice shifting again, from cold-hearted bringer of truth to a man who's got a way out for us, a man with a ticket to redemption.

"Now I want yall to do something for me. And for Karen-Anne. I want everybody to bow their heads and close their eyes."

As one, the room concedes. I bow my head but don't close my eyes.

"Now, I want to see a show of hands—no one's going to look—who among you wants a personal relationship with Jesus Christ? Who wants to see Karen-Anne again in heaven?"

With that, I stand up, look deep into BP's eyes. He smirks—smirks!—at me. I walk out.

I'm outside before I realize two things.

I've dragged Catherine out with me.

And Kendra-Sue has followed us.

"Can you believe that?" I ask? "What an asshole! Who does he think he is?"

Kendra-Sue says nothing. She just walks over and snatches Catherine away from me.

"Owww, Mawmaw," she protests.

"Get back inside."

"Kendra-Sue," I stammer.

"You shut your face," she says. "You shut it right now."

"I don't under—"

"Shut. Up," she screams, her voice bounding through the parking lot, across the highway, out into the fields, where the cows look up to see if the noise is a threat.

"Katie-Lee, look at me," she says in a singsong voice. "Prom queen. Cheerleader. Sorority girl. Big city lady. Can't sit still for a single sermon.

"You have no right," she continues. "None. You ran away Katie-Lee. Ran away and left us all behind. Left me alone. And now you just waltz back in and think you're in some position to make a grand gesture, to make this all about you?"

"Bullshit, Kendra-Sue." I find my voice. "You know it was never like that. I didn't want to leave. I didn't. You were the one wanted to leave. But you went and got knocked up. I didn't want to leave. I didn't have a choice."

"Yes you did. You weren't a kid. You always have a choice and you made yours back then. And made it again every day after that. But you know what you can't choose? You can't choose to drag my grandbaby into your drama."

"What? I didn't even realize—"

"Typical Katie-Lee. Not realizing what she's doing to other people, that her actions have consequences."

We're both red-faced and breathing heavy. If I'm not mistaken, we may be on the verge of coming to blows.

A shrill whistle cuts through the air.

"Yall stop it! Right now!"

Clovis. Standing outside the doors of the funeral home, a bottleneck of people behind him, staring out in horror at the two of us.

"Yall crazy or something?" he asks.

Kurt Junior steps outside and they walk toward us, looking like pest control come to subdue two fighting dogs.

Clovis takes Kendra-Sue by the arm. She pulls away, but he insists. "Shit," she says and starts crying onto his shoulder. "Come on, baby," he says and walks her to their truck.

"Come on Katie-Lee," Kurt Junior says. "You can ride with us, I guess."

People start slipping out from the funeral home, giving me wide berth. They shake their heads, whisper. What I want to do most at the moment is scream, "She started it!" My feet don't seem to want to move. Maybe I'll just stand here in the parking lot for all eternity, turn into a light post or a tree or something.

"Katie-Lee," Kurt Junior says again. He walks away without another word, shaking his head.

Hot-faced and ashamed, I sit in the back of their minivan,

watching the countryside roll by as we make our way to the cemetery. In a bend in the road, somewhere between an abandoned house and the remains of an old general store, my phone vibrates to life. Six voicemail messages and 16 texts, a few from Candy, two from Danielle.

"Hope ur ok," the first from Danielle reads. "Call if you need."

Her second text reads. "Layoffs? You ok?"

I'd forgotten that it was Monday.

CHAPTER FOURTEEN

Laying Karen-Anne's body to rest, putting the shiny silver box into the ground, seems almost an afterthought, as if all of our emotions have been spent. Under a cloudless December sky, we stand in a stupor, paying no heed to the words of BP. He keeps the service short. Perhaps he senses he's pushed too far. Maybe he's discovered in himself one last ounce of shame. Could be he's figured the family has suffered enough.

Or maybe all of his graveside services are this short, a ripping off of the bandage. Get her in the ground and get out. Fine by me. It's one thing to contemplate the glories of heaven or ravages of hell under soft lighting, surrounded by wreaths and your feet planted on carpet, another thing entirely in the middle of a South Louisiana pasture, a gaping hole in the earth that, at some primitive level, I feel won't be satisfied with Karen-Anne alone. Having tasted one dead body, it's going to spread wider and swallow us all, tumbling us into a mass grave, closing over us. Would that be so bad, really? Fall right in. A brief struggle, then troubles over. Darkness. Peace.

The ground, saturated by winter rains, squishes under my feet and a shudder runs through me.

No. I'm not ready yet. Not even close. I may have little, but I have life. Good enough for me. And, selfish as it is to be dwelling on myself at a time like this, it occurs to me that getting laid off has freed me from my one earthly obligation. I could step out of this graveyard into the field beyond and just keep going. Go walkabout. Find myself. Or just drink my way across the country. Is this a good thing or a bad thing? I don't know. Will I wither without a place to show up every day? Or will I flourish, finding at fifty things in me that I've buried since I was twenty?

The whine of the little motors lowering Karen-Anne's casket signals the end is near, and I return to reality. Surrounded by my past, our one future certainty staring us in the face, I return to the present. I have no idea where I am. Literally. If Kurt Junior left me out here, I wouldn't know how to get home, wherever that is. People get intimidated by New York, but it's easy to master, especially in Manhattan with its numbered grid. Everything has its box. And even off the grid, in the West Village or Brooklyn, there is always a recognizable landmark to guide you. Here? There's not even a church to serve as a marker. The charred remains of a structure that burned to the ground ten years ago rest just over the fence line—a century of community up in smoke and no longer enough people out here to justify rebuilding.

This is where Sonny's family is interred. Karen-Anne will spend eternity as she spent most of her life—with him. Which is good. Good for her. Good for him.

The service over, people fan out among the headstones, alone and in bunches, some visiting their thoughts and their God, others visiting old family or friends buried here. The women's heels punch holes into the wet dirt, the men's voices carry in low murmurs as they comment on their discoveries.

"He's dead? I didn't know that," someone says.

"About three years ago. Caught a stroke," someone responds.

They might not have all known each other, but they all knew *of* each other, grew up in the woods and pastures and bayous together, the last generation cut off from the wider world, before the interstate and cable and Internet reached out and absorbed their children into the rest of this thing called America. There will always be differences, of course. The accent. The food. The graves. Headstones aren't enough in this part of Louisiana. We may not have to store our dead above ground as they do in New Orleans, but we must install concrete roofs over our coffins lest a flash flood float them free from their dirt prisons. And, of course, there are unique local touches. I find myself standing at the foot of one of these seven-foot-long concrete slabs, upon which is perched a pig carved from solid marble. The pig is adorned with a wreath. At her marble teats suckle little marble piglets. Embedded in her side is a photo of a smiling man in a white shirt and white cowboy hat.

I smell Kendra-Sue's perfume—something popular in the '90s, Eternity, maybe—before she slides up next to me and reads aloud the words engraved on the pig.

"Enios 'Speedy' Comeaux. A man who loved his farm and animals. May he rest in peace."

"At least he was sure of something," I say.

"You don't know that," she says. "Maybe he hated pigs. Maybe when he died, his older sister was so mad at him, she decided to put a pig on his grave."

I look away from the pig and up to her. But before I can determine if she's starting another fight or trying to apologize, something—someone—catches my eye. Over her shoulder, near the dirt road where the cars are lined up, I see him turn from Karla-Jean and Gene, who are pointing in my direction. He seems a shambling, broken thing—thinning hair, teeth so yellowed from years of smoking I notice it even from this distance as he offers me something meant to be a smile.

"No," I say.

"Don't start again," Kendra-Sue says.

She doesn't see what I see, this ghost approaching me. My knees wobble and I reach out and grab her for support.

"No," I say again, louder now.

"Damn it, Katie-Lee," she says as I fall to my knees. I feel the damp ground through my pants.

"Nooooooo!" I'm screaming now, I think. A long, sustained howl. Heads turn toward me. I grasp the hem of Kendra-Sue's jacket, gasp for air.

The man stops. "Katie-Lee," he says. "Look."

"Noooooo," I scream again.

The last thing I hear before the world goes dark is Kendra-Sue's voice, burning with rage. "You son of a bitch, what the hell are you doing here?"

▫ ▫ ▫

New Year's Day 1980 started out as the happiest day of my young life. I was hung over, but it didn't matter. I was a sophomore at USL, had aced the Fall semester's finals, was working my way up the chain of command at the Tri-Delta sorority, had finally decided on elementary education as my major. Everything was in its rightful place. And at the stroke of midnight the night before, at a house party in Lafayette, Lawrence dropped to one knee and, while Kane played guitar, sang to me in a wavering voice.

"A long, long time ago,
While we sat in my Bronco,
I kissed you hard and swore I wouldn't let you go.
And then the next year."

He stopped, but Kane kept going on guitar, prompting Lawrence, "We went to the dance . . ."

"We went to the dance," Lawrence sang, and they both started laughing.

"Something, something, almost peed my pants," he continued.

Kane stopped playing. "Aw, hell, Lawrence, just do it."

Lawrence looked at me and out the words came. "Katie-Lee, will you marry me?"

The squeals of my sorority sisters drowned out my response. It was an enthusiastic and unqualified yes, followed by an enthusiastic and unquantifiable amount of drinking. At some point, Kane, Lawrence, and I called it a night and somehow made our way back to Opelousas without killing ourselves or anyone else. Conventional wisdom dictated that with everyone else on the road as drunk as we were, it was probably more dangerous to drive sober. We sat under the carport on rickety old lawn chairs waiting for the sun to rise. It was a warm New Year's Eve, unseasonable even by Louisiana standards. We didn't need a fire, but we lit one. We didn't need any more to drink, but we each cracked an ice cold Miller High Life, the champagne of beers, fit for celebrating our conquest of the future. We talked vaguely about the wedding. St. Landry Church for the ceremony. That was a no-brainer. But where to have the reception? Two choices: the country club or the Knights of Columbus hall—hall being a grand name for a wooden structure that might once have been a barn.

"I'm sure Mama's going to insist on the country club," Lawrence said.

"Then I'm sure she's gonna be happy paying for it," I answered.

"Who's going to be your best woman?" Kane asked.

"My best woman?" I shrieked, finding this hilarious.

"Maid of honor," Lawrence said by way of assistance.

"Yall know what I meant," he said. "Shut up."

"I don't know," I said. I tried to focus on the question. Despite having three real sisters and a house full of the sorority sort, I never had latched onto a best girlfriend. Best friend? I had two. Lawrence and Kane. A little triumvirate. Best girlfriend?

Only one name came to mind, though it surprised me as it left my mouth. "Kendra-Sue, I guess." She was a pain in the ass. I hardly saw her anymore. Between school, sorority life, and her moving out to the country with Brent when they'd saved up enough to escape the trailer, we already lived in separate worlds. But it felt right. Neither Kane nor Lawrence seemed shocked by the answer. "Who's going to be your best man?" I asked.

"Who the hell you think?" Lawrence asked. "My man, Kane."

"Really?" I shrieked. I was a shrieker then. A squealer. A girl given to emotional exclamations. If I'd had a mobile phone, I'd have been a chronic LOLer and emoticon abuser. "Awwwww. Yall!" I teared up, even.

"But you gotta wait until I turn eighteen," Kane said. "Best man gotta do a bachelor party."

"Hell yeah," Lawrence cheered.

"I catch yall in a titty bar, I'll kick both your butts."

As the sun climbed into the sky, we fell silent. I climbed out of my seat and onto Lawrence's lap, the chair creaking in protest. I reached out and put a hand on Kane's head.

Mama shuffled out of the house, wrapped in her ratty old house robe, her hair a mess. If my sorority sisters had been around, I'd have died of embarrassment. But in front of Lawrence, such things no longer mattered.

"What yall crazies doing out here?"

Lawrence spoke for us. "Just watching the sun rise, Miss Beverly."

I stuck my hand up at her, brandishing it as if it was topped by the Hope diamond instead of a half-carat chip. "Lawrence asked me to marry him, Mama."

She put a Winston between her lips and lit it with Daddy's old Zippo. "Yall gonna wait till after college?" she asked, her voice flat, worry in her eyes. Much as she might have wanted to, she wasn't going to ask me if I was pregnant right in front of Lawrence.

"Yes, Mama," I said.

"Yes, ma'am," Lawrence said.

She smiled real big then. "Congratulations, then. You a fine young man, Lawrence, and I'm happy to call you a son."

"Awww, Mama," I cried, hopping up and wrapping my arms around her.

Uncharacteristically, she hugged me back, which only made me want to squeeze her harder.

"Lord, Katie-Lee, you gonna break my ribs. And you stink. Yall smell like a bunch of winos. Kane, you been drinking?"

He held his beer up to her. "Yup."

"Shame on yall," she said to Lawrence and me.

"Mama, it's New Year's," I said, as if Kane hadn't been drinking every weekend since he'd turned fourteen. As if she didn't know that.

"That's right," she answered. "So how about you go take a bath and then come help me in the kitchen."

So there I was, hungover, sleepy-eyed and smiling while I stirred a pot of black-eyed peas. Not even the stench of the smothered cabbage bubbling on the next burner could bring me down. That was New Year's in Louisiana: pork roast, black-eyed peas, and cabbage for luck and health and riches or whatever superstition we wanted to attach to it. Same thing cooking in every house in Acadiana. The whole family was coming over for lunch. Kurt Junior and Melinda, and Kendra-Sue and Brent from Grand Prairie. Karla-Jean from the trailer in the back yard. She and Harold had divorced about five minutes after their second child was born and Harold decided that if a bottle was good enough for the baby, it was good enough for him. Karen-Anne was helping me in the kitchen, hustling around the house, sweating in ratty old clothes, completely unaware she'd turned into a raven-haired beauty. Kane had gone down for a nap. I was too excited to sleep, too full of good news.

Lawrence had gone home. He'd pop in at some point in the afternoon. His parents still had a standing invite, one they never accepted. I wondered if they'd at least stop by, to congratulate me on the good news.

When Kendra-Sue and her gang arrived, the two boys—T-Brent and Timmy—went straight for their favorite aunt, Karen-Anne.

"Yall not gonna say hi to me?" I protested. "Breaking my heart." I knew I'd have kids someday. Two, maybe three if the first one wasn't a girl. I definitely wanted a girl and she was going to be named Whitney. The boy we'd name after Daddy. If we had a third, Lawrence could name him or her.

"They hardly ever see you," Kendra-Sue said as she came through the door. She'd lost a lot of the baby weight. She'd never get back to the pre-T-Brent form—she was fifteen when she had him. But she looked good. And her home-set perm looked, as the commercial had promised, like it had been done in a salon. "What do you expect?"

"Happy New Year," I shouted at her, smiling.

"What's the matter with you?"

I stuck my hand in her face.

"Your nails are dirty," she said, playing it cool, though she had to have been surprised. Mama hadn't called her. Back then it was still long distance to call Grand Prairie and there was no point wasting money to call someone you were going to see later that day anyway.

"Kendra-Sue!"

She took my hand, looked at the ring.

"You better name it after me if it's a girl."

"I'm gonna slap you," I laughed.

"Better not hit me with that hand. That ring falls off, you might not find it, it's so small."

I yanked my hand back. "Keep it up, I won't ask you to be my maid of honor."

She squinted. "Me?"

"Yeah you. Who else?"

She took my hand back and pulled me in, hugged me for a whole second and let me go. "I'm not wearing pink," she said.

"How about sea foam?"

"I don't know what that is, but I like the sound of it. Sounds classy. Can we wear shoulder pads?"

"Wouldn't have it any other way."

And lo, peace reigned in the House of Fontenot, even through lunch. It helped that Karla-Jean's two girls were spending the day with their daddy, and she sat sulking in the corner, all two hundred pounds of her. After we were done eating, Lawrence showed up—without his parents—and suffered a good half hour of teasing for having the audacity to propose to me. We settled in the living room, where I started to nod off in his arms.

"You haven't slept yet?"

"No."

"I guess we're not going out tonight, then?"

"I don't think I can, baby," I said. "That okay?"

He brushed my hair back from my temple and kissed it.

"I guess. I kinda wanted to take you around and show off my fee-yonce."

"Sorry."

"I'll forgive you if you let Kane come to the camp with me tonight." He turned to Kane. "You wanna go?"

"Don't need to ask me twice," Kane said, hopping up and heading for his room to get his gun and change into camouflage.

"The camp?" I whined. "Really?" It could have been worse. The camp wasn't that far away. And the two of them had a spontaneous streak that often made me nervous. It wasn't uncommon to come back from a week at school without seeing Lawrence even once, to find that the two of them had picked up and gone fishing at Grand Isle or crabbing at Holly Beach or hunting God knows where.

"Yeah. Cold front coming through tonight. Ducks might come in tomorrow."

Kendra-Sue jumped in. "Ducks my ass. Yall just gonna drive out to the bayou and jackass around. Play cards and get shit-faced all night and sleep all day tomorrow."

Kane stuck his head out of his bedroom. "She's not as stupid as she looks, hunh, brother-in-law?"

"I'm not answering that," Lawrence said.

"That's good, Lawrence. You're not as stupid as *you* look," she said.

Kane came out of his room, dressed head to toe in camo, Daddy's 12-gauge slung over his shoulder. "Mama, I could go to the camp with Lawrence?"

"I'm sure glad you asked," she said.

He bent down and kissed her on the cheek.

"You the best Mama in the world," he said.

"Yall just be careful. No drinking and driving."

I followed them out to the carport, barely able to keep my eyes open. We kissed good-bye and Lawrence and Kane walked off across the gravel road toward that ugly old Bronco.

"Love you!" I called out.

"Love you, too!" he called back, turning around and waving.

"Gross!" Kane shouted, louder than either of us.

I had just put head to pillow, eyes already closed, when the Bronco's engine roared to life and they crunched down the road. I fell into a deep, peaceful sleep, the kind known only to exhausted little girls, secure in their knowledge that everything was right in the world—and that tomorrow would be more of the same.

What woke me up? It was Mama, shaking me.

"Katie-Lee," she said, "Katie-Lee," my name elbowing its way into whatever foolish wedding-flavored dream I was having at the moment. I drifted up to find Mama standing over me backlit by an alternating flash of blue and red lights.

That was strange.

"Mama, what time is it? What are those lights?"

She stood there, just looking at me. She opened her mouth to speak, but nothing came. She looked toward the window, at the curtain flapping in the breeze. The squelch of a police radio carried through the night.

"Mama." I tugged on her robe. "You're scaring me."

She looked back at me, something about her eyes sending a black finger of dread into my chest, touching my heart.

"Mama," I said, starting to cry, but unsure why.

I never did know if what she did next, she did on purpose or because her legs simply buckled. Either way, she went down to her knees—they smacked on the hard tile floor and they'd be bruised for a week. She buried her face in my mattress, reached up her hands to the blanket wrapped around me and clutched onto it as if for dear life.

I didn't move. Couldn't. Never in my life had I seen her in such a state. I wasn't even sure she was breathing, it looked so much like she was trying to suffocate herself with my bed.

Finally, I reached out and touched her hair. "Mama," I whispered.

She breathed then, one long deep breath, as if she'd just surfaced from the bottom of a dark lake. And then? Then, without picking up her head, she started screaming, sobbing, wailing—I don't know. I didn't have a word for what she was doing. All I knew was that I could feel the mattress vibrate from her anguish, feel her fingers digging into my flesh even through the blanket. I don't know how long it went on, but eventually her breathing returned to normal. My sense of terror, though, only grew as she calmed down.

She looked up at me, her eyes shot through, snot on her nose.

"Mama," I whispered.

"Baby," she said. "Oh, baby. It hurts so bad. My heart hurts so bad."

Lawrence and Kane had driven into the evening, toward the darkness, stopping at a gas station on 190 to pick up a case of beer and bottle of whiskey. There, they met with another carload of Lawrence's friends. Driving the speed limit, it would have taken them thirty minutes to get to the levee on Bayou Courtableau, then another twenty to get down to the camp Lawrence's daddy had built somewhere back in the woods.

They unloaded the car and then what? What did men do at the camp? In those days before cable was run out that far, before the Internet and cell service and emails and updates? Before girls were invited to such places and before boys started posting real-time pictures of their stupidity, collapsing the distance between their foolish antics and the stories those antics would produce?

They jackassed around.

What was jackassing around, exactly? Like pornography, you know it when you see it.

They drank. They played cards. They drank some more. They played drinking games. Quarters. Asshole. Three-man. Those, I'd seen at house parties closer to home, versions of them at any rate, no doubt subdued by the presence of girls.

And that night, jackassing around for some reason involved a 12-gauge shotgun. Daddy's. Kane's. Unloaded, to be sure. These weren't dumb-shit city boys unwise in the ways of the gun. They'd grown up with guns. Had killed things with guns. Squirrels. Rabbits. Ducks. Dove. Deer. And they'd heard the stories.

They knew better than to play around with a loaded gun. Of course it wasn't loaded.

Except they didn't. And it was. How it got that way no one knew, no one knows, no one will ever know. But there's no denying it was, because somehow it went off. Inside the camp. A 12-gauge shotgun loaded with No. 6 lead shot. It discharged. That was the word in the police report. The word used later in *The Daily World*.

On one end of the shotgun, the business end, the barrel end, was my brother Kane, Baby Joey.

On the other, holding the smoking thing, was Lawrence.

Twenty years later, things would have been different. There would have been a phone in the camp. And phones in the pocket of each guy there. 911 would have been dialed. At the very least, they could have met an EMT somewhere in Port Barre. And they could have made good time because much of the levee road would have been paved. This one night of stupidity might have turned into one of those close-to-unbelievable stories that, with time, became family lore, something approaching a knee-slapper. "Hey, brother-in-law, remember that time you shot me? Man, that was crazy."

But no such luck.

By the time they recovered enough from the shock and horror and impossibility of what they'd just seen, by the time they drove down the levee road, holding towels and clothes and whatever they could find to Kane's chest, while whoever had the wheel tried valiantly not to fishtail off the gravel road and into the bayou, by the time they made it to Opelousas General, even after making record time down 190, thirty long minutes had elapsed and it was too late.

Too late for Kane, who died that night.

Too late for Lawrence. He would do no prison time, but he'd become a prisoner of his own actions.

Too late for me. Shattered. A wreck. Unable to look people in the eye, much less talk or go to school. I don't remember much of it—not the versions of stories swirling around, not the empty words trying to soothe me. I remember the police report, what ran of it in *The Daily World*—its cold, distant language the closest I could get to the story. The sedation, I remember. Taking the pills, at any rate. The funeral. Bits of that come through. The wake I didn't go to at all, but they wouldn't let me skip the funeral. So out of my mind with grief and drugs, all I knew for certain was that Kane was placed into a hole at St. Peter's Catholic Church in Grand Prairie, next to Daddy, while St. Pete, hanging upside down on his cross, looked on.

Kurt Junior shepherded us through it all. He had his hands full. Kendra-Sue alternated between tears and rage, at one point crossing the lane to Lawrence's house and pounding on the door until her knuckles bled and the cops arrived. Karla-Jean sat in the corner muttering prayers to herself. Karen-Anne, unable to find words adequate enough to bring peace, fell silent.

I clung to Mama, she to me, both of us under the illusion that we were propping the other up. But it was too late for her, too, and six months after her baby boy's death, she simply gave up. Having seen enough of this world, she left.

And so did I. I climbed aboard a Greyhound bus and rode it to New York without telling anyone, without so much as a good-bye. What was I thinking? I wasn't. I was young and stupid and broken. I knew from watching movies that broken people hopped on buses and disappeared. New York seemed far away, geographically, mentally. When I bought the ticket, the woman behind the counter, before taking my money, asked, "You sure you want to do this, honey?" I shrugged, mumbled a "yes," and shoved the crisp bills at her, hoping she wouldn't call the police and, even though I wasn't a minor, report me as a runaway. Or perhaps I hoped she would. Instead, she shook her head, whispered, "Lord have mercy," and took my money.

I called Kendra-Sue when I arrived at Port Authority. Called collect from the dirtiest pay phone I'd ever seen.

"Come back, Katie-Lee," she said, too sad even to be angry with me, which only made me sadder. “Katie-Lee,” she cried into the phone. “Come back. Please come back.”

▫ ▫ ▫

“Katie-Lee.”

I hear my voice as if from the bottom of an open grave. Sensation comes back in stages. Through wet clothes, I feel a cold granite slab pressing against my back. Kurt Junior has lowered me onto one of the better graves in the yard. I smell the stale cigarette smoke on his shirt, this morning’s coffee on his breath. His face comes into view.

“Katie-Lee,” he says, lightly slapping my cheeks. “You okay?”

“Not really,” I say.

I can’t have been out long, because Kendra-Sue is still shouting.

“Get out of here. Go on. Get out.”

My head swivels to the right and there she is confronting him. Lawrence. What’s left of him after all these years. She’s shooing him off as if he were a cow that had gotten into the garden.

“You ol’ drunk. Get out!”

“I cleaned up,” he stammers. “I changed. I found Jesus.”

“You found Jesus? Yeah? And what did Jesus say about what you did to Kane? To Katie-Lee? To Mama?”

At this, his head goes down, eyes locked on the tips of his muddy shoes. For the first time in thirty years I feel something for him. Not much, but a little. As much as I wish the ground would swallow him up, take him out of my sight, I realize, judging by the sight of him, that Kendra-Sue’s condemnation is redundant, a bucket of cold, dirty water dumped on a man who’s finally trying to get out of the rain. He mumbles something.

“What was that, Lawrence?” she demands. “What did you say?”

He looks up, crying, a child who’s learning all over again that in the real world apologies don’t right wrongs. They might bandage hurt feelings, but they can’t undo actions.

“I said I was sorry.” He wipes his nose with his hand. “I know it doesn’t help you any.” It looks like a lesson he’s been learning every day for decades—before drinking the education away by the time the sun went down. "My heart hurts, Kendra-Sue." He looks to me and I flinch, as if the evil eye has been cast upon me. Those words. That phrase. Did he have to put it that way? "My heart hurts so bad, Katie-Lee. All the time. It won't stop." He's blubbering now. "He was my friend, too, Katie-Lee. He was gonna be my best man."

At this, I turn my head away.

"Yall gotta know how sorry I am. And I never got a chance to say it in person. Thirty years it's been eating me up. So I thought." He trails off now, confused, perhaps realizing the futility of it all. "Karla-Jean and Brother Gene said maybe if I came down here—"

Kendra-Sue raises a hand, cuts him off. "Karla-Jean and Gene? I should have known."

The pair, as if summoned, materialize on either side of Lawrence.

"Sister Kendra-Sue," Gene says in that singsong voice of his, the one that puts you in mind of a man, a van, a bag of candy and unfortunate happenings at a playground.

She points a finger at him. "Call me sister one more time, Gene, and I will slap the Holy Ghost right out of you."

"Now look here, Kendra-Sue," Karla-Jean says. "Jesus Christ asks us to forgive. Lawrence has been suffering all these years and Jesus would want—"

"What?" Kendra-Sue asks, walking toward Karla-Jean. "What would Jesus want?"

Gene and Zombie Lawrence back away as Kendra-Sue draws closer.

"He'd want some half-ass preacher to come to your baby sister's funeral and crap on her grave? Scare the kids? Convert the Catholics?"

They're nose to nose now.

"He'd want you to bring your brother's murderer?" The way she says murderer makes it sound like Lawrence planned the whole thing, waited in the bushes and shot Kane. "Bring him, of all people, to the graveyard to traumatize your other baby sister? If Jesus was as dumb as you, he'd have rounded up only two apostles and we'd all be

Muslims right now."

As if to prove just how dumb she is, Karla-Jean, instead of turning tail and getting while the getting is good, opens her mouth.

"You don't scare me, Kendra-Sue. Not one little bit."

"No?"

"Never have. Never will. I got Jesus on my side."

"Well you better start praying," Kendra-Sue says and, faster than anyone her age has a right to move, her hand whips up and grabs Karla-Jean by her hair. In one swift motion she pulls her to the ground, landing on top of her.

Karla-Jean, whose ribs somehow survive this impact, calls out not to Jesus but Gene. Neither Jesus nor Gene is stupid enough to intervene at this point. Clovis rushes over, whistles, shouts out Kendra-Sue's name, but to no avail.

I push up into a sitting position, give my head a chance to settle. I stand, wait another moment. I force myself to look at Lawrence. I look at Karla-Jean and Kendra-Sue. I turn to the fence and consider the horizon, the fields beyond, open and inviting and quiet.

"Katie-Lee," Kurt Junior says.

"Somebody's got to stop it," I say.

I walk over to where my sisters are wrestling in the mud, indistinct now from each other, looking less like two women fighting than one cow in its death throes. A purple and black cow that grunts in English.

I look away from them and up at Lawrence. "Lawrence," I try, but his name gets stuck in my throat. I clear it. He turns to me. "Lawrence," I manage. "You can go now. Go on." These are the first words I've spoken to him since New Year's Day in 1980, when I said "I love you" and he drove off and shot my brother. Whether or not he had the courage to apologize in the months before I left for New York, I don't know. Mama wouldn't let him near me. And I wouldn't have talked to him if she had. Looking at him standing here, I realize he's suffered as much as me, maybe more. He's had to live with the guilt. It was an accident. Kane was his best friend. Logically, I know this. On some level, I can almost touch the pain Lawrence must be feeling at this moment. I walk over to him. He takes a step back, cringing like a kicked dog. I touch him on the arm, surprised that it doesn't physically hurt, and try to find some words of forgiveness, try to release him from his hell, but the only words that will come out are, "Just go. It's okay." I hope for his sake they're enough.

Neither of my sisters witnesses this scene, busy as they are defiling the eternal resting place of Karen-Anne. I walk back to them.

By this point, the other attendees have recovered from their initial shock. I see more than a few of them looking at their phones, thinking hard about taking a picture or two.

"Kurt Junior, you gonna help or what?" I ask.

"Aw hell," he says, almost smiling. "Too bad we don't have a pineapple."

"That would be inappropriate. Pineapples are for wedding receptions, not funerals."

Then, imagining myself as Jesus breaking up the perpetually brawling apostle brothers, James and John, I reach into the scrum with one free hand, find their shoulders, call their names loudly.

And just like that, I'm at the bottom of the pile, mud in my mouth, a finger in my nostril, my hair being used as reins by one if not both of them. At this point, none of us are sure why we fight. We're sisters. We need no good reason to fight, even though we have plenty of them. I fight because I'm scared of growing old. Kendra-Sue fights because I left her all those years ago. Karla-Jean fights because we abandoned her to Jesus. We all fight because Karen-Anne was taken.

I hear someone, probably a kid, shout, "Keee-yawwww. Look at 'em go."

"Shut up or I'll slap you," he's told immediately. "And put that phone away."

"Kurt Junior," I yell. Through the flying limbs I see that he's standing over us, trying to find a break in the action. I reach out a hand. When he grabs it, I pull hard. "Get your ass in here," I tell him.

I'm not sure how long we fight but it can't be for very long. As old as we are, it's a miracle no one breaks a hip or has a heart attack. It dies out of its own accord. We're sitting there, panting in the mud, when Sonny and the kids walk over, stare at us in silence for a bit. Sonny finally speaks.

"Everybody's coming to the house. Mama made some gumbo last night. Tina's picking up some Popeyes. Appreciate it if yall come." He turns to Kurt Junior. "Can you pick up a few cases of beer and some ice?"

"Yeah," Kurt Junior says when he catches his breath, embarrassed for us all.

Sonny turns to go.

"Sonny," I call out. "I'm sorry. We're sorry."

He smiles for the first time since I've been here.

"Shit, Katie-Lee," he says. "Karen-Anne woulda loved to see that."

CHAPTER FIFTEEN

I ride with Clovis and Kendra-Sue back to their house. Catherine sits next to me in silence, perhaps afraid to speak until she can figure out what the mood is.

Clovis, shaking his head, is the first to say anything. "I'd say yall should be ashamed of yourselves, but I don't think either of you is capable of shame."

Getting no response, he continues. "All them people there to pay respects to your baby sister. And yall acting the fool. What people going to say?"

"Oh shove it, Clovis," Kendra-Sue says, slapping him on the knee. She then leans over and kisses him on the cheek. "Them people should send us thank-you cards. They going to be telling that story to their grandchildren."

"Yall crazy," he says.

Kendra-Sue turns around. "Catherine, if you put this on YouTube, you better write that Mawmaw won."

By the way she blushes, I can tell that Catherine indeed shot video of at least part of it. If this trend continues, my third YouTube appearance will involve a knife fight.

"Let's not get carried away," I say. "Looked more like a draw to me."

"You want a rematch?" Kendra-Sue asks.

"No."

"Didn't think so."

Not until after a shower and a change of clothes, while sitting in Kendra-Sue's bedroom, am I able to start sorting things out. Last week I lost my job. My sister Karen-Anne joined the ranks of the dead. I flew home to Louisiana. Was all but told I'd spend eternity in hell. Came face to face with what remained of Lawrence—and the ghost of Kane he carried with him. And I ended up wrestling in the mud of a graveyard with my two remaining sisters.

And I survived. Somehow.

But that doesn't do much to stop the sensation that I'm going to shake apart at the seams. Now that the adrenaline has worn off, the drama has died down, I feel like I've been drinking gallons of coffee on an empty stomach. Wired, exhausted, trembling, nauseated.

And now we have to go to Sonny's and confront all those people.

And then what? I lie down on Kendra-Sue's bed, close my eyes, and try to talk myself out of puking. What do I do next? Board a plane, go back to Brooklyn and start looking for work? At my age? Sit alone in my apartment until I justify going down to the Brazen Head and bringing someone else home from the bar? Get a cat?

"You okay?" Kendra Sue asks when she comes out of the bathroom.

"I guess. I thought I'd be worse." I open one eye.

She's standing over me, looking down at me. "Me too."

"But I would make out with Brother Gene for one of those Valiums you got hidden somewhere."

"How you know I'm hiding them?"

"I checked your medicine cabinet."

"You little bitch," she says, snapping her towel at me. She disappears into her closet, a walk-in that's slightly bigger than my

Brooklyn bedroom. "Tell you what. You get that wet hair of yours off my bed and I'll hook you up."

I sit up as if spring loaded. She doesn't have to tell me twice.

On her way back to the bathroom, she tosses a travel bag onto the bed. It rattles like a snake—a big, camouflaged, pill-filled happy snake.

"Go crazy," she says.

"Already there," I say.

I unzip the bag, expecting one brown bottle tucked in between sunblock and bug spray and deodorant. Instead, I find a treasure trove. Valium. Lexapro. Ambien. Xanax. Abilify. Even good ol' Prozac.

"Damn, Kendra-Sue!"

She steps back into the room, working a Q-tip in her ear. "Don't judge me, Katie-Lee," she says and points the Q-tip at me. "Don't you dare."

"Judge you? I've been on all of these and then some. I left mine at home. I've been going batty since yesterday."

I look down at the stash and back at her.

"But why?"

"You don't hold a patent on crazy, Katie-Lee."

Pig-headed, first-to-fight Kendra-Sue. Rock solid and practical. Queen of common sense, vanquisher of nonsense. Backbone of the family.

"I had no idea."

"How could you?" The edge has returned to her voice. "You never asked."

I deserved that. "I deserved that," I say. "But, shit, Kendra-Sue, one of the reasons I never wanted to ask is because I thought you'd think I was weak. I mean weaker than you already thought I was. You were the strong one. You didn't run away."

She sighs. "Honestly, Katie-Lee?"

"What?"

"If I didn't have them two kids at the time, I'da run away, too. Hell,

I'da run away before that. Like you said, I wanted to get out, see the world. But, also like you said—and thanks for reminding me because I almost forgot—I got knocked up. And it was husband and kids, then another husband and another kid. For what? Twenty, twenty-five years? Making ends meet. Getting by. Noise and commotion. This and that. School. Work. Exams. More school. Baseball. Football. Basketball. Homecoming. Prom. Girlfriends. Fights. Damn, those boys fought. Beat the snot out of each other. Broken furniture. Blood. Stitches. I thought it'd be easier without girls involved. But drama, drama, and more drama. Every day. Twenty-four, seven."

Just imagining all that chaos, the noise, the inescapable commotion. Sisyphus pushing that rock of his never had it so bad. "Calgon, take me away," I say. "No wonder you turned to the marvels of modern medicine."

She shakes her head. "No," she says. "That's not it at all. One day they were just gone. Poof! The kids were out of the house. And I had all the silence I ever could have asked for, all the time in the world to think. Jesus. When T-Brent and Tammy had Catherine, I almost kidnapped that child to give me something to occupy my mind when I wasn't at work, give me something to worry over. But I couldn't keep her all the time. Next thing you know, I'm at work, start sweating, chest starts hurting, and I'm pretty sure I'm having a heart attack."

"Anxiety," I say.

"Sounds like you been down this road."

"Yeah, well."

"Why?" She pauses. "Was it the stuff with Kane?"

"What?" For some reason, the question strikes me as ludicrous. I was twenty when that happened. After I moved, it never occurred to me to get pills. Not legal ones. Get drunk, smoke weed, sure. Pills? Psychotherapy? No. Just move along. Keep moving forward. Let the pain dull with time.

"No, it wasn't that." Which is most likely a lie of epic proportions. "Well, sure, that's probably at the bottom of it all, if we wanted to really dig deep." But that's not what triggered the actual trip to the doctor. "I guess I woke up one day and wondered where my life went, what I'd done with it. Which led to a more depressing question. How much is left? I swear to God, Kendra-Sue, that's what it boils down to. That one question. And when I'm alone at night? Or when I see a nineteen-year-old girl primping in a restaurant bathroom? Or a little kid crying? They've got life ahead of them. But me? I've lived over half my life already! I can't breathe just thinking about it."

"Jesus," she says, "that's depressing."

"You think? I told you I was crazy."

"But Katie-Lee, you're not unique. You're not the only one. I'm the same. Hell, maybe we all are. What other question is there? How much is left? I don't know how you do it. Facing that all alone. I don't know if the pills would be enough. Hell, even Karla-Jean has creepy old Gene."

"And Jesus," I say.

"Oh yeah. Mustn't forget Jesus. She needs two men to keep her demons at bay. She's got religion and we got pills."

"What about Karen-Anne?" I ask.

"What about her?" Kendra-Sue says, a defensive edge in her voice. "I don't want to cry, Katie-Lee. Not right now."

"I mean, did she have these issues? Was she taking pills? Was she staying up at night?"

Looking away from me, she sighs—a long one that sounds like all the air going out of a balloon.

"Honestly? She was miserable."

"What? Karen-Anne? She always was the only one with any sense. She struck me as so together." How had I come to that conclusion? Because she had finished college? Was a scientist? Had a job? A nuclear family? Didn't post prayers or passive-aggressive attacks on friends or family or ex-lovers on Facebook?

"Oh, sure. She held it together. She was always good at that. But she needed to get out of here so bad, get away."

"Like leave Sonny and the kids?" This is a shock. "Was she having an affair?"

A weak smile comes to Kendra-Sue's lips. "You're so dramatic sometimes. No, it's just that she always had these plans. She'd go to college, get married, get a job, have kids, save up and when the kids were off, she'd see the world. She wanted to see Paris. She wanted to see Egypt. She wanted to go here, do this, do that. She talked and talked about going to New York to visit you."

That hurt. Just a little. "But why didn't she?"

"You never invited us," she says, her smile a little bigger.

"You can't help yourself, can you?"

"Okay, that was cheap, but you sort of walked right into it," she says. "But Karen-Anne had one son in Afghanistan and worried every weekend that some homophobe redneck was going to get his hands on her daughter. She kind of took it out on Lucy at first because, well, you can't yell at a soldier protecting your freedom. And it was Sonny Junior she was really worried about. She locked herself in her room for a week when he re-upped. I wanted to kill him. I told her, I said, 'What? You're gonna sit watching CNN and Fox News, surfing the web, waiting for something bad to happen? Nothing you can do about it. Get out there while you can. At this rate, you'll be in an old-folks home and he'll still be at war.' Anyway, she said she just couldn't travel with him off at war like that. I didn't push too hard because. But I sure as hell was going to sit his ass down and tell him something next time he was in." She sits down next to me. "And now it's too late. Guess he can go back off to war. Hell, at least if he gets his dumb ass killed now, it won't destroy his mama . . . shit."

She breaks off. She isn't really angry at Sonny Junior. Or she isn't angry *only* at him. She's angry at life, nature, politicians, God, Baby Jesus, Karen-Anne, and all the things we could have done, should have been.

"I didn't even know her," I say. "My own sister and I didn't even know her."

I unscrew the cap on the Lexapro and raise the bottle as if in a toast, then take a pill. Just to be sure, I chase it with a Valium.

"So why hide them?" I ask, anxious to change the subject away from Karen-Anne. "Kids get into them?"

"Nah," she says. "It's for Clovis."

"Clovis?"

"Prideful fool. It hurt his feelings that he couldn't make my crazy go away. You know how men are. Always trying to fix things can't be fixed. So I told him it was work-related. The stresses of nursing. All that. And I'd go off the pills when I quit. So when I quit last year, I just moved them to the closet."

She takes a Lexapro herself.

"And don't say shit about me going behind his back. Little white lie. Won't hurt anybody."

"I wouldn't know the first thing about holding a marriage together."

I put my forehead on her shoulder. She rests her cheek on my head. I feel like a girl again, as if I'd been dreaming for half an eternity and only now come to. Which, of course, is nonsense, as she and I have never in our lives sat like this. Not even after Kane died. But we should have. It should have been like this always. We should have grown old together, our kids playing and fighting and raising hell. Going down to Grand Isle together or out to Gulf Shores. Squabbling over who would host Thanksgiving and Christmas. Sure, I'm idealizing it. But maybe I could cope with idealizing things in life rather than writing them off from the get go.

"I got fired Friday," I say.

"Just like that?"

"Fifteen years and just like that."

"Ain't that some shit."

"But there's a year's severance. Imagine. A full year's salary, no work."

"That's something at least. What are you gonna do?"

"I don't know," I say. "Maybe I'll move back here." I don't know why I say it. This is the first time the thought has crossed my mind.

"Are you crazy?"

"What?"

She knocks on my head with her knuckles. "Helloooo. We're not always together like this. Holidays, weddings, and funerals. You think it's tough being alone in New York, being alone down here is going to be worse. And you ain't exactly of marrying age or type. Especially now that you're a big-city librul."

"I only play one on TV," I laugh. "Yall seemed to handle Lucy and Tina well enough. Hope for yall yet." My accent is coming back.

"Lord, Katie-Lee. When you're not underestimating us, you're overestimating us. It's a funeral. Soon enough, they'll be gossiping and judging and praying for Jesus to rescue Lucy's eternal soul. More than a few of them have slipped Sonny brochures for Pray the Gay Away Camps. But for now, they're all on their best behavior."

"Except us."

She laughs. But she's right. Deep down I know it. Been here two days and haven't heard one racially tinged comment. Has to be some kind of record. Especially considering who the president is.

"I think you'd be of more use to us up in New York. Year off? Me and Catherine can come visit. Show us the world. Take us to one of those real local pizza joints in Brooklyn or something."

And what was I going to do the rest of the time? Take up macramé or crochet or knitting? Become one of those old ladies who spends her days in the locker room at the gym just for the companionship? I could freelance. I'd always been too scared. Fancy that. Ran away to New York City, spent the first ten years or so working this job and screwing that guy. But when I finally found my way into full-time America, I became too scared to give up my health insurance ever again. But this way, I'd be covered, salary-wise, for a year at least. There was money to be made freelancing for an enterprising person with half a brain and no sense of shame when it came to overcharging.

"I guess I could get a full-time job. Double up on salary. Save up a huge chunk of money."

Kendra-Sue pulls away from me, takes me by the shoulders as she's about to shake me until my head falls off. "Really, Katie-Lee?

Really?"

"What?"

She shakes me until it feels like my head might fall off.

"Owwww. What?" I laugh.

"It's not funny. You're worried so much about how much life you have left? What if you died next week? Run over by a circus elephant or hit by a bus or something?"

"Wow. Thanks a lot."

"No, but really. We of all people should know Death doesn't wait politely for you to tidy up loose ends. Hell, Karen-Anne should have known that. You want to have spent your last days sending out resumes, kissing ass, sitting in a cubicle—saving up money for what? A nice casket? Everyone's always saying, 'One day when . . .' Well, honey, looks like one day is here. You said half your life is over? Katie-Lee, who says that has to be the better half?"

I can see her point. But I also know myself. "I need some kind of structure to my days," I say.

"Seems airline schedules and hotel checkouts and check-ins could give you plenty of structure. Maybe you can even put away the laptop and the smartphone."

My thumbs start to itch and the mere suggestion of it.

"Christ," she says, laughing. "Look at you. I've worked with crackheads who hid their addictions better. But, c'mon, Katie-Lee. You have a year of freedom. At least a year. Don't waste it. All these years I'm supposed to be living vicariously through you and, I gotta be honest, you haven't exactly held up your end of the bargain."

I could travel, finally, like a European. Weeks of vacation at a time instead of seven rushed days. Maybe I could fly around with Harriet the Pentecostal. Despite her religion I bet she'd be fun.

So many damn decisions. I'd be starting in on a panic attack if the Valium hadn't kicked in already.

"Can I stay through Christmas at least?" I ask.

"That would be nice," she says, then stands up. "Come on. Before we start playing Faith Hill songs and singing into our hair brushes."

We haven't even made it to the bedroom door when we hear a commotion from the front of the house, staring with Clovis wildly proclaiming, "Mais, goddam, I can't believe this right here. What you doin' here, boy?"

It's hard to tell from the tone of his voice if he's angry, happy, worried, or what.

"God. I hope it's not Lawrence," I say.

"He's not that stupid, Katie-Lee."

Then from the front, Clovis says, "Get your ass in the house. Come on."

"Obviously not him," I say. "Let's go see."

Kendra-Sue puts a hand on my shoulder to stop me. "Look, I don't want to start anything. But it wouldn't kill you to try to forgive him."

"Him who? Him Lawrence?" I want to get defensive, want to accuse her of betrayal, but I realize there's nothing in the tank.

"You saw him out there. He's trying to get his act together. But he's had a hard few decades."

"I told him it was okay," I say. "While yall were on the ground fighting."

I brace myself for whatever it is she's going to say next. "Good," she says. "That probably wasn't easy. But good." She yanks the bedroom door open. "Now let's go see what this fool is going on about."

What Clovis is going on about is standing in the middle of the living room, smiling nervously, hands in his pockets, watching me walk into the room and waiting for a reaction.

It's Howie.

And my reaction? I stop. Stop walking. Stop breathing. And because I'm flooded with approximately five trillion thoughts and emotions, I stop thinking as well.

"Hey, Katie-Lee," he says, unsure of himself.

Kendra-Sue elbows me in the back.

"Howie," I say back. What the hell is he doing here? "What the hell are you doing here?"

Did that sound bitchy? I'm not sure. It wasn't meant to. I really just want to know what the hell he's doing here, in my sister's house, thousands of miles from wherever it is he's supposed to be.

"You hadn't updated your Facebook status since the airport, so I thought you might be dead or something. Figured I'd come down and check."

"And that," says Kendra-Sue, "is why we like Howie. Come here, you." She wraps him up in a hug, pats his back, as if they're lifelong friends.

I haven't moved yet.

"Kendra-Sue, come help me load the car," Clovis says.

"Load it with what?" she counters.

"Just come on."

Left alone, Howie and I stand facing one another until his smile falters, replaced by worry. "Well say *something*, Katie-Lee."

So I say the first thing that pops into my mind. "You're not going to ask me to marry you again, are you?" For the life of me, I have no idea where it came from.

He laughs. Loudly. "What? God no. Are you crazy? Or just an egomaniac?"

"Sorry," I say, protesting. "I'm a little freaked out, that's all."

"Look, after I saw you in the airport, I was worried. So I called Candy."

"Wait. What? You called Candy? Are you two sleeping together?"

He gives me his smart-ass smile. "None of your business. But no. Never. We just talk sometimes, is all. She helped me through the, well, you know." Like he can't even say the word *divorce*.

"Anyway, I called her. And she said if I was thinking about coming down, then I should. That you would never ask for help, even if you actually needed it. That sounded like you, so here I am."

"There you are," I say, and instead of being pissed that they were discussing me, I'm touched. It's sweet.

"Yup. Here I am. And Candy's on her way. Couldn't get here until tomorrow, though."

"What?"

"And Danielle, too."

"I don't—" I don't what? Don't want this? No, that's not true. In fact, I'm crying, now, so moved that not even the mood stabilizers are stabilizing me. "I don't understand. How did you even get in touch with Danielle?"

"C'mon," he says. "Really?"

"Facebook," I say, when the answer dawns on me.

"Sorry we missed the funeral," he says. "But by the time we got our crap together . . ."

"No. Don't apologize. God. I just can't believe yall would do this. I mean send flowers, that's what people do, right? Sorry for your loss, call me when you're no longer a wreck. You know?"

"The Fontenots didn't strike me as the flowers type." He shrugs.

Then he opens his arms, and just like that I fall into them and close my eyes. It doesn't feel like fate or destiny or anything like that. But it does feel good. Solid. Something to hold on to.

"But, this doesn't mean we're getting back together or anything, right?" I say. "That's not what this is about?"

He pauses. "To be honest, I hadn't thought about any of that. I sort of surprised myself when I offered. I thought I still hated you."

"Gee. Thanks."

"But you can't carry that kind of grudge around forever. It's not good for you." He pauses, shifts gears. "And, hey, if you do want to have some funeral sex, just let me know. I hear funeral sex is even better than make-up sex."

I can't help but laugh. "You are so disgusting."

When I open my eyes finally, I see Kendra-Sue and Clovis standing outside, staring into the window and waving, not a half ounce of shame between them.

◘ ◘ ◘

Sonny and Karen-Anne's yard looks like the parking lot outside Tiger Stadium on homecoming day. Trucks and cars parked three deep in the grass, people milling about in clusters, everyone now changed out of their dress clothes and back into hunting or football garb.

The mood is schizophrenic. When we arrive, Kendra-Sue and I are greeted with rowdy applause.

"Let's get ready to rumble," someone calls out.

But it quickly dies down. We're probably the most somber group of beer-drinking Cajuns—and one Asian man—a person has ever seen. We form a tight knot around Sonny and the kids, Kurt Junior, Kendra-Sue, and I sitting on the tailgate of Sonny's ridiculous wide-bodied truck. We tell jokes, remember Karen-Anne's life, starting with the tale of the Tooth Fairy and working our way forward.

"Remember when she fell out the peach tree in Grand Prairie?" a voice says from outside the circle.

Karla-Jean.

A path opens up between her and me, as if it's my decision to forgive her or not. My anger's gone, I think. But I'm not going to let her off the hook that easily.

"Where's Gene?" I ask.

She swallows. "He stayed home. With Lawrence. He wants to make sure he doesn't go on a bender and drink himself to death."

No one says a word. Not a cough, a snicker, a smart-ass remark. Christ. Lawrence. All these years I've left him twisting in the wind. I fish my phone out of my pocket and find it's got two full bars of service.

"Would you put that damn thing away?" Kurt Junior says.

Kendra-Sue, perhaps knowing what I'm doing before I do, tells him to shut up. "Just give her a second," she adds.

I pull up Facebook and search for Lawrence's profile, then send a friend request. "It's not much, but this is the best I can do for now," I type. "Try to forgive yourself." In a million years I couldn't have said that to his face, but maybe this will free him.

"I want to apologize, Katie-Lee," Karla-Jean says.

I put my phone away and reach into a cooler behind me, grab a beer and shove it toward Karla-Jean. I'm all but asking her to decide between her religion and us. It's not fair of me, especially considering my own past, but such is life.

"Okay," she says. "But just one."

I hop off the tailgate to make room for her and stand next to Kendra-Sue, leaning against her. Karla-Jean tells the story of the peach tree—funny now, but not at the time—when Karen-Anne fell out of the damn thing and came terrifyingly close to losing her virginity to a fence post. Missed it by inches, but the gash left an eight-inch scar on her inner thigh that lasted for life.

"That girl was always an accident waiting to happen," Kurt Junior says. "Lucky she didn't bleed to death while we were trying to untangle her from the barbed wire."

Howie clears his throat. For the life of me, I can't imagine what he might add to this discussion, unless he and Karen-Anne had been conducting some really in-depth correspondence on Facebook.

"Hey, Katie-Lee, tell that one about the toilet paper."

"What?" I say, drawing a blank.

"Well, not the toilet paper. That story your daddy used to tell you guys. The one with the burning grass."

"Oh," I say. I know what he's talking about, but I'm still a little confused. "I don't remember telling you that."

"But you did," he says. "See, I paid attention."

Kendra-Sue raises an eyebrow at me.

"It's not really about Karen-Anne," I say.

"Mais, just shut up and tell it," Kurt Junior offers.

So I start talking. It's really not much of a story, just a memory, one of my favorite that's stuck with me all these years, of us—all of us—sitting on the porch at that little house in Grand Prairie.

◻ ◻ ◻

After a long day of working in the dirt or in the kitchen, the porch was where we'd gather after supper. Especially during the summer, when we chose the mosquitoes over the sweltering house. The other kids lay about the porch, sated, looking for all the world like lions lazing on the savanna after a kill—Karla-Jean, the poor thing, practically an albino one, almost glowing in the night. I sat with my back against a support post, holding Baby Joey in my arms, wondering when and if I'd ever have a baby like this, if I'd marry somebody like Daddy, live on a farm all my life like him and Mama. Mama and Daddy still had life in them, youth and vitality lingering as if drawn from being so close to the land.

Or maybe it was just that the lighting then—moonlight and cigarettes—was more forgiving.

"Going to be another hot one," Daddy would say.

"You a regular almanac," Mama would answer.

And we'd all chuckle at a joke we'd heard at least twice a week, five months a year, for all of our lives up to that point.

Mosquitoes buzzed, June bugs and moths clicked against the screen door, chickens slept under the house making that purring sound. Karen-Anne claimed it was because they were dreaming they were cats, the sort of thing that made sense to her and her alone.

She came skipping from around the house. "Mama, we outta toilet paper," she said, unembarrassed by such a proclamation. Bathroom functions weren't something any of us kids felt particular shame about.

"That's what that Sears catalog is in there for," Mama said. "Just in case."

"Them Sears pages hurt my butt-hole," she complained.

"Oh well, listen to her majesty," Daddy teased.

"But Daddy, it does," she said.

"You know what your old Daddy had to use when he was your age? You want to know what hurts?"

"What?" she asked, climbing into his lap, leaning into his chest. She knew. We all did. But that wasn't going to stop Daddy from telling us anyway. Besides, we liked the sound of his voice in the night air, our entertainment in those days before we moved to town and got a TV.

"An old corn cob," he said. "An old dried-out cob. You pass that on your little hiney one time and you be begging for Sears. And

Roebuck, too. Heck, even the Montgomery Ward catalog'll feel like clouds on your butt after a corn cob or two."

"Awww, Daddy," she said, giggling.

"But that's not the worst I ever had," he went on. "One time, when I was just a little thing—about knee-high to a chicken—I woke up in the middle of the night and had to go bad-bad. Shoooo, I tell you what. But it was dark and cloudy and I was scared to walk all the way to the outhouse."

Karen-Anne interrupted. This was her first time hearing the story. "Why didn't you just go in the pot-chambre?"

Yes, we were still a people who used chamber pots.

Mama chimed in. "I better not catch any of yall shitting in the house. Not until we get indoor plumbing. I don't care if it's raining hell-fire outside."

"Indoor plumbing?" Daddy shouted. "Your Mama sure got some fancy ideas, huh? Anyway, *my* mama felt the same way. Besides, she'd taken our pot-chambre out the room because your Uncle Brian kept falling out of bed and knocking it over in the middle of the night. After it was full."

"Gross, Daddy!" we all shouted.

"It's for true," he said, his English getting away from him a little. "One time he fell in head first. His eyes was yellow for a week after that."

"You lie," Karen-Anne said, so pleased with this embellishment she almost squirmed out of his lap. If she hadn't just been to the outhouse, she might have peed herself.

"Your old Daddy wouldn't lie to you," he said. "But like I was saying, I was too scared to walk to the outhouse. So I went outside and squatted right on the side of the porch and did my business. Well, of course, there was no corn cob right there. And I hadn't thought to bring any newspaper. I was going to use the cat's tail, but it wouldn't come when I called."

"DADDY!" Karen-Anne shouted. We all laughed with her.

He didn't stop. "So I figured I'd use some leaves. Well, I reached out in the dark for the first bit of grass I could find and had passed it on my little old butt before that first bite of pain could even start up."

"What you mean, Daddy?" she asked. "Why it hurt?"

"Your Daddy had grabbed a clump of burning grass. Shoooooo. I think it started burning my butt before I even felt it on my hand."

Karen-Anne's eyes went wide. She was young enough she hadn't learned how to identify burning grass and had fallen into a patch of it not two weeks before, the stinging little fibers along the stalks and leaves grabbing hold of her skin and marking it a flaming red.

"Keee-yawwwwww, Daddy. That musta burned bad, hunh?"

"Tell you what," he said. "I woke up all of Grand Prairie, and they heard me all the way in Ville Platte and Washington, too. Mama said she thought the Angel Gabriel was blowing his judgment trumpet, I hollered so loud."

▫ ▫ ▫

Just like that, the story was over, and after our laughter trailed off, we lapsed into silence, secure in the knowledge that Daddy was always going to be there to protect us.

I like to think of Karen-Anne and Daddy like they were that night, still in that rocking chair, two peas in a pod the way they were meant to be.

And here we all are, in a line, what's left of us, oldest to youngest. Kurt Junior, Karla-Jean, Kendra-Sue, and me.

Something occurs to me. "Well, shit on me," I say.

"What?" Kendra-Sue asks.

I should be terrified by what I'm about to say, but I'm not. For this one moment I feel surrounded, protected. Safe enough to joke.

I shrug. "Looks like I'm next."

Clovis shakes his head. "Yall ain't right," he says.

The four of us, all at the same time, just laugh and laugh.

ACKNOWLEDGMENTS

Many thanks to Jason Primm, Jacquelin Cangro and Amy Holman for first reads—and second and third reads. My gratitude to Cynthia Manson, for hooking me up with Premier Digital Publishing—and PDP for taking another shot with a guy who refuses to stick to one genre. Thanks as well to Caitlin Alexander, for tackling editing duties on this book and saving me from my worst excesses, and to Nancee Adams-Taylor who did a hell of a copyediting job. Any mistakes still in the book are mine and mine alone.

On a personal note, thanks to Cara Carline for packing up the car and the poodles and moving to Brooklyn, bringing a daily dose of South Louisiana back into my life. I owe you at least one bestseller.

There aren't enough trees in the world to properly acknowledge the entire extended family back home. I'd name you all, but that would take another book entirely.

Thanks for raising me right and thanks for a lifetime of stories.

ABOUT THE AUTHOR

Ken Wheaton was born in Opelousas, Louisiana, in 1973. Raised Catholic and Cajun, Wheaton aspired to one day be a navy pilot but was sidelined by bad eyesight and poor math skills. He graduated from Opelousas Catholic School in 1991 and went off to Southampton College–Long Island University in Southampton, New York, intending to study marine biology. An excess of drinking and (again) a dearth of math skills led him to become an English major. From there he returned to Louisiana, where he received an MA in creative writing from the University of Southwestern Louisiana (now the University of Louisiana at Lafayette).

Wheaton is the author of *The First Annual Grand Prairie Rab-bit Festival* and *Bacon and Egg Man*, and is the managing editor of the trade publication *Advertising Age.* A Louisiana native, he lives in Brooklyn, New York.

Said Dave Barry of Wheaton's second novel: "I had several drinks with the author at a party, and based on that experience, I would rank this novel right up there with anything by Marcel Proust."

CPSIA information can be obtained at www.ICGtesting.com
Printed in the USA
LVOW08s2004250714

396042LV00001B/221/P